Acclaim for Maisonvide

'Maybe print about 20 copies and let's see what happens'
— Ben Clark, Short Run Press Ltd.

'Just because we knew each other as children, doesn't mean I can
help you with this literary disaster'
— Rachel Joyce, Author

'I knew he wasn't marking assignments' *— Mark Burrough, Exeter College*

'Do you understand what libel means?'
— Jane Wills, Paul Taylor Solicitors

'I literally soiled myself'
— Andy Charlton, Love Devon, (yet to read Maisonvide)

'The only award this book will get is The Cats Arse Trophy
— Steve Price, Riviera FM

'Look will you stop hanging around the shop, the answer is no!'
— Manager, Waterstones

'There are more twists and turns on the road across the Nullarbor plain'
— The Australian Tourist Board

'I couldn't wait to put it down'
— Trish Millinson, The Beekeeping Times (A hive of activity)

MAISONVIDE

Nicholas Thom

Published in 2019 by The Old Forge Book Company

ISBN 978-1-5272-4841-0

Printed in Great Britain by
Short Run Press Ltd, Exeter, Devon

For my girls Julie and Tabitha

This book is dedicated to the memory of my Father
David Michael Hooton Thom (1938–2014)
Who loved a trip to France

Acknowledgements

Thank you to Peter Bryson (uncle) for supporting this whim.

To Julie for everything she has done to help bring this to print.

To Glyn, what a talent, you're wasted in the shop.

And to Pam for dropping back my key two months after we had returned from holiday.

Dear reader,

Picture if you may your own headstone. On it, just below your name and your dates are some numbers. These numbers represent the amount of time you have spent either watching television, playing with your mobile or been sat in front of a computer.

What would you like yours to say?

Below the first set are another. These numbers represent the amount of time you spent properly being alive, experiencing everything that life and the world have to offer.

Sadly, you can't offset the second figure against the first, the damage is already done.

However, it is never too late to change and make sure that the second number totally dwarfs the first. Be more Pam and Bob about life, be a bit dodge, be unpredictable and above all else never conform to what society dictates you should be doing.

One thing my friend, that my late father and I can categorically guarantee is that you will only be here on this mortal coil once.

Leave a bright and lasting light not a dull and diminishing shadow.

Now get on with it!

Prologue

"What the hell am I doing?" Bob asked himself, aloud, when he caught sight of his pathetic reflection in the half glazed front door of Dr. Roberts' house.

He had his wife Pam's coat on, covering his pyjamas and was wearing wellies, without socks. Bob had nodded off during The Antiques Roadshow and came to as Pam closed the bathroom door.

"Bugger! I've forgotten to feed that bloody cat!" He was vaguely talking to Pam; who couldn't hear him as she was running a bath.

Bob grabbed all the keys from the hall table and set off up the road. It was raining. The village was quiet with most of its residents shut in against the elements. He could make out the odd glow of an oversized television and the occasional bedroom light.

Bob was trudging up the only road in the small Devonshire village of Whiterock. The settlement was split into three parts; the old section went with the church, high on a hill about a mile away. The newer part where Bob and Pam lived, with maybe 30 other houses, and then the last part of the village which was situated down over the hill on the main road and contained the local pub.

As he walked up towards Dr. Roberts' house he reflected on his neighbours and their lives. Over the years he had been into nearly all of the houses he now passed in his capacity as the official "go-to" man when people went on holiday and were too tight to use kennels or the cattery.

He turned into Dr. Roberts' short driveway. Hers was almost the last house in the middle village, a funny building in the 1960's style, trying too hard to be of architectural note, failing to do so, and actually looking a bit out of place.

The PIR light came on, its low energy lamp beam barely illuminated the cat but Bob could still make out the look of complete contempt aimed in his direction. This is the moment when he caught his reflection in the door; wet, in his sleep gear, wearing his wife's coat. The cat head-butted him. Bob was brought to focus and reached into his pocket. He pulled out 6 sets of keys, selected the key with the "Monaco" fob, and pushed open the door. The cat sped past him and he tripped over trying to avoid it, fell, and landed in the spare cat bowl area.

The cat's face did the almost impossible and showed even more contempt.

Holiday Job ...

Every village, street or small urban community have a "Pam and Bob". Often taken for granted and always taken advantage of. These folk are poorly rewarded but utterly needed; for those weeks away or the last minute weekend break – good old Pam and Bob would step up to the plate.

Like all these things it started on a small scale and developed over the years into quite a concern.

"If this was a business, we could float it on the stock market" Bob had remarked on more than one occasion. First had been their direct neighbour, Mary Braces. She had been difficult to say "no" to as the first favour involved direct eye contact and therefore no time to think of an excuse.

Pam could remember the exact moment she had first said yes to feeding Mary's cat and looking after her small flock of hens. They had only moved in three weeks before, had barely met any neighbours and Mary had come around with a Trojan horse of a pot plant. After ten minutes of stunted small talk Pam had agreed to feed the cat, keep an eye on the fish, feed and clean out the hens, take in – but not read the newspaper and the post, so that Mary could have a short mid-week break; much needed, by all accounts, due to the stress of being on the Parish Council.

"If I had said no to her back then, none of this would be happening! Mary would have gone elsewhere, forgotten about it and probably never asked us again!" Pam had mused more than once.

From this critical moment, events of house sitting had escalated to the now quite ridiculous situation they found themselves in. Hanging on the wall at Bob and Pam's house was one of those large wooden fun-keys popular in the Seventies – covered in hooks for real keys. Theirs was full, but none of these door openers was for Chez Pam and Bob.

For one insane three-week period the year before, Pam and Bob had simultaneously looked after seven houses, containing a total of 4 dogs, 18 cats, 5 Guinea pigs, 8 rabbits (17 by the end of the time), 1 tortoise, 12 chickens (in three different establishments), 2 snakes and 1 African grey parrot with Tourettes. This assorted menagerie was accompanied by the usual day to day requirements of post and parcel handling, 2 meter readings, and to accommodate a visit from a building surveyor from a mortgage company.

In the middle section of this mad period, Bob had even taken some time off from his part-time job to cover all the responsibilities.

Their reward for all this work – four tea towels, one bottle of a never-before-heard-of yellow liquor, a fridge magnet and the promise of a bottle of wine when the unpacking was done – it never materialized.

Pam worked out that they had done four hours extra a day that week. To make sure he got to every house in time; especially the ones with the chickens who got very vocal and grumpy if not let out soon enough, Bob had been getting up at 5.30 am, staggering around the houses, walking old dogs between venues, collecting eggs and cleaning out hutches.

To be honest they didn't think that everyone in the village realized they were away at the same time and that basically Pam and Bob were in charge of everything. It was a massive pain in the backside but not done deliberately.

One of the only remaining residents at that time was old Mr. Baker; rattling around in his immaculate bungalow. Pam visited him as a matter of course every morning to reassure him that he was still alive. He had asked her to check once and this had worried her; so now she did it every day.

They hadn't really had a holiday that year, or, in fact any year since the initial Mary house-sit. In between looking after everyone else's pets and homes, they had both put in extra hours at their normal work to make up the shortfall.

Bob had worked part-time for a delivery company and Pam had taken on extra cleaning. In the past they had both had good jobs, the mortgage had come down so they had both decided to go part-time and take things easier! Yeah right, that had happened!

Their two children had come and gone, no real dramas, both had settled down within a couple of hours' drive, no grandchildren yet, good job too, neither would have had the time.

The village had a thriving social life, well they say thriving, there seemed to be a hell of a lot on in the village hall, but as to attendance figures at these clubs and events, nobody knows.

Bob and Pam attended a few – the social club held every third Monday, bring and share talks about bees or the love lives of beavers. Bob went to a music club; he was pretty good on guitar. Pam went to Pilates even though the teacher always arrived late and then clock-watched the entire session.

Despite being asked on several occasions, they had both sensibly declined the offer of being co-opted onto the Parish Council, mind you, with the wonderful gift of hindsight it might have been a good idea; make a few contentious planning decisions and the house sitting workload might have dropped due to pissing a few people off.

So, really without actually knowing it, this quiet, humble, unassuming couple were the glue that held the village together.

Dr. Roberts ...

Bob's eyes came to focus on the cat food bowl, less than six inches from his face.

He recognized the pattern and the shape but couldn't place it. He got up, brushed off Pam's coat and made his way to the downstairs cloakroom where the alarm consul was housed.

He typed in the code, which was his own birthday as Dr. Roberts had asked him to set up the system last year as she would be away on a Rhine cruise. On her return from this Germanic quest she bought Bob a lovely tea towel with the image of a lederhosen clad bear eating a large slice of Schwarzwalder kirschtorte. More than enough reward for a week's house sitting and setting up a complex alarm system!

He bundled along the hallway and through the sitting room, unlocked the internal kitchen back door and went into the utility room. The other cat was there, waiting, not for Bob to make a mistake, but just waiting for him to breathe so that it could pour looks of scorn, hatred and contempt at him.

Of all his neighbours, Dr. Roberts had at least made an effort to ease Bob's pain; she had bought two cat food dispensers fitted with timers.

These she had acquired via a catalogue from Shites of Stow, 'Delivering poorly thought out crap since 1967'. The design looked like a collaboration between the makers of Lego and Heath Robinson and it didn't work.

The timers were very loud and probably scared the cats, the catches became sticky due to the food so the flip-up lids only half opened; exposing part of a tray of stale food.

Neither the cats nor Bob were impressed by this haphazard contraption, so he bypassed the system and used a couple of bowls instead, until the day

4

before the return of the occupant, bearing yet another forgettable gift from the arse end of Europe.

Pam had once been given a box of fudge with a stuck-on postcard stating that it was a gift from Devon (bought from a petrol station near Plymouth, about 30 miles away) in gratitude for over two weeks' worth of house and pet sitting.

I mean if these ungrateful people had used an agency or a cattery it would have cost hundreds of pounds. Tight gits.

Bob doled out the cat food.

Antiques Roadshow!

That was it! That's where he had seen the bowl before or one very like it, he couldn't really bring the details to mind now or the value but it was one of the later items so was probably worth a bit.

He put the bowl's contents into the semi-automated machine and carefully put it to one side. The cats slowly circled the offerings, looked at him, and disappeared out through the cat flap. They weren't going to lower themselves and actually eat in front of him.

Only once in the past had Bob abused the trust of a neighbour. They had gone away on holiday and insisted that their cat, Prince, would only eat a gourmet tin of food mixed with some line caught Tuna. Pam and Bob's, now departed cat, Graham, had the gourmet food. Bob had Tuna sandwiches for lunch and Prince eventually ate Sainsbury's own brand fish selection to ward off feline starvation.

Bob put fresh water down for the ungrateful felines, turned and locked his way back through the house. The walls were covered in paintings, not really to his taste, a bit too Turner prize meets African beach art.

In the main sitting room area there were shelves from floor to ceiling, full of books. Bob touched some of the spines as if he could read using his fingertips. Most of the titles were children's books such as the complete Beatrix Potter set, every Enid Blyton, full set of Biggles and Tintin. "Strange", he mused aloud to himself.

Dr. Roberts never had any children of her own, although she was renowned for having delivered every person under the age of 50 in the area. This would have been done in a no nonsense manner, probably on a cold stone floor with cold water and no encouragement, it wouldn't have been just the babies that got a slap.

He pulled out a copy of Peter Rabbit and opened it; a first edition.

He did the same with Tintin and The Black Island, again a first edition.

They all were; every box set here was a first edition. Wow! Quite a collection.

He replaced the copies, went to the alarm and tapped in his date of birth. He would be 55 next birthday – was this really it for him?

He shut the door and made his way home in the dark.

"Alright darling?" asked Pam.

"Is this it for us?" replied Bob but Pam wasn't really listening.

"Don't forget that Mary goes away tomorrow for a week."

'For Christ's sake' thought Bob. 'I really hate that cat.'

Mary Braces ...

Their next door neighbour, Mary, had been the first person to ask about house sitting. She was the cow who had started it all. Bob had never liked her cat since he saw it spray on his rose bush during the week they moved in to the village.

To go with the cat, Mary had four chickens and two fish.

Chickens really added to the workload when you were house sitting, I mean you had to open up the hen house really early and close it at dusk, and if you didn't the fox would definitely take advantage, it would kill all four in moments.

Yes, the eggs were a bonus, but Mary seemed to think this was payment enough. The four girls laid on average two eggs per day between them, so when Mary went away for two weeks in the summer they would get about two dozen, equal to £5 wow!

They used to split the work between the two of them. Pam would open up one week at about 6.15am with Bob shutting them in before the fox did his rounds. Unlike other animals in their care you had to clean the house out every morning, the droppings soon build up.

There always seemed to be a greater responsibility with hens, more so than with cats and dogs. Fish were pretty easy – a bit of food and a glass clean every few days would suffice and if one died, it didn't really matter.

The same could be said of cats, it had never happened on their watch, but cats could be, well, "disposed of" and a car could be blamed, but a chicken felt different.

This was probably because the total care rested with you. They didn't wander off, you supplied all sustenance, cleaned them out, woke them and put them to bed, if one died, even of natural causes, then the blame would squarely land at your feet.

Mary didn't even bother to call in before she left for her short break, Bob always felt her holidays fell somewhere between old singles, club 60/80, wife swap and dogging. She told them it was a short escorted tour of historical European capitals. Bob imagined different.

"Bob, don't be so naughty, Mary isn't like that!" Pam would say.

"I bet she is" Bob quietly replied.

Pam was cooking when she saw Mary walk past the window. She heard something land on the mat.

Mary went back past the window. 'Bit rude', thought Pam.

In the envelope that Mary had dropped on the mat were the house keys and a list of instructions. The cat was on medication (probably for feline stress bought on by watching Mary's holiday videos, suggested Bob), one of the chickens was looking a bit off colour and the fish tank may need a clean!

Pam had sort of accepted her lot and it didn't really affect her but Bob was showing signs of stress and rebellion. He was getting really pissed off with his village life. He was putting his coat on and sifting through the keys looking for the ones to the big house, he was having to let in a smart meter installer at the Smartin's place.

"Silly cow! two weeks away and she doesn't even bother to say goodbye, leaves us with more pet issues than the super vet could cope with and she doesn't even say thank you on the note, cheeky mare!" he snorted.

"Don't be like that darling, she's alright Mary, maybe just in a hurry to get off?"

Bob smiled at the double entendre

"No Bob, not that, she might be in a hurry to get to the station, she would help us out."

Bob interrupted.

"No she bloody wouldn't, she wouldn't even sign for that parcel for us last week, it went back to the depot and I had to pick it up, our names on the delivery ticket and she still didn't take it, you asked her once to have old Daisy (their recently departed dog) for one evening so we could meet up with the children in a pub, but she said no as there was a double EastEnders on and the dog might upset the calm of her house."

Pam stopped and took on board what Bob was saying and actually he did have a point.

"Right Love, see you later, I am off up to the big house."

Bob left and set off walking up the road. As he did, he saw Mary saunter out of her house and into a taxi. 'She wasn't in a hurry at all, see she is a silly cow' thought Bob.

Pam went to Mary's house to check on things, she let herself in and was met by the emaciated cat hoping for some food, she went past the fish tank, 'might need a clean'. Jesus it was filthy! Probably hadn't been cleaned since Bob did it last time that Mary went away. Pam went into the back garden, the chicken run had not been moved for some time, which Pam did now, the area they had been in looked like it had been treated with agent orange.

She tried to seek out the one that looked a bit off colour but they all looked the same so she checked for eggs. There were none. Perhaps she had left them inside so that Bob could have some for his tea, she had a look around and 'OMG she must have taken the day's eggs with her, what a tight arse'. Pam took a very deep breath and sighed, she decided to clean the tank out now so as not to put Bob over the edge.

In all, after she had found the equipment, it took her the best part of two hours. She would go on to spend the rest of the day worrying that the water was too cold or had too much chlorine in and she hadn't added enough Fish Safe liquid or even put too much in and the fish would grow an extra fin or flap around with their swim bladders trailing behind.

She finished cleaning up. At least the fish did look happier. Mary would probably not even notice.

Pam headed home, without any eggs.

The Smartins ...

Either Bob was early or the EDF installer was late. He let himself into the big house. It wasn't the biggest house in the village anymore but for a long time it had been and the name had stuck.

He didn't mind the cat here, mainly due to the fact he rarely saw it. During this week's duties and the whole of the last big-house-watch stint he hadn't even seen the cat; the food disappeared but no cat ever showed itself.

Bob wandered around the downstairs rooms. The house was a Georgian style pile, not too grand but big enough. Apparently a farmer had come good back in the 1800's, knocked down the existing old cob farmhouse and replaced it with quite a tasteful and well-proportioned country house. Seven bedrooms, an elegant hallway, and a staircase of national renown; mentioned in various architectural articles as an excellent example of a Devon vernacular staircase.

The current occupiers were the Smartins; a lovely, large family with now grown up children. They also had a house in London where Mrs. Smartin spent much of her time so she could be close to various grandchildren.

Bob heard the gravel crunching as a van entered the driveway and headed towards the front of the house. Bob made his way to the back door and around the side of the house to direct the engineer to the electric meter cupboard.

The van driver introduced herself as Viv and proceeded to show Bob her ID badge, which made her look like she was about to commence a ten-stretch for crimes against personal hygiene.

Viv asked Bob if she could see the existing installation so she could make her assessment. Bob decided against sarcasm as a form of wit and took her inside.

The electric distribution board and meter were situated in the back kitchen. Viv followed Bob through the hall and into the rear of the house. He pointed to the small cupboard and Viv turned on her head torch. She took some readings and wrote down the box number.

"He grew up here didn't he?" Viv asked already knowing the answer. Maybe Bob had been here before or he was just tired and wanted to get home and try and get on with a bit of his own life.

"Yes, he did," replied Bob.

The 'he' in question was one of the Smartin brood, who had become, and I am not over exaggerating here, one of the most famous musicians in the world. His band had sold tens of millions of albums, they played to sell-out crowds at some of the largest venues on the planet. Mr Smartin spent a lot of his time touring with the band and acting as a meeter and greeter to the more famous guests at the gigs. In fact, Mr. Smartin was with the band at the moment on the New Zealand leg of their latest sell-out world tour, hence why Bob was stood there with Viv in the electric cupboard.

"I'm such a fan!" exclaimed Viv. "I have seen them three times in concert. When I saw the name and address appear on my job list this week, well I just couldn't believe it. I haven't slept much, been so excited, then I said "come on Vivian, it is still just another smart meter upgrade, he won't be there, he's on tour. Just make sure you do a brilliant job with the installation, no mistakes, we can't have any issues at this address, he might need the electricity for his guitar to help him write more fantastic songs."

Bob thought that Viv might soon pass out with swooning so he brought her out of her train of thought.

"Do you want to see the music room?" he asked. Viv turned, open mouthed. She just nodded with her mouth still open.

"I will show you as soon as you finish your job, so that you can just concentrate on the work in hand, ok?"

"Ok, I will get my stuff!" Viv left, almost in a trance and headed back to her van.

Bob and Pam had been briefed many years before about the expected level of privacy in connection with the famous son. Most people in the village stuck to the unwritten rules. One lady who used to babysit for the family did sell her over-elaborated story to a Sunday tabloid for £10,000, she was completely ostracized and eventually left the village – the stories she told weren't that interesting either. Some obsessed fans did still make a pilgrimage to the house just to get a photo of themselves outside.

Bob didn't really understand it, but then again, the only thing he was really obsessed with was Pam – and he could get a photo of her anytime.

Mr. Smartin had replaced the house name sign so many times he gave up in the end. Someone had even taken the wheelie bin as a souvenir, the wheelie bin for god's sake!

Bob didn't think that the Smartins would mind if he let Viv see the music room, it might get him out of here quicker. Viv returned with her tools, did a very professional and speedy install with no chat. Bob sat out in the hall and waited for her to finish. On a side board was a photo of the band members surrounding the piano in the music room with Elton John at the keys, 'that's pretty cool' thought Bob. Then Viv reappeared.

"All done, checked and working" she beamed, Bob thought he saw her actually shaking with anticipation.

"This way to the music room" invited Bob as he went down the smaller hall way with Viv in a trance behind.

He opened the door to quite a non-descript room that badly needed re-decorating, but all Viv could see was bank of gold and platinum discs that filled the walls.

Since the very beginning of the band's formation they had agreed to do two main things, one was to put back 20% of any profits into a charitable foundation.

The other was to give Mrs Smartin any awards and album sale discs they received; as a thank you for the endless driving of the minibus and the support she had given in the founding years of the band's history. Every award and trophy was here, and there were hundreds.

Viv's face didn't know what to do. Her mouth remained open, and as she slowly walked around the golden walls, she started to read some of the inscriptions.

"In recognition of 1,000,000 sales worldwide" and "Album of the year!"

She probably would have stayed in that room until the day she died so Bob coughed to bring her back to planet Earth.

"Sorry, I just can't believe that this is actually happening to me, would you mind taking a picture of me in front of the wall?"

Bob thought about it for a minute, what harm can it do, the boy hasn't been here for a while. I will tell Mr Smartin when he returns I am sure he won't mind.

"Viv, can I ask you to keep it to yourself, close friends and family? I don't want to get into trouble!"

Viv turned to him and almost standing to attention said with the sincerest voice:

"I wouldn't do that. I am a real fan and besides my company probably would not be too happy if I started posting pictures taken from inside a customer's home, I will keep the images to myself mate – trust me."

Bob smiled and took Viv's phone, he went to work with Viv beaming in every shot. When lots of pictures had been taken in front of the discs and trophies, Bob returned her equipment and they headed for the door; where Viv turned and took a last look.

"Bugger, this lot would be worth a small fortune to a collector!"

"Really?" said Bob, not totally shocked by the language. "What sort of money do you think?"

"To the right person, tens of thousands of pounds, maybe over a hundred bags of sand, some anonymous collector, someone who would only take them out every now and then, really covet them, thousands and thousands …" Viv had started to sound a bit creepy towards the end.

"Bugger!" said Bob, he had never even thought about it before. After he had taken a last picture of Viv outside the house, he watched her leave the drive and without seeing the cat yet again he locked up and started walking home. Further down the road he met up with, and fell alongside, Pam as she was leaving Mary's. Bob tapped his watch and rolled his eyes.

"Tell me about it, nearly three hours we have done each and for no reward. The tight cow even took this morning's eggs with her, what was she going to do with them? Give them to the taxi driver as a tip?!"

Bob held her hand until they reached their gate, where, under his breath he said to her …

"I don't want to do this anymore my darling. I didn't see my retirement as being subservient to the village, how can we get out of this relentless cycle?"

They both left this hanging in the air, entered the house, made some lunch and then went out to do some work that paid. That night they finally collapsed in a heap together at 9.50 pm.

Pam had had trouble at Mary's with a rogue hen not wanting to join the others instead opting to roost in a bush. Pam couldn't take the risk. A farming neighbour had once told her that the fox went past the hen house every night to check you hadn't forgotten. Pam had to get her safely tucked up, all the bush scrabbling had alerted the rest of the flock who then proceeded to exit the coop to see what all the fuss was about. All this for one late egg, Mary would be gutted she had left this one.

It was too late to do anything for themselves and Bob was too tired to even make a joke about Pam fiddling about in Mary's bush. Bob had an early start in the morning; another of the villagers was off on holiday and had asked Bob to be there at 6.00am for the handover.

Peter Henson ...

As a very tired and forlorn Bob approached the house at 6.05am Peter Henson actually tapped his watch face and shook his head.

"Cheeky bastard" muttered Bob under his breath. He was a little tardy because he had let Mary's chickens out on the way down. Pam and Bob had Peter down as an early retired civil servant who took redundancy from a post his colleagues had conspired to remove from the company structure as a way of getting rid of the annoying git. Boy could he be annoying. Well maybe not annoying as such, just a bit too involved in everything.

The energy he had once put into local governance he now channelled into the village community. He ran several groups at the local hall, which now had something on every day and evening. He was Chairman of the Social Club – in charge of securing guest speakers with topics ranging from the love life of a woodlouse to 'I was the cleaner for Princess Diana's Butler'. Thrilling!

He organized and attended (wearing Lycra), a Pilates group on a Tuesday, table tennis on a Wednesday, art club on Thursday and a craft social club on Fridays (yes ... ALL in Lycra).

In the village he crossed paths with most people. He had also set up the community website, chaired the Sustainable Whiterock group and contributed regularly to the Parish Magazine with many column inches about how awful we all are towards the planet. Fair point.

Peter's house was a reflection of the fact that early retirement meant that he had rather a lot of time on his hands. Everything was over engineered; labelled, sorted by alphabet, or sell by date, or level of toxicity. All his logs were stacked dependent on size and date cut. Maybe he wasn't annoying but people were just a bit envious of his lifestyle being in such good order.

"Morning to you good neighbour!" Peter laughed as he handed Bob a laminated copy of the instructions and method statements required for the following week. Peter was off on a yoghurt weaving course in the Balkans or something similar. From Bob's face it was clear that the number of tasks and duties being asked to be performed had been grossly understated by Peter.

There was the normal cat feeding to do plus the two giant Russian lop eared rabbits that Peter had bought for his daughter of 28 years – despite her not really living at home anymore.

Rose, his eternally prodigal daughter, visited the house on a regular basis sporting some new strange piece of artwork fashioned out of her own bodily waste products and of course when she ran out of money. 'Why couldn't she look after the bloody house with her stupid rabbits in?' thought Bob. Almost like Peter had heard this he spoke.

"Rose is away on a meditation retreat in mid-Wales for a month, but has left you her own list of rabbit care tips."

"How kind." Replied Bob as he took hold of yet more laminated instructions. Annoyingly, Peter tapped his watch again and led Bob into the house. All boots and shoes were arranged in seasonable use order, as were the coats. In the kitchen Peter had constructed a pigeonhole style storage system out of old cereal boxes. In each box was the allotted food for the cats/rabbits plus an envelope for each day.

"The recycled envelopes contain a key code for the village hall, and all the details of whoever is holding an event. If you wouldn't mind putting any received post into the correct box on the day of its arrival, it will be easier for me to catch up with and prioritise on communication upon my return," Peter said this like it was normal behaviour.

"I have tried to make it fool proof."

'Charming.' Thought Bob.

"For example, Monday – take out pet food and dispense, distribute packaging to correct recycle box, pick up envelope with key code, replace with day's post, and so on …"

"Twat!" Bob had thought that this was just inside his head but actually it was on his tongue.

"I'm sorry?" questioned Peter.

"Oh, urm, THAT is a great system!" Bob, with great expertise, recovered.

"Why are there two envelopes for Thursday?"

"Oh, it's no biggy, don't worry it's not two hall events, it is just a reminder for you. My main compost heap needs turning on Thursday night; I am running an experiment. The compost heap in question is aligned to the moon cycles. I think that the bacteria run to the lunar cycle and not our human calendar. It must be turned right over on Thursday late evening after sundown. Please try and stick to this – the gardening club are really getting excited about the results."

"I bet they are!" Bob replied in his best unsarcastic tone. He glanced at the sheet of instructions. It was going to be a very busy week.

"Show me the correct compost bin before I leave Peter?"

With the gift of hindsight this was a stupid thing to say. Peter took him outside where, behind a shed, stood a large box made out of pallets with a large cut out painted moon hovering over it.

Peter was explaining his preferred compost turning technique as Bob switched off and started glancing around the garden. It was then that he spotted it, a camouflaged camera, fixed to a tree and pointing at the compost bin. For the second time that morning Bob muttered the words "cheeky bastard". Peter was actually going to film the compo turning event on Thursday evening.

They returned to the house.

"Alexa, how long before I need to leave?" asked Peter.

"*You have 20 minutes before you need to leave*" replied an animated female Tupperware container on the kitchen work top.

"Alexa, are you sure?" queried Peter.

"*I have calculated some current traffic issues on your journey planner and to maintain your preferred ETA, you will need to leave within the next 19 minutes.*"

"Thank you Alexa. Well Bob, you heard the lady, time to wrap this up. I need to get going." Peter ushered Bob to the door, gave him a set of colour coded keys, nodded then turned back inside. Bob heard his voice in the hallway.

"Alexa, what's on my packing list?"

"Alexa, did I wipe my arse this morning" muttered Bob, under his breath. He was trudging homeward now. He was very unhappy. He was at breaking point. One more thing, just one more thing …

A car horn blared very close by to the depressed Bob. No need really; he was walking close to the hedge. The offending car pulled alongside him, a window was wound down, it was the new chap from the old Barton. Bob couldn't even recall his name.

"There you are Bob! Thank god I have found you! A real emergency! We have been asked out to a ball tonight and might have a drink or two, so thought we would stay over. Mary said you would be good enough to check on things, you know the cat and the house."

Bob was speechless; his jaw was almost on the floor. The lady in the passenger seat was applying industrial quantities of make-up and didn't even bother to look over and acknowledge Bob's presence. The driver, Terry, then proceeded to actually throw some keys in Bob's direction. He missed them and the bundle dropped to the ground.

"We will be back tomorrow afternoon or whenever the alcohol level in my bloodstream drops to a vaguely legal percentage. You could drop the keys back any time after 3 o'clock. There's a good chap."

The car pulled away with a small wheel spin. Some gravel flew back and hit Bob as he bent down to retrieve the keys.

That was the one more thing.

A Retirement Plan …

Bob was sat in a crumpled and dejected heap. The Channel 5 documentary washed in and out of his consciousness. He was knackered.

He had been down to Peter's and to the old Barton. Terry (Bob had checked some post to confirm his name) hadn't even left any food out so he had spent half an hour traipsing around the house looking for cat food. The cat had followed him with a 'I know where the food is kept you twat!' look on its face.

He had found it in a cupboard in the old back kitchen, four rooms away from the actual cat bowls. The cupboard was situated next to a gun cabinet which, worryingly, was wide open. Inside was a fine pair of old shotguns. Bob wasn't an expert, but he knew quality when he saw it. Having fed the cat, he took the guns out to feel the weight and balance. 'Perfect' he thought as he bought the cat into his sights. He put the gun maker's name into his memory bank, put the guns back, pushed the cabinet door to a little, and left the Barton to go home.

"You heard this love?"

"I'm not really watching to be honest darling."

"Well the man's a bloody fool if you ask me. If I had to disappear, no-one, and I mean no-one would ever see me or hear from me ever, ever again. I would dissolve into the World and never make any mistakes, unlike this idiot!"

The program that Bob was referring to was about a husband and wife who had faked a disappearance and death involving a sea canoe incident. The wife had feigned grief and heartbreak whilst cashing in an enormous life insurance pay out. The couple had got away with the hard bit, until years later when, unbelievably, they had got involved in some publicity photographs for a holiday scheme in Panama. Someone had recognised his image and the game was up.

"They would never find us my darling, never."

Pam raised her eyes. "It's not that bad is it lover?"

"I don't mean the fake death part; I mean the disappearing bit. If you are going to do it, then do it in style, big time, leave a legacy, something that would enter folklore, do something that the village would talk about for generations. They would sit their grandchildren down and say "Once upon a time there was a couple called Pam and Bob". And yes my love, for me it has got that bad." Bob hung his head.

"Well let's do something about it then, bugger the lot of them, the ungrateful sods!" Pam almost shouted this out.

Bob sat bolt upright, only once or twice before had Pam exhibited this level of fire and passion (fortunately for Bob it had been in the bedroom). Bob wasn't tired anymore.

"Ok love, we need a plan. A Whiterock exit strategy so cunning that no one will ever believe it could have been possible. We don't need to rush, we have time and above all we have the element of surprise "nah, not old Pam and Bob, they would never do anything like that" the neighbours will say."

Pam nudged Bob at about 1 am, she had nodded off in the chair. Bob had entered a new state of consciousness. He was wide awake – well his brain was – this was exciting, something really could be happening. He went to bed but could not sleep, his thought strands taking him to endless possibilities, most of them fruitless, but a vague Venn diagram/flow chart was forming; the first 2 boxes were filled and his mind could follow the 'yes' arrow course to a conclusion.

In the morning over breakfast, Bob had a new enthusiasm for life which he not felt since he and Pam had first moved in together.

"We would need enough funds to live well, in comfort, and never need to come back" said Pam between mouthfuls of Special P. Bob had bought her a box of promotional cereal to make up for the fact that there wasn't a can of Coke with Pam's name on it.

A huge smile of relief came over Bob's face, he leant forward, covered her spare hand and gave it a gentle squeeze.

"I love you Pam, I am so glad you remembered. I was worried it was just me, but together we can achieve anything."

Pam turned to him and smiled.

"Convince me" she purred and returned to her Special P. Bob had been thinking about little else all night.

"I have roughly worked out that at our age and with our current state of health coupled with our estimated life expectancy, we would need about £1,200,000! That would buy us a modest house with plenty of cash to live a humble but good life. I don't want to be watching the Euros in my old age."

"So you fancy Europe then, to settle down in? Me too, warm, sunny, good food, sorry, do go on darling" Pam mused thoughtfully.

Bob continued "As you know love we have no mortgage and I reckon our old house is probably worth getting on for about £350,000, so we have a shortfall of about £800,000 … Which I am working on."

"I am sure you will sort it out darling, now don't forget to turn Peter's moonlight compost."

"On my way gorgeous." Bob leapt up and with real enthusiasm headed off to Peter's house. He was a bit early to turn over the lunar heap but he had to the feed the cat and spend some time with himself to solve the large gap in his retirement fund. He arrived and let himself in. The cat was waiting with its tail draped over the bowl as if indicating where it wanted the food to be placed.

"Alexa, why is Peter such a twat?" Bob said out loud.

"*I don't understand the question*" came back an attractive but tinny voice. Bob jumped – not expecting the thing to be switched on let alone being able to activate it. Bob just threw a question out there; well you never know unless you ask.

"Alexa, how much money is in my bank account?"

"*As of close of business today you have £3,872.41 in your current account*"

'That won't get me far' thought Bob.

"*You have £86,600 in your savings account, £22,025.25 in NSI premium bonds and as of 4.00pm yesterday your share portfolio was worth £42,320; down 0.27% on the day.*'

'Wow, now you are talking, a good start for my nest egg' Bob thought about asking Alexa if Peter had any money hidden under the bed, but instead asked:

"Alexa, I would like to transfer some funds."

"*Please provide the sort code and account number of where you would like to transfer the funds*" the disembodied voice replied.

Bob didn't take it any further this time. He glanced at the cat and put his finger to his lips. On his return that evening after feeding the cat and avoiding temptation with Alexa, he went outside as the light was fading and under the early glow of the moon started to turn things over both in his mind and the compost heap.

He didn't know what time it was when he finished at the heap but it was late. Peter would be very pleased with Bob's attention to detail. He had gone into autopilot and come out the other side with some very interesting and very dark ideas. Over the years he had never really broken the law. The odd speeding offence and had accidentally lifted the odd item of shopping without taking it back, but that night he had realised that the only way this was going to work was by going over to the dark side; not just dipping a toe in but full body and soul submersion.

He walked home by the light of the compost moon in high spirits; even if this didn't come to anything, he was enjoying the game.

Pam had gone to bed but Bob stayed up at the table, writing down his mental notes. Over the last few days he had seen some items of real value and with that day's revelations from Alexa a list was forming. Dr Roberts' extensive first edition book collection, Terry's pair of shotguns and the platinum disc collection at the big house, that lot would make a sizeable dent in the pension shortfall.

Over the next few days he carried out some initial research into some values and into the workings of voice activated computer systems. He started to put down on paper his Venn/Gantt/Flow diagram, a plan was forming. One evening later that week when this particular period of pet sitting had quietened down, Bob was sat in his armchair mulling over the shortfall when an advertisement on the television pricked his attention. Pam was about to turn it over.

"Wait" gasped Bob "I want to see this!"

"You want to watch an advert for some finance scam targeting the elderly? Ok darling, whatever you say."

That was it; Equity Release. That could be Mary's contribution to Bob's retirement package. He was wondering how she was going to pay back for all that free house-sitting. The doorbell rang. Bob got up, still deep in thought and went and opened the front door, to Terry.

"Hello Bobby!"

Christ, Bob hated that. "Sorry for the late notice again, but something has come up." Bob wasn't really listening; he was looking beyond Terry at the mother of all campervans. Terry's wife was in the passenger seat applying makeup. Terry clocked Bob looking over.

"She's a beauty, isn't she? The van I mean. 6 berth, bathroom, moped, the lot. I was just going to test her out – the van I mean, just for one night. Do you mind holding the fort mate?"

"No problem MATE!" replied Bob enthusiastically. He caught the keys this time "No problem at all!" He watched them drive away in style then grabbed his coat and called back to Pam.

"I'm off to feed Terry's cat love, I won't be long."

"But he isn't away, is he?" called Pam from the kitchen.

"He is now, see you in a bit."

It was too early to feed the cat but Bob wasn't really interested in the animal; he was more interested in the serial numbers of the guns – he would need them for his possible upcoming shotgun licence application.

Bon Chance … !

Bob sat Pam down. For the last few weeks he had been hard at it doing lots of research and at last he was ready to show Pam the fruits of his labour. He placed an exploded Venn diagram in front of her at the dining room table.

He had been careful not to leave any ghosts or trails during his research journey. Using a burner phone for the internet, he could destroy this if the idea came to nothing.

Pam studied all of her man's efforts; she carefully followed the various scenarios and flows until she reached the last box, entitled "Escape".

Underneath this box were the all-important figures.

Our house	–	£360,000
Smartin's disc collection	–	£120,000
Dr Roberts' books	–	£95,000
Mary Braces' equity release	–	£290,000
Peter Henson – Bank account	–	£150,000
Terry's guns and camper	–	£155,000
Various loans and credit cards for Pam and Bob	–	£120,000
Total	–	**£1,290,000**

"Haven't you worked hard my darling, is that really what the disc collection is worth? Well, there is only one small problem I can see with this brilliant plan, how can we ensure that they are all away on holiday at the same time?"

"I know my lover; I am working on it."

There had been several times in the past when at least 3 of these pension providers had simultaneously been away, and once 4 were absent during the same period but even with that rare overlap it would have only given Bob four days to get everything done. He could do loads of prep work and apply for the loans and credit cards but he would need longer, it would take at least a clear week to be able to carry out all the deceptions. Something would turn up, and besides, Bob was enjoying the chase. Pam sat back from the table.

"The other thing of course is the children and any possible future grandchildren; it would be hard not seeing them again."

"I know love, I am working on it and hadn't forgotten them, would you like a cup of tea?"

"Oh, yes please darling. I will get my thinking cap on."

Pam returned to the paperwork and Bob headed for the kitchen. He was pleased that Pam hadn't rubbished his ideas, she was his best and most honest critic and would have said so if he was in cloud cuckoo land. He put the kettle on. No bloody tea bags left.

"Love, we are out of tea bags, do you want something else?" he called from the kitchen.

"No we're not darling, there are some in the drawer, the ones we took from that Premier Inn last year."

Bob looked through the drawer and found a small selection of paper sachets in a sandwich bag. "English Breakfast Tea and Lady Grey by Twinnings" he murmured aloud to himself.

The slightly agricultural way in which he pronounced the name of the tea company triggered an epiphany.

Twinning!

That was it!

That's how he could guarantee that all the neighbours were all away at the same time; they could all go on holiday together!

Pam could go with them. Bob stood there, and as the kettle switched itself off, the first cog in the massive mental flow diagram machine slowly turned and put the ideas into motion. This was going to happen and it really could work.

Maisonvide …

It was mid-September by the time Bob received a response from someone at the European Commission Headquarters. Bob had asked for somewhere in the South of France, a long coach journey away, but not too far that flying would be an option. The letter contained a list of small villages who were without a suitable Twin community in the UK.

Bob knew he had to research them carefully. They would have to be appealing, have a bar, and a limited phone signal. Over the next few days, Bob worked through the list making a tick sheet of positive and negatives, and at last, one clear favourite emerged; "Maisonvide".

It was almost perfect. A little like Whiterock, and one major advantage it had over its rivals was a historical resistance to any form of union and so had very challenging communication issues.

From what Bob could glean from his research, most French communities had been actively encouraged by the central government to embrace the European ideal and link with a likeminded community in England. Looking back at Maisonvide's efforts it seemed like they didn't want to be part of the European Union and had rejected or thwarted several approaches in the past. This narrow minded outlook fitted in very well with Bob's master plan. Try as he might he couldn't even get the place on Google street view. The village had a website but this saw very little traffic.

Bob did find the place on an old French road atlas; it was a good two days' drive from the channel ports and high up in the mountains between France and Spain with only one road in and out. The road seemed to be a bit of an ongoing theme in the history of the village, it had not been maintained for many years and had proved the undoing of many previous attempts to partner-up. This was music to Bob's ears and could prove crucial if his plan was to ultimately succeed.

Bob hadn't told Pam about the teabag revelation as he had wanted to get everything sorted in his head. That isn't to say she had forgotten, far from it she had some brilliant suggestions and had found three equity release mortgage companies, two slightly dodgy antiques dealers, and she had joined the fan club of the boy Smartin's band.

The day arrived when Bob was ready to reveal his master plan. He had been waiting for a booking to be confirmed and it came whilst Bob was doing some paid work. Bob sent Pam a text GET A COUPLE OF SPECIAL BOTTLES IN X I THINK I HAVE IT! X

A single *X* back from Pam was quickly received.

They only had Mary's cat and some chickens to sort out that night. Bob was actually being nice to the cat. He had cleaned out the fishtank and didn't mind that there weren't any eggs.

Back at home, Bob had moved the flow diagram up to A3 size and Pam brought in the wine. She sat down, poured the glasses full and waited for Bob, who cleared his throat.

On the table were two copies of Bob's master flow chart. It was very professional, thought and said Pam. It ran along a weekly timescale from the social club meeting of the 3rd October, which according to the chart Bob had booked himself as the guest speaker.

From what Pam could see her brilliant husband had thought of everything. Wherever she traced her finger along the yes/no lines of his plan it always came good. She couldn't fault it. He seemed to have considered every last case scenario, the Twinning was brilliant, Pam looked up and smiled and she raised her glass to her man.

"Cheers, darling, I think you really may have something here." She smiled and sipped her wine.

Bob's face lit up, Pam was his greatest foil and the real brains behind the unit. If she thought it was good, then it might just work.

"I see you have even thought of any future grandchildren, good, I would have missed them."

The Social Club ...

Pam and Bob surveyed the inside of the Parish Hall – it was packed. Everyone they had hoped would come, had.

Pam had gone the extra mile with the catering; Vol-au-vents, quiche, baguettes, basically anything French she could think of and make.

Bob had acquired some lovely wine from a couple at the top end of the village who had shares in a vineyard. The man was a solicitor who spoke fluent French and his wife would be suspicious of anything organised by a male, so Bob had not put them on the escape plan hit list. He felt a tap on his shoulder – it was Peter, without Alexa.

"Hi Bob, well I am intrigued, I sense a French undertone? A talk about your holidays maybe?"

"No, not really Peter" replied Bob "not long now and you will find out along with everyone else – how is the compost?"

"Yes, um, sorry, yes, meant to say thank you for turning it in the night – made a big difference, tracking results with yield size alongside the rest of the gardening club, looks exciting."

"Well, I think we are nearly all here, if you don't mind Peter I would like to make a start."

Peter had a look of jealousy in his face, he wasn't involved enough and he didn't like it.

'You will be heavily involved soon enough' thought Bob.

Bob clapped his hands together and nodded at Pam (who was now sporting a striped jersey and beret). She turned off the lights and put on the PowerPoint. The background noise changed from chatting to the classic theme music from 'Allo 'Allo, they had everyone's attention.

"Madam et Monsieur's, welcome to Whiterock social evening. Pam, first frame please."

An image of an idyllic fortified French hilltop village appeared on the screen.

"Ladies and Gentleman, I give you Maisonvide. A beautiful French community high on a hill in South Western France. It has a population of some 420 souls plus a few Donkeys" (Pam changed the frame to a Donkey – everyone loves a Donkey).

"It boasts a shop, a restaurant, café, bakery, and most importantly; two bars."

(Pam continued to change the images to match Bob's speech.)

"Maisonvide, like Whiterock is missing one thing – a Twin village in the UK".

He let that hang in the air and looked around … he had all of them by les boules.

With the well-chosen PowerPoint pictures, the food and the wine, they were all sold and wanted to be in France right now. It was a cold and wet October evening outside but inside the Parish Hall it was a warm summer's days with the smell of croissants in the air.

Bob went on.

"Now Pam and I have lived here for many years and do love it but we have always felt that we as a community were missing something. We all drive through many places abroad; all proudly displaying the name of their European Twin. Some places are smaller than our own village and have much less to offer."

He paused. They were all hanging on his every word.

Pam continued with the images of France and the region around Maisonvide, the music had changed to the French national anthem.

"I would like to apologise in advance if you feel I am being too pushy or presumptuous, I just wanted to make sure that this could happen rather than disappoint everyone with false promises."

"Like the Parish Council!" someone shouted in a false voice. The hall collapsed into laughter; except for the members of the Parish Council. Bob didn't crack his face – he let the noise subside and then continued.

"I've been in contact with the European Council for Communities who put me in touch with several villages. Apologies again, but instead of endless debates and dates not matching etc. I whittled the list down to the one most similar to ourselves, hence, let me introduce: Maisonvide!"

"Good one Bob, you should be on the Council, might get some stuff done!" Came the same made up voice that sounded a lot like a falsetto Mr Smartin.

"No thanks, I don't have enough spare time after feeding all your pets to serve on the Parish Council!"

They all laughed, it went right over their heads. 'You won't find it very funny soon' smiled Bob to himself.

"I have also made first contact with the Mayor's office to express an interest in Twinning. The Mayor has replied and would love the union to take place – he has invited all of us over to his village next Easter to exchange signs and formally reach an accord".

Bob stopped as the slideshow returned to a shot of a French village square with its fountain and terraced bar in the background. Cheers and Whoops rang out accompanied by applause.

"Nice one Bob!"

"Tres Bien Pam!"

"Merci beaucoup mon ami!"

Were amongst many of the statements that could be heard coming from the audience, the place was buzzing, the village was sold on it. Peter leapt to his feet just ahead of Dr Roberts, both wanting to ride on Bob's wave.

"Ladies and gentlemen" he started "well, I am sure you will all be joining me in thanking Pam and Bob for both an amazing presentation and an incredible opportunity for the community of Whiterock."

God, he sounded like a politician. He had always seen himself as the Mayor of the village in all but name and this was his ticket. Mr Smartin was having none of it, he stood up and made his way to the front, the hall was still buzzing and the occupants were cheering the golden couple. This had drowned out most of what Peter had said, his timing was wrong, everyone had seen right through it. Mr Smartin approached Bob.

"So Bob, good show, good man, now do you want to see this through, you've done all the leg work and I wouldn't want to have anyone, including the mayor of Trumpton over there stealing your thunder."

This precise conversation had appeared on Bob's latest version of the flow chart.

"Pam and I have enjoyed doing this but it has been quite time consuming, so we are happy to take a back seat now and let someone else actually organise the trip." Replied Bob.

"Right you are Bob, message received and understood, let me sort this out, by the way, top man Bob, top man!" Mr Smartin turned to the still wildly excited crowd and called for some semblance of order.

"Fellow Whiterockians, I have just had a chat with Bob here and to keep this very exciting momentum going he would like to hand over the reins, now I suggest we do it here and now. Who amongst you is interested in taking on the mantle?"

Surprise, surprise Peter put his hand up, new man Terry put his up too.

"Right then, that is two nominations, we will do this on a show of hands, all those in favour of Peter please raise your right arm ..."

Four people, including Peter, put up an arm.

"All those for Terry?"

The remaining 37 right arms in the room went up and 1 left arm from Clive who had been involved in a nasty strimming incident a few years back. Bob and Pam didn't vote.

"Right, there we have it, the baton is passed to Terry."

A ripple of applause sprang up, more out of relief that Peter wasn't holding the baton than for the newcomer himself. Terry and his glamorous wife made their way to the front, she was called Jean and was more than happy to help; as a trip abroad meant lots of duty free makeup. Terry was about to speak when Bob tapped him on the shoulder.

"May I just finish up please Terry?"

"Bob, mate, you can do just about anything you want right now, knock yourself out."

Bob cleared his throat, ready to cast out his last tasty fly.

"My friends, just a last couple of bits before Pam and I hand over. I will of course be around to help Terry and Jean get up to speed, my last contact with the Mayor of Maisonvide brought up a possible date for our first visit during the Easter holidays, the week beginning April the 10th. I went out on a limb and said yes, it is a special time in their village as they have a festival of flowers and wine."

A huge cheer went up and people started checking their phones for clashes and booking it in the diary section. Jean was nodding and making notes.

"Now, please don't feel bad about this last bit of news as it actually benefits you all, my dear mother needs to have a very serious operation, (she had died some 6 years before this meeting), it is booked for early April and I need to be here to help her through the early recovery period so I won't be coming with you on the first visit. Pam of course will be going, however, it does mean that I will be available for pet feeding and house guarding.

A combination of cheers and 'Ah's' went up. All this work and then not able to come but Bob could still look after the pets; what a guy! And caring for his poorly mum too – wow he is the man!

Terry and Jean stepped forwards and Bob moved back and went to Pam's side. He squeezed her hand and smiled.

"This is it my darling. The game's afoot!"

Terry cleared his throat.

"Well folks, you heard the man, April 10th it is. Those who are interested in making the trip please leave all your details with Jean on the way out. I would also like to continue Bob's most welcome change in the way he deals with matters and invite Peter to act as Vice-Chair of the new Twinning Group 'Entente cordiale!' I believe is the phrase".

Peter nearly fell off his stool. Terry continued:

"Peter, Jean and I will get some prices on transport and confirmed dates by the end of November, it only remains for me to say don't forget to renew any passports and three cheers for Bob and Pam! Hip Hip …"

Last Christmas … ?

Bob and Pam had been invited to no less than fourteen Christmas parties that year. There was one evening with three on at the same time, Bob went to one, Pam the other and then they met up together at the third venue; Terry and Jean's.

The house was a reflection of Jean's beauty regime; a lot of make-up hiding a bit of a wreck.

Whenever Bob appeared it was always accompanied by much back-slapping, he was still King of the Village.

Pam was always greeted with a double-cheek continental kiss, which had now become the norm for the village, much to the delight of the postman.

Terry made his way over to greet the king.

"Bob mate, thanks so much for coming tonight, and honouring us with your presence!" Bob smiled "Now I wonder if I might show you something? Let me get you a drink first." he motioned for Bob to follow him, got him a mulled wine and went into the kitchen.

Terry handed Bob a fancy bit of paper, it was an invitation letter confirming all the details of the forthcoming Twinning trip.

The Whiterock Twinning Group
Departing the Parish
10th April 2020
To Maisonvide:
Return coach, ferry, and all hotels £490
All interested parties must register with Madame Jean
By the last day of January with payment in full.
Please complete the personal information section on the back.
Merci pour votre compréhension

"We have had an amazing response to this – nearly half the village seems to be coming!"

"I know" said Bob "I'm looking after all the pets!"

"Oh, would you do ours? Sorry to ask but I probably need to get in there quick. Peter has had to book an extra-large coach to accommodate everyone. The Parish Hall Committee has subsidised some of the cost so we are able to keep things cheap. I have spoken to the Mayor of Maisonvide, very good English, he mentioned something about the roads and suggested we all stayed in a hotel this time and then partner up with host families on the next visit."

Bob knew this already as the contact number for the Mayor of Maisonvide was the number of his own new phone which he had bought on the internet from a French Telecoms site, he was pleased that his accent had been so convincing.

"Terry, I wonder if I could ask your advice on something?"

"Fire away Bob, anything for you."

"I am thinking about getting a campervan and wondered if I could have a look at yours?"

"No problem mate, come on let's take our drinks out to the old girl now!"

Terry showed Bob through to the internal garage and there she stood; an enormous Florium something or other. What a beauty; six berth, shower room, separate WC, better TV and sound system than Bob's house.

"What's the security system like?" Bob asked; taking everything in.

"Amazing mate, it has an enhanced alarm system for any forced entry but best of all is a discreet tracking system linked to the company's own satellite so it can be followed on my phone."

"Wow!" said Bob "Can I see it? I mean is it easy to install and … can I afford it?"

"It's tiny, ours is fixed to the top of the front glovebox, it's wireless but it wasn't cheap. Two grand plus and an annual members' fee, but what price can you put on peace of mind? Come on Bob, let's get back and join the others before tongues start wagging!"

Bob winced and followed Terry back watching carefully where he put the keys to the van. He then caught Pam's eye, went to her side and gave her a gentle squeeze.

"Hello lover, I think I may have got transport sorted, how are you getting on?"

Pam smiled. "Almost there, we have done well tonight. Got Dr Roberts and her cats, Peter and his compost heap, his unusual daughter is going to

France too. Mary Braces already in the bag, just Mr Smartin and Terry to go."

Bob beamed.

"Just got Terry and Jean, so only one left. I will go up and see him over Christmas. Shouldn't be too difficult. Shall we make a move?"

They left quickly and were not missed. As they walked the short distance home, Bob turned to Pam and looked straight into her eyes.

"Darling, the beauty of this is that we can stop any time before April 10th and no one will ever know we were even planning anything. So if you are having any doubts, tell me. We are only doing this as a team."

Pam gave him a kiss on the cheek.

"My lovely man, we have lived among these people for years and tonight at the party Mr Mangoe called me Pat! So no, I am not having any doubts, let's screw the lot of them over."

They carried on walking, and didn't need to say anything else. At home Pam filled in her Twinning trip application form.

"Feels funny just doing this for me, are you sure you can handle everything here?"

"It will be tight darling, so it will be good to know you're with them, my insider knowledge girl. We will only be apart for a week, then we will be stuck together forever, you will soon be sick of me."

"Never!"

Pam put the form in an envelope addressed to Peter.

"There, too late now."

The next day, another piece of the jigsaw was turned and slotted into its place. All the edge pieces of the retirement puzzle were now complete. Pam and Bob had been invited to Christmas Eve drinks with the Smartin's up at the big house. A real honour. The famous son and his current beau would be there. Bob embraced this news and adjusted his flow chart to suit. 'The boy coming home for Christmas, Bonus' he thought.

Mr Smartin met them both at the grand front door.

"Lovely to see you Bob, and you've brought your daughter along I see!"

He had said this the last time they had seen him, and the time before that. What a turkey.

Pam giggled like she hadn't heard it before.

"Pam, go on through would you, I need to run something past your man here, won't be a jiffy. The boy is through there with some ghastly vacant Dutch girl, be right behind you."

Pam smiled and went through to join the throng.

"Now Bob, listen, couple of things, never a good time, so here it is. Could you look after The Major, you know, when we hop over the Briney, don't want to rub it in or anything what with your mother etcetera … how is the old girl?"

"Very still." Replied Bob.

"Yes, I'm sure she is, anyway, you know the rules, press and suchlike, thanks, anyway, second thing is good news, had a chat with the other Twinners and we would all like to pay for young Pam's trip, on us you know, told Peter, already squared it, ok, least we could do, come on, no words needed, let's drink enough to not let anything really matter!"

He slapped Bob on the back and practically pushed him through the door.

Everyone who was anyone was there, only a very select few from the village had been invited. Terry, Jean, and Dr Roberts.

All the members of the band were there, and the WAGs. What a golden opportunity. Bob didn't mind tugging his yokel forelock. He was thinking of the bigger picture and at the moment he meant that literally. It would probably be better coming from the head of the household so Bob, drink in hand, sidled up to Mr Smartin.

"Look neighbour, straight bat and all that, in exchange for all my cat-sitting duties over the years, please can I ask just one favour of you and your son? One photo of just me in the middle of the band and all their autographs? I know it sounds like a really peasant thing but I doubt I will ever get the chance again, something for the grandchildren."

Mr Smartin smiled at Bob. "For you Bob, not a problem, I am sure the boys will be delighted, to be honest most people are afraid to ask. I will set it up for you, anywhere in particular? Music room perhaps?"

'Aligning planets or what?' thought Bob as he stood in the middle of the band in front of the awards wall, holding a piece of paper with all the group's autographs, you couldn't have made it up. Pam took loads of pictures. They thanked the band members and moved on through to the sitting room to make small talk with the various guests, the majority envious of Bob's photo shoot. Terry and Jean made a bee line for them. The pair were almost overawed by so many celebrities and so much glamour; Terry had had a few sherbets and was in a good festive mood.

"Evening you two, wow what a do, I love a nibble or three, don't I love?"

Jean had so much foundation on you couldn't tell if she was blushing or not.

"Now, if you will excuse me, I need to make a very important phone call before it gets too late."

The assembled group all nodded their approval, Terry reached for his phone and brought it close to his mouth.

"The Mayor" he said to it.

Bobs left pocket started to vibrate violently, he nudged Pam who sensed he needed a distraction. She dropped her vol-au-vent on the floor and Bob used this minor savoury food incident as cover and excused himself. He dived out into the hallway to answer his second phone.

"Oui, Allo!" He blurted out.

"Ah, bonsoir monsieur Marie" Terry began, "I just wanted to wish you une joyous Noel from everyone here in Whiterock!"

"Ah, merci Monsieur Terry, a very 'appy Christmas to you all aussi" replied Bob, in the hallway, in his very best French accent. "We are all looking forward to your visit in the new year."

"Thank you, your worship, I hope it's not too late over there, I must say it is a very good line, you could be in the next room – isn't technology amazing. I will let you get back to your festive party; it sounds like a fun one."

"Oui, oui, tres bien, you too and thank you for calling, bon soiree!" Bob hung up. Phew that was close. He took a deep breath and returned to the fray.

"Here you go love, another Vol-au-vent, everything ok here?"

Terry looked up from checking his emails and the status of his campervan on his phone.

"Ah Bob, the Mayor of Maisonvide sends his regards to one and all, he was at a Christmas party, sounded like a riot."

"Excellent news Terry and thank you and the all the others for your special gift to Pam, I haven't told her yet, would you do the honours?"

"Of course. Pam, the Twinning committee all agreed that we should cover the cost of your trip to France, after all your hard work in setting it up and of course for Bob agreeing to hold the fort back here."

Pam smiled. "Well that is so kind of you all, I feel very moved. Thank you Terry and all the committee, now I am sorry but we will have to make a move, we have an early start tomorrow. Mary is away for Christmas day and we are doing the stockings for the hens!"

All the farewells and season's greetings took well over an hour, and as they left the big house it was starting to snow. Pam cuddled up to Bob as they walked home together.

"Won't you miss all this?" Although directed at Bob she was actually asking herself.

"No love, I won't. I have been really careful in choosing our final destination, they have all the seasons there, just much longer and hotter summer days. They enjoy Christmas like us, the only thing to miss will be the people and let's face it after the number we are about to do on them, I can't imagine anyone in the village would want to see us again, unless we were strung up in the Twisted Oak." Bob replied.

"You are right of course my darling; it will just take some getting used to that's all. I mean after all these years in the village we don't really have any good friends, they have all just taken advantage of our good nature, to hell with them all."

Bob squeezed her hand, he would really miss England, especially at this time of year, no one really did Christmas quite like the British. He awoke early on Christmas day, he went around to Mary's place, did all the chores and was home putting together Pam's stocking before she had even stirred. He always did a stocking for Pam, even now, well after the children and Father Christmas had left the building. He enjoyed buying things for her, because he loved her.

A New Year's Revolution ...

"Happy New Year my darling!" whispered Pam.

The fireworks were going nuts in front of Big Ben on the television.

"I think that apart from the year I met you this is going to be the best year ever" replied Bob "I am so excited about the future, not many people have the chance to start out all over again, a whole new life, woo hoo! A Happy New Year to you too gorgeous" he chinked glasses with Pam.

They had been invited to numerous parties to welcome in the New Year, but now the work really started so they had declined all but one, a first footing to Mary's open house tomorrow.

They both arrived purposefully early and caught Mary doing the finishing touches to her outfit.

"Happy New Year neighbour" said Bob as he offered her a lump of coal, "sorry we are so early but we have a favour to ask of you."

Mary declined to handle the coal and motioned Bob's hand towards the hall table, she did look a bit put out and an audible tut escaped from her hens' arse mouth.

"What is it that you want from me?" she almost snapped at them.

"Oh, sorry Mary" Bob offered before he turned on the charm machine "it's quite personal and what with your high standing in the village, Pam and I were wondering if you would witness our wills, it is one of our New Year's resolutions to get our house in order."

Mary changed her outlook and tone almost immediately; she loved being bigged up.

"No problem, what a good idea, of course I will, everyone can take me as I am for the party. Bring the paperwork through to the withdrawing room."

They all sat down at the table and Bob placed a couple of sheets of paper in front of Mary.

"These are the two wills, Mary, and I also have the deeds to our house. There is a cover note to witness as well, thank you so much for doing this for us."

Mary made a big scene of putting on her reading glasses and carefully going through the papers, trying to give the impression that she had done this before on numerous occasions which she hadn't! She then signed the wills and moved them towards Pam, before replacing her pen lid with a theatrical flourish.

"Now what is it about your deeds I need to address?"

"Well Mary, I am sure I don't need to tell you that the government recently issued some advice that if you no longer had a mortgage and held your own deeds then you need to put them with your last will and testament. This will ensure that all the estate is considered and makes things easier for the ones you leave behind". Bob placed on form on the table.

Mary wasn't going to have this told to her without saying anything, she reacted exactly as Bob and his flow chart had predicted and hoped for.

"Of course I realised that's what you were after, I remember my accountant, John Wilson sending me an email to that effect some time ago. I finished paying off my mortgage some seven years ago now, look let's kill two birds with one stone. So to speak, let me take a copy of your form as I have filed mine away somewhere or the cleaner has destroyed it. I will attach it to my deeds, just to keep the money people happy of course."

"No problem Mary, help yourself" Bob handed her the form that he had produced over Christmas, it looked very professional. Mary took the form and went over to her desk and placed it on the scanner/printer, which she turned on and set to work, she then ran her fingers along the bookshelf until she came to a book titled 'There's no place like home'. She pulled the hollow tome from the shelf, it was one of those false books that turned into a secret box file. She reached inside and pulled out the deeds to her house. The printer spat out a copy of the form and Mary retrieved it and put it with her deeds. She wasn't however going to lose the higher ground and let Bob or Pam witness her form, she had a friend from the bridge club who had been awarded a BEM in recognition of all the countless people she had bored into an early grave, Mary would get them to witness her form instead.

She returned with the original form and placed it on the table, Bob marked the page with a cross and Mary signed it in an overly elaborate manner. It wouldn't matter, the carbon inlay paper would capture it for future use.

Someone coughed at the door, it was Peter Henson.

"Happy New Year one and all!"

Bob and Pam got up.

"What an exciting year it will be too, only four months until the big adventure!" exclaimed Peter excitedly. "Nearly everything is confirmed now, just a few glitches with accessing their website, you still up for minding the house Bob, no compost this time!"

"Yes, no problem at all Peter, Pam is getting very excited and a Happy New Year to you too."

Bob made a mental note about the website. The house started filling up, it felt like the entire village had been invited and turned up in pairs or small groups. There was a real buzz about the place, all talk was about France, not Christmas past or even pot-holes.

Dr Roberts had raised the excitement levels even more by announcing the arrival of the official Twinning signs. These were to be placed at either end of the parish boundary on the side of the main road. A date was set for a small ceremony early in the New Year, before the visit, so that pictures could be taken on the trip to show the inhabitants of Maisonvide.

Bob and Pam stayed for about an hour, wished everyone a happy New Year, made their excuses, and left for the very short journey home.

Bob closed the front door behind them and made for the hall cupboard to retrieve the master flow chart.

"Right my love, that was a job well done. I knew Mary would fall for it. Now the work really starts, a new year, a new updated flow chart. No mistakes, always an alternative route, always a get out clause and never be the canoe couple."

Bob got out his large flip chart pad and set to work with Pam by his side, checking it and questioning it. Together they spent the whole of the rest of New Year's day on the plan and as night crept on it really took shape and looked like it might even work. Pam poured out a large glass of Pendryn whisky for Bob and they sat back to admire their labours.

1. **Dr Roberts.** Sell the entire book collection to one main dealer. Back story is that her house is actually Bob's Mum's place, and that Bob is having to sell the house and majority of the contents to fund his elderly mother's care. Contact already made with a Mr Bird, a specialist dealer,

who has been invited to view and make a cash offer on the 12th Feb as Dr Roberts is to be away at a nursing college reunion in Buxton for five days. Alternative route – Bob to photograph the collection ready to send to the dealer in case the reunion was cancelled. Dealer to pay for and collect books the day after the Twinning trip leaves England. Cash on collection estimated to be around £80-90,000.

2. **Mary Braces.** Sell 90% equity in house to Key Equity Release. All legal works to be completed beforehand, signing and contract exchange during week leading up to Twinning trip, money to be cleared through Bob's new French account at Credit Agricole. Back story: Pam is Mary! Key Equity Advisor knows that Mary lives abroad and wishes to release capital to continue with this lifestyle. The agent, called Mark, understands that Mary is often in Spain and only pops back now and again to check on things but is happy to be there for valuation and contract signing. Next time Mary goes away Pam will call to arrange the home visit and show the deeds etc. all communication to be through Pam's mobile, signature from Bob's last will and testament being practised and looking good. Initial valuation carried out at £340,000. Mary to settle for around £290,000. Key ER quite greedy and can't believe people actually go ahead with their deals, so not really looking in much detail – back story not in place yet as quite low risk, but Bob to work on something.

3. **The Smartins.** Band memorabilia from music room, to date the most difficult to execute due to the high profile of the seller. Via contact with an agent from the Fanzone, a wealthy collector from the Far East has been identified. Bob to pursue, language barrier a bit of an issue but progress being made. Mr Smartin away quite a lot so the actual deal can be sorted in the days after the Twinning party set off for Maisonvide. Back story is that Bob is the main assistant to the band's manager but keeps out of the limelight (the Christmas group photo will add credence). The group are about to enter an exciting new creative phase and need to separate themselves from the past. They want a conscious uncoupling. Total discretion is required from the buyer or no deal. Any leak in the run up to the transaction will make the sale null and void. The handover will take place at the Smartin's house to add authenticity; transaction in cash – figure in the region of £120,000. A presale viewing from the buyer is acceptable by arrangement with Bob.

4. **Peter Henson.** Clear out all accessible funds using Alexa. Explore

early cash-in of pension and possible equity release? Hopefully no back story needed as all can be completed during the Twinning trip, will need to get to Alexa as soon as practicable and after Pam gives the all clear from the ferry. All funds to be transferred directly to Bob's new account. Need to try and restrict Peter's access to phone and internet whilst away as he is probably up to speed with technology and internet banking. Fortunately phone signal quite unreliable for most of the trip. Financial outcome dependant on stock market and pension cash in offer, but hope to realise in excess of £150,000.

5. **Terry and Jean.** Sale of shotguns and campervan, so far quite straight forward, two potential buyers sourced from gun collector magazine, buyers known to each other so a bidding war has started. BACs transfer or cash on collection. Bob to pose as Terry, signature practised and looking good. Back story is that Terry (Bob) is finally selling the gun collection that belonged to his late father as they bring back too many memories. Bob to use the campervan as the means to leave Whiterock for the last time. During the lead up to Bob's departure the campervan's advanced tracking system is to be removed and hidden aboard a suitable decoy which can be chosen from the nearby service station. The campervan itself will be part exchanged at the earliest opportunity once safely on French soil. The sale of the shotguns should produce around £130,000 at current market estimates and a quick scan of garages close to the port of Roscoff shows that a decent onward vehicle could be had with up to €30,000 cash back. New part-exchanged vehicle needs to be capable of transporting the small amount of personal items that Pam deems essential.

Bob put his marker pen down with conviction.

"God, this really is it, we are going to do this aren't we?"

Pam said in a tone that Bob didn't recognise, it had a realisation in it. This was it. No going back unless to prison; never to return to Devonshire. Bob firmly squeezed his partner's hand.

"Are you having second thoughts love?" He enquired softly.

"No, absolutely not my darling, just taking it all on board. This is really going to hurt these people, isn't it? I mean what will Mary do? We are practically selling her house."

Bob folded away the master chart, sat down, took both her hands across the table and looked straight into her eyes.

"Look love, I know these people have never really done anything bad to us apart from taking advantage of our generous nature and at times being down right rude. They are only things; objects. I am sure the equity release contract won't go through, Terry could get his guns back and the band could get replacement discs if they wanted. Yes, I grant you it might be tricky for Peter getting his money back but you never know he might get some compensation from Microsoft or Google for showing them a glitch in their technology."

He paused as if he needed to convince himself, to try and justify it all, but he couldn't and didn't really need to.

"Pam love, it is theft, and of the worst kind. I am not going to try and excuse it. We have decided on this path, never to return, and yes that will be hard and yes for a long time we will be watching over our shoulders, but it will be worth it. This could add years to our lives, never have to work again, never have to feed another bloody animal except our own, but we can stop now if you want, all this is undoable. I will do what you want."

The pause was short before Pam spoke.

"Bob, we are only here once darling, one shot, let's do it. It's actually very exciting. If we do this properly we will be the envy of many people. So no canoe man! The perfect crime please."

Bob smiled.

"For you my love, it will be perfect."

Family matters ...

"Bugger me it's cold." Bob spluttered as he entered the hallway. Pam bought the kettle to the boil.

"Mary's going away for a long Valentine weekend and asked, well, told me we were to watch the house."

"Watch the house, cheeky cow. Sell the house more like!" Pam scoffed.

Bob chuckled. "Good timing though. I will firm up the retirement equity company, what day is she off?"

"She goes on the 12th and back on the 15th, should be enough to confirm the details, don't you think?"

"Plenty" replied Bob "these equity release vultures can't wait to tie you down to a death grip. Any post?"

"Yes, one for you, looks French."

All Bob's new bank account details had turned up. French bank "Credit Agricole" with British and European streams based in Jersey, would be difficult to unpick for a while.

"Excellent, now we need to start filling it." Said Bob with a twinkle in his eye..

Their own house had sold very quickly. No signs had been placed outside, obviously, yes they had received slightly less than the market value but they needed it to be discreet.

The contracts were to be exchanged on April 1st, money transfer on the 4th and vacant possession on 16th. Time was moving fast. Bob still needed to get away to France for a few days in early March to carry out a recce of Maisonvide and the surrounding area. The first and second week of April was flat out, he had bought them six days minimum, eight at the most. As long as no one let them down he should be able to do it.

"I will see if I can book a ferry for the 2nd March and be away for five days. I shouldn't think anyone will notice, did you manage to book one of those storage units?"

Pam nodded "I paid them a year's rent in advance. Put it all in the children's names, well we won't need any of it. I will start to box things up next week and we can slowly start to shift it down there."

"Nice one darling, what shall we tell the children? I thought about saying we were selling up and travelling the world before we retired to somewhere smaller near Dawlish or Sidmouth."

Pam thought about this for a while.

"Yes, good idea, and let's get them both here for a meal, for old time's sake sort of thing. I will arrange for it to happen before you go to France."

Bob got out the laptop and went straight to the Maisonvide website; the one he had recently taken over after a new set up.

Two messages to check. Now the main reason Maisonvide was on the European Commission Twinning website and had remained on there for over 15 years without a bite was due to its location; yes, it was lovely, untouched, very French but quite cut off. The only road to the hilltop was precarious to say the least. The track clung to the contours of a steep sided canyon. It had little or no safety barriers along its nine-mile length. Deep below at river level lay the decaying rusted remains of several vehicles – mostly French, but with the odd smattering of ill-advised hire cars.

Bob had tried to follow the route on Google Earth before, but even the camera car had given up halfway. A small portable version had made it to the village square on foot or hoof to record images of this isolated community.

An enthusiastic newcomer to the village had, some time ago, put Maisonvide onto the list of potential Twinning partners in line with government guidelines; but without success, much to the relief of most of the locals.

The village website, like some of its houses had fallen into disrepair. Bob, with help from some IT geeks on a website development evening class at the local college, had resurrected it. He was now the controller.

Back in the early days of his escape plan he had extensively researched the village. The website had a clock that had stopped and it had had only 167 views in its twelve years of existence. Bob had taken the site contents along to the evening class as a working example. The lecturer, Dr Price, and class, had seized on his initiative, made it bloom and handed it back to Bob, who then went on to delete all contents about the precarious roads, accident numbers, and an article on dwindling population figures.

There had obviously been a rise in recent visits and traffic to the website. Bob was having to work quite hard at keeping it ticking over; especially where Peter was concerned. Christ, he'd even followed links from the main site to a fictitious doctors' surgery and had asked a question on access to drugs for his various conditions. Bob got Pam to answer these questions as she was more medically orientated.

Pam looked around the corner.

"The children will be over next Sunday for lunch so book your ticket for any time after that love."

Bob returned to the website questions. Big surprise, one from Peter to the Twinning chairman.

"Can I have the details of my Twin, so to speak, so that I can contact them prior to my arrival with some advanced medical/health requirements?"

Awkward, thought Bob. I need to be careful here. If I give him contact details he will spread the word and everyone will want one. Too much to set up and work on. If I fob him off he might smell a rat. His hands hovered over the keyboard.

Mon amis, I am afeared that we cannot assist you, this visit will be mostly based around the hotel. We do have a potential link family, who you will meet. Perhaps you can speak with them around your concerns.

That will do for now, thought Bob and moved to the second enquiry.

Would there be any chance of any fishing nearby? Asked Mr Mangoe.

Bob replied.

Yes of course Monsieur. The region is blessed by many clean and rich rivers; I am sure we can accommodate this. Please make this request aware with the hotel on your arrival.

Bob went to the Brittany Ferries website and booked his ticket for the following week; a five-day return. Seemed strange going without Pam, but it had to be done.

"Right darling, all set for tomorrow's sign unveiling?"

Anyone who was interested met at the Parish Hall the next evening, Dr Roberts had raided her own extensive wine cellar and supplied the drinks.

"Good turnout on such a crap night." Terry offered to anyone who was listening. At least forty souls had ventured out for the unveiling. The two signs had been propped up on chairs and hastily covered in some old stage curtains, Dr Roberts coughed. She had a heavy cold, but it served to get everyone's attention.

"Madam et Monsieur, thank you all for coming out on such a foul evening. As promised, the committee have acquired the relevant signage to the current European standard. Now I haven't asked him yet but I would like to move that Bob do the honours and unveil the official Twinning signs."

Bob was momentarily caught out, but to great applause he stepped forward and surveyed the room. Little did they know, he thought to himself.

"Dr Roberts, well, this is a genuine surprise and I would like to thank you all for your kindness. Fortunately for you all I am a man of few words so without further ado I would like to officially unveil your new signage, not long now and you will all be there!"

To heightened cheers and applause he pulled the old stage curtains aside to reveal two lovely new Devon County Council standard road signs.

"Welcome to Whiterock
Twinned with Maisonvide"

Dr Roberts stepped forward.

"Thank you Bob, well I am sure you will all agree that these will lift our community to new heights of international friendship and they are a lot smarter than the ones down the road at Tedborn St Marjory. The highways officer says we can erect them on our return from France, when we have the official paperwork."

The gathering all clapped and went to charge their glasses while Peter organised a photo shoot ready for the Parish magazine. Some strange, and until now deeply hidden, dark part of Bob's soul put its hand up and nudged him.

"Peter, can I have a photo please, just me and the signs?" He blurted out.

"But of course Bob, I was going to ask you anyway." (He wasn't)

Peter sidled the committee members out of the way and moved Bob into position. Bob put on his most enigmatic smile 'this is the one that all the press will want to use when the true story breaks out' thought Bob. He was a little shocked that his personality contained such a bad section but he supposed that in the scheme of completely wiping out your neighbours it wasn't actually that surprising.

Bob's shotgun licence application form came back the day before the children returned to the nest. A home visit was needed to check he had a secure cabinet fixed to a wall, he put a call in to Terry.

"Result love, Terry has a spare gun cabinet (Bob knew this from a cat feeding nose about), he says I can borrow it for the visit of the licencing officer and he might sell it to me if I am successful, the cheeky git! Anyway ironic or what?"

Bob updated his flow chart with the date of the visit, he then spent a while on his Maisonvide website. He added a few details about the upcoming wine festival and noticed that there had been 18 more visits to the site since he had last checked in. Peter had not added any stupid questions about the availability of corn plasters. The website was looking good; he was proud of himself. 'Looks like a nice place to visit' he thought to himself.

Both children arrived within fifteen minutes of each other. Pam had never really been much of a clucker around the pair, which had paid off as they were both very independent. The whole family loved each other deeply, all conversation was sincere and listened to, which was refreshing. Both respective partners were good people and they were well matched. Following the normal greetings, catch up and small talk, they all drifted towards the table.

"Right then oldies, what's all this about?" Their son Andrew got there first.

"Well, you four, firstly we are not that old and secondly we have some important news …"

Bob was about to continue when his daughter Andrea, (Bob and Pam both really liked the name Andrew) interrupted.

"Mum, Dad and big bro, we too have news, shall we go first? (She carried on anyway) It's in two parts. David has been offered a promotion, but it will mean moving to Brussels for at least five years and so your first grandchild will be half Belgium!"

There was silence for a moment.

"I have bought a new motorbike!"

Offered Andrew to break the spell.

"Look mum, I was sure you wouldn't be offended in the slightest, I don't want you to think that I don't want you or Dad involved with the upbringing." Continued a concerned Andrea.

Pam moved across the room and gave her daughter a huge, lingering hug, the type where you become one entity.

"Darling, we are so happy for you and for your promotion David, we are both very proud … What bike did you get son?"

Everyone laughed.

"An old Enfield, anyway, what was your news?"

Pam smiled, becoming a Grandmother wasn't going to change anything about the escape plan, the children had to make their own journey through life. In fact, her resolve was steeled even more, she and Bob could provide financially for the new comer and forever more they would be known as the exciting, notorious, adventurous but a bit naughty Grandparents.

"Your father and I ..."

"Who are you? The bloody Queen?!" Andrew put in.

"Sorry, me and your Dad have decided to take a change of direction in life, we have found ourselves in a bit of a rut. The rut was in a road heading downhill and at the end was sheltered accommodation. We have had an epiphany. We are currently making arrangements to leave on a big trip, before it is too late. When we go we will give Andrew some keys and a note. We ask only two things of you all, first, don't ask us any questions and second, trust us that even if you don't hear from us for a long time all will be ok in time, how does that sound?"

Pam was aware that this all sounded very odd and waited for the reaction, Andrew went first.

"Wow! Mysterious or what, but it suits me and as long as you two are happy and safe then I really don't mind what you get up to. So, sis, I am to be an Uncle, cool beans, when is the baby due?"

That was it, no questions were asked, it was forgotten, they were trusted.

All talk was of babies, Belgium, Tintin (possible baby name) and Royal Enfield motorcycles. Bob and Pam watched their little brood and were pleased with the way they had turned out.

They both realised that the consequences of their near future actions would be water off a duck's back. A grandchild growing up in Belgium would be better off and a little bit closer to them and Andrew could always take Emma off for a long bike ride.

Bob's Brexit ...

"You be alright to feed the cat love?" Bob had his small bag packed and ready in the hall.

"Sod off you saucy git."

Came the retort from Pam.

"I am away my love. I have hidden all the planning charts and just put a couple of things down on a to do list for you. Don't forget to sign those forms from the equity release company and send them off, I will keep an eye on the website and while I am away I might even call Terry or Peter from a French phone to add some real authenticity."

They met in the hallway and held each other deeply and closely, Pam kissed her man.

"Away quick, return quicker."

This was only the second time he had been away without Pam in their entire relationship. It was only an hour to Plymouth in his old but trusty Volvo estate, and he went straight through check in and border control. It was very quiet; only the seasoned Francophiles were booked on this March crossing.

The pop-up coffee van was shut so Bob stayed in the car listening through gritted ears to Radio Devon. The traffic news had just reported that a trailer parked in a layby near Kingsteignton was sticking out a bit and might cause an accident. "Yes, thanks for that important update Bill you dickhead!" Uttered Bob to his empty car.

He had already spotted two likely contenders for the 'I can't remember where I parked my car, despite being told twice and been given a card with the deck and door number on it' competition that would be held the following morning during disembarkation.

Just as his line was about to move forward for embarkation, one of the contenders, a halfwit driving a Rover pulling a caravan, decided that now was a good time to check the inner workings of his chemical toilet. Bob didn't mind waiting as he loved to watch people.

"Bon soir Monsieur, you are parked near to the D5 exit."

The heavily made up French girl, who was in this job as she was clearly too short to be considered for aircraft cabin crew, handed him a card with this information stated on it.

Bob said thanks and made his way up to the bar. It was very quiet, probably running at only 40% capacity. Pierre Bear, the Brittany Ferries' mascot was half-heartedly greeting the few children that were travelling.

Bob ordered himself a pint of Guinness and oddly a packet of Marlboro; less than a fiver a packet and an unhealthy holiday treat. He took his purchases out on to the deck as the engines powered up to sailing speed. He set himself up on a table overlooking the harbour. The boat did its signature lurch as the massive ropes let go their tautness. Like a giant spider releasing its prey from the clutches of a sticky web.

The Armourique slipped out of her berth and headed for the breakwater past Drake's Island. Bob lit a cigarette, had a sup, and settled back to savour his own company as the ship left the beautiful Devonshire coast and headed into the Channel. The next time he did this, next month, could be the last time he ever did. It felt strange being on his own. He was completely anonymous.

The entertainment made a meek start, the holiday season hadn't really started so it must be hard trying to work the depleted crowd. The person who had dressed up as a slightly sinister looking bear was also the magician and ran the colouring competition.

Bob returned to the bar via the stage area. He carefully picked up a cup of crayons and the colouring contest sheet. He ordered another Guinness and took it to a quiet corner to complete his entry; his dark side was showing again.

He drew and coloured exactly what the judges would want to see; the company logo on a sailing ship passing in front of Mont St Michel on a sunny day. Brilliant! He dropped it on to the table by the small stage without anyone seeing and headed for the bar to buy a nightcap to take to his cabin.

He called Pam and told her he loved and missed her, then followed up the call with a text saying much the same; just before the British signal was lost. The ships intercom crackled into life.

"Madame, Monsieur et les enfants, there were lots of very high quality entries for the colouring competition, but I am afraid there can be only one winner. The winner is Bobby, will little Bobby please come to the stage and collect his prize, that's Bobby to the stage area please."

Little Bobby turned off his light and drifted off deep into the land of nod.

If you have never done it, then you need to do it before you die; that is to be woken up on a Brittany ferries ship. A beautiful, haunting and hypnotic Gaelic ballad brings you back from the depths of seaborn sleep. It slowly increases in volume and tempo to raise you from your pit.

Bob awoke, washed, and headed for his breakfast of a large coffee, OJ and a warm croissant. The Tannoy system announced that they would be arriving shortly at the port of Roscoff. It went on to say that Bobby mustn't be shy and that he could still pick up his prize should he wish.

He made his way to D5 with another large coffee, disappointingly two of his three contenders had already found their vehicles, but there was always hope. Sure enough his favourites for the prize were nowhere to be seen. He felt the ship docking and before long the cars up ahead of him started up their engines and put on the lights.

A couple appeared at the door marked D5 about six cars down from where Bob was sitting, they looked around, couldn't see their car and went back inside again. Less than a minute later they reappeared and filed passed Bob. She was holding the card given to her and was shouting at her partner. He was carrying an unfeasibly large Toblerone and was gesticulating madly towards the far corner. They had clearly won the prize.

Bob subtly checked their progress in his rear view mirror and witnessed them actually walk past their own car before double backing and finally getting in just as the queue moved off. 'What a couple of twats', thought Bob. Had mankind really reached this level? And these two idiots were about to be released onto the French road network.

Although he realised that next time would be very different, Bob left the port without incident; security and border control were barely in evidence. He carefully positioned himself on the right hand lane of the road and headed for Morlaix, which was the first big centre of commerce in this otherwise sparsely populated agricultural part of North Western France.

Before he entered the town he turned off and drove around the main industrial estate looking for a large unit that sold campervans. It didn't take long to find it and there was a massive selection of vehicles; although none looked as large as Terry's. Bob pulled in and parked up. A dapper looking middle aged man with fashionable blue rimmed spectacles appeared out of the showroom and approached.

"Parles vous Anglais Monsieur?" Bob enquired.

"Un peu Monsieur." Came the response.

Bob's French was pretty good and always improved as the trips went on. He understood perhaps 80% as long as they didn't talk too quickly. With their combination of linguistic skills, the pair got along well and Bob outlined his requirements. He had bought with him lots of pictures of Terry's van, plus he had downloaded various brochures to help with negotiations.

He explained to his new friend that he would be returning to France in one month's time and that he wished to part exchange the van in the pictures for something more suitable for driving through the Alps, hopefully LHD, and maybe even a 4x4.

Monsieur Champs-Blancs spoke better English than he had originally let on, he did have a very nice LHD Land Rover county TDI that he would be willing to negotiate on, he took Bob to the rear of the unit to check it over. It was immaculate and had Bob's name all over it. Bob explained that he realised he knew he wouldn't get top Euros for his very impressive camper van but didn't mind.

Monsieur Champs-Blancs did raise his Gaelic monobrow at the final agreement; probably because he couldn't believe his good fortune. They shook hands on 25,000 Euros and the Land Rover in exchange for the beast of a campervan. Bob offered a deposit as a guarantee of his word, but none was taken.

Details were exchanged, and a date and time was fixed for the swop, which Bob requested should take place somewhere near to the ferry terminal at Roscoff, at a venue to be confirmed by Bob and then sent by text within a week. Both men departed happy and confident with each other's integrity. They both knew that the deal would take place, Bob just had to tie up a few things first!

It was 658 miles from Roscoff to Maisonvide via the West coast. He had banked on one stopover with a sleep in the car. He stuck to the Route Nationales, not to be tight, just to enjoy France. He got six hours' sleep just North of Bordeaux in a busy and well equipped service station. It served delicious, fresh, strong coffee 24 hours a day, 7 days a week.

He left well refreshed and ready for the last leg. A good two hours before the Maisonvide turning the road started to steadily climb. He had left the main road and was heading along an ancient border route. He became aware of the occasional roadside altitude sign, it was telling him he was at 800m above sea level then 840m and still the road twisted and turned ever upwards until at last he hit 1000m above.

The spectacular views offset the precariousness of the tarmacadam. The countryside was arid with only sparse habitation. Any livestock he spotted looked hungry and thirsty. It felt like he was travelling through a different continent, it felt reassuringly a long way from Devon.

After what felt like a gap year he entered the small mountainside village where he had booked himself in for the night. A sign informed him it was at 1080m above mean sea level which for some unknown reason gave him immense comfort. Bob would visit Maisonvide the following day.

He was hoping the place he had booked would be suitable as a base for the Whiterockians when they turned up next month. From the outside it looked perfect, large enough and very 1970's. It was quiet with only a few walkers and die-hard border castle baggers booked in. Bob had read about this odd group whilst he had done his research on the place.

He signed in and reserved a table for his evening meal, which was delicious, as was the entire bottle of a local grape. After his meal he ventured outside for a smoke and to contact Pam, which he couldn't due to the lack of signal. 'Excellent', he thought, and returned inside to use the hotel landline. Pam was in good spirits, all was well. He slept like the dead.

He was awoken by a text from Pam next morning, that had found its way through the mountain passes. She had signed and sent off the forms, hoped he had slept well and that he must take good care of himself. He got up, dressed and went downstairs for his petite dejeuner. There were four other guests at breakfast, two German and two English, he was fully aware of possible future events so he kept himself as nondescript as possible and made it through the meal without incident. Unfortunately, he bumped into the two Brits in reception.

"Which one are you bagging today?" One of the couple politely asked Bob.

"I'm sorry?" Bob replied, feigning no idea what the question meant.

"Border forts, that's why you are here isn't it?" Came back the over enthusiastic man.

"No, sorry, I am not bagging anything, just on a short stopover on the way to Spain, the name's Peter, where are you from?" He held out his hand.

"Me and the wife hail from god's own county, I'm Ted."

Bob hated the expression 'the wife' as did 'the wife' who visibly recoiled when her husband uttered it.

"You're from Devon are you?"

Bob regretted this the moment he said it, but he already didn't really like Ted and was giving him one from 'the wife'.

"Sorry Ted, I didn't catch the name of the lady to your left." Bob continued.

She smiled,

"It's Lyn and we are from Yorkshire, although I hear that Devon is just as beautiful."

Ted looked put out as it dawned on him that he had just been got at twice.

"Yes, well, have a good day Peter and enjoy your stopover, come on love we have two to get today."

He grabbed his wife by the arm and moved off, as they got to the hotel door, Lyn turned and smiled at Bob, the smile said 'thanks'.

'Careful', thought Bob. 'I don't really want to be recognised,' but Ted struck him as the type of man that didn't take a daily newspaper as it wouldn't be able to tell him anything he didn't already know.

He made his way to reception to look at the leaflets and flyers and the places of interest to visit nearby. They were pleasingly few and far between. A goat farm offering tours of a pungent cheese shed, a honey farm and a few small vineyards. Bob was bought back by a cough. He turned.

"Monsieur, can I offer you some advicement?"

The young receptionist/cleaner/waitress/barkeeper smiled.

"Um yes please. Do you have any local maps, pardon, avez vous notre carte pour local?"

Bob always thought it better to try and speak French, even if very Pidgin with the English first. The multi-tasker smiled again and found a simplistic map with various local trails and paths, Bob opened it and had a look.

"Ah, maybe I will visit Maisonvide ..."

"En voiture? Bonne chance Monsieur, perhaps you might prefer to walk and save your car and your life."

Bob nodded and thanked her for the advice and asked for a packed lunch. He went to his room and packed up his small rucksack ready for the day's adventure. He was very excited. When he returned to the entrance hall of the hotel he saw that his packed lunch had been prepared and placed on a table, it looked delicious and included a small bottle of local wine, he picked it up and headed for his car.

Before he started the engine, he sat there and cleared his mind. "Think like the Twinning committee", he muttered aloud to himself. He wanted to imagine what was going to happen next month when the coach arrived. He had decided to drive the short distance out of the village to the junction where the road to Maisonvide turned off.

It was quiet when he drove slowly along the main street. Many years ago this village had been the centre of a prosperous farming community. It held a weekly market and supported a range of shops; alas no more. As the road left the deserted village centre it was flanked by locked up shops and abandoned homes. The old market hall was slowly dissolving in the mountain weather. A vain attempt had been made to give the village a heart, an obscure fountain bubbled unenthusiastically within a well-kept small formal garden. Bob couldn't really see what the fountain was trying to represent, maybe some kind of recumbent animal or maybe just a lump of the Pyrenees, whatever it was it flowed like it knew no one was watching.

Just as he left the village outskirts a sign appeared on his left pointing out the road to Maisonvide. He indicated to nobody and pulled into a layby just beyond, parked up and set off on foot.

Highway to Heaven …

The road started off in relatively good order. It climbed steadily and headed towards the sound of running water, but within the space of 500m everything changed. The road veered sharply to the left and then quickly corrected itself to fall in line alongside a tumbling river. It was quite a drop and some half-hearted crash barriers had been erected, but after a while they petered out, as did the quality of the road surface. It was like the contractors had all decided not to go any further. The coach wouldn't make it any higher than this, thought Bob, he made a mental note and carried on.

The environment was beautiful, the air was thick with new smells for Bob's nose, heather, grasses, fresh mountain water. A road sign indicating that there was a possibility of rock falls had ironically been hit by a rock and now, severely dented, had been propped up against a post.

The sides of the valley had been steadily coming closer together as Bob continued his climb. It was like the tops of the mountains were trying to touch each other again having been parted by the river thousands of years ago. The road levelled out a fraction and the surrounding land opened out a little, an ancient shepherd's hut held its own just feet away from the roadside. The small but robust building had a faded advertisement painted on its gable wall. It was directing people to a hypermarket in the nearest large town. "I expect they all went there and stayed" mused Bob out loud.

It was then that something came into earshot that wasn't the turbulent rock filled river or the large number of excitable birds, it was the unmistakeable sound of a 2HP engine being driven to within an inch of its next service.

Bob leaned against a warm wall of the old hut and waited for it to pass. Around the corner, just down the track, appeared a bright yellow Citroen Mehari. The powered front wheels were only intermittently gaining purchase

58

on the dusty ground. The two occupants seemed blissfully unaware that they were taking part in a near death experience. If the journey from the main road to the shepherd's hut was offered at Alton Towers even the most hardened of thrill seekers would deem it too dangerous.

The yellow, plastic, mechanical lunchbox came to an abrupt halt alongside the hut.

The driver enthusiastically motioned at a now frozen Bob towards the death trap. He was speaking French at a high rate of knots and the lady sat in the passenger seat of the oversized Tupperware container smiled warmly.

Bob's lack of motion and bloodless head was interpreted as a sign that he clearly wanted a lift to Maisonvide. Bob came back to his senses as he was being ushered into the back seat, he used the classic British device to slow a fast speaking foreign person down,

"Je suis Anglais, I am English!"

To Bob at that moment it felt like he was showing them a diabetes card or the 'I suffer from occasional fits' necklace. The man looked at Bob then at his passenger and raised his generous eyebrow (he had one large continuous one similar to Monsieur Champs-Blancs).

"Oh Anglais, welcome, welcome, bon chance, you are 'aving a good trip?"

He smiled and with more luck than judgement engaged the lunch box into gear. Bob frantically scanned the rear of the car for some form of safety equipment, he could only see a baguette, he grabbed it.

The car leapt into action and careered itself up the hill, the driver who had introduced himself as Robert, turned himself through 180 degrees too many times for Bob's liking, his quite good broken Franglais was used to explain some of the highlights of the trip, about the various last resting places of vehicles, where the highest drop into the ravine was, that there were only 2 passing places along the entire 9km route and how difficult it was to dig deep graves in the village cemetery due to certain geological conditions (it was bloody rocky). Bob was seriously beginning to question the whole plan when Robert lowered the revs and the car slowed, they were approaching Maisonvide.

Bob loosened his grip on the baguette, which by now had now become a collection of rolls and croutons. He looked about him and was transfixed. It was beautiful, truly beautiful, World heritage site beautiful.

Robert guided the car through an ancient stone archway and into a narrow network of streets. They passed houses bedecked with fresh, drying laundry, and lush hidden gardens. The vernacular was part alpine ski lodge, part barn, part ancient farmhouse. Nearly all buildings had a balcony. They had a style that Bob had only seen in magazines. He hadn't really thought that they existed and that the images were photo shopped, but here it was.

Robert's lovely passenger, Belle, was pointing out various items of interest and a bit about the history, but most of it was passing over Bob's head. He was already both in love and lost in this place.

The Mehari picked its way through a variety of wandering livestock, chickens scratching at seeds, and the odd baby goat warming itself in the morning sun.

The end of the street they had arrived upon opened up into a picture perfect French village square. A café without boundaries spilled over the pavement and onto the road metal, with tables being added or removed as required; resembling a sort of catering draughts game.

The café itself, with a change of paint tone at one end, became a bar and Tabac. Three other buildings in the square exhibited signs of being commercial outlets rather than houses. A restaurant, a bakery and a small "super" Marché.

Robert rallied the car around the square and came to rest outside the sprawling café. He had the air of a hunter who was bringing his quarry back to the fold to share with the tribe. The café owner and five clientele stopped what they were doing and turned towards the new arrivals to assess the offering. A man sporting a white apron approached the car, he offered his hand to Robert, his cheeks to Belle and took Bob's rucksack, without asking, towards a neatly laid table at his establishment.

"We don't 'ave many visitors!" Belle said whilst rolling her eyes at the waiter's rucksack manoeuvre,

"The road here is tres dangerous, n'est pas?"

Bob nodded, although the near fatal experience of getting to this Nirvana had all but faded from memory. The Apron was beckoning Bob towards the prepared table with large gestures, and he made a point of relaying the already laid table by lifting each item, inspecting it, and then replacing it in the exact same spot.

Bob turned to thank his driver and guide but they had already departed for the bar. He made his way to the table and with an elaborate swirl of a tea towel Bob was seated. The Apron produced a menu.

"Bonjour Monsieur, my name is Raphael and I will be your waiter today, apologies for my English, you are an English aren't you? "

Not for the first time that day Bob just nodded and Raphael continued

"Oui, I am thinking so, you have that English colour about your face, would you like a coffee?"

Without waiting for another nod, Raphael disappeared with yet another Gaelic flourish. Bob reached for his rucksack and took out his glasses and mobile phone. Still no signal. 'Excellent' he thought.

He glanced at the menu, crepes seemed to be the main event here. Bob bloody loved crepes, he looked up from the menu and tried to take in all that surrounded him.

"I shall end my days here" he vocalised to no one in particular. It came from a place that he didn't use very often. Only when he first met Pam and knew that he was going to be with her forever had he felt like this before.

Café de Reves …

Raphael with a near ballet dance move produced a coffee. It was normal French coffee but tasted like only something a god would be served. The Apron hovered; pen and paper at the ready.

"Raphael, je voudrais trois crepe, une entre, une crepe du jour et une crepe dessert, s'il vous plait, please you choose the contents."

Bob closed the menu. Raphael smiled warmly, relieved Bob of his carte, did a solo pas de deux and disappeared with a flourish.

Bob sat back and savoured his coffee. Another car arrived in the square, an old 4x4 Lada, the occupant got out not far from the café and made his way over.

Despite numerous empty tables the man gestured at the chair opposite where Bob was sitting. Bob nodded his approval, the new arrival accepted the offer with a side nod and took his seat. He then emptied the contents of his pockets until eventually he had produced all the requisite components needed to make a roll up cigarette, which he did and offered it to Bob, who took it, placed it in his mouth and waited for his new assertive friend to make his own before they were both lit.

Without any obvious signals, Raphael arrived with a small dark coffee. The man carefully placed two brown sugar lumps into the rich liquid and stirred it thoughtfully. He then took a large toke on his roll up and held the thick smoke in his mouth whilst he poured in his drink, both stimulants entered his body simultaneously, he obviously enjoyed the experience as a warm glow filled his expression.

"C'est une belle village, n'est pas Monsieur?"

"Yes, it is very beautiful, c'est parfait in fact" responded Bob.

"You are not a journalist are you Monsieur?" Bob's table guest spoke, like so many of his countryman, with impeccable English; putting Bob and his nation to shame yet again. The man was now looking straight at Bob awaiting the response.

"No sir, I am not and my name is Bob," he offered his hand across the table which was accepted.

"And you are not from a British holiday companies' association are you?"

"Again, no, why do you ask?"

The first of the crepes arrived, and although simple fare, it smelt of lavender, honey and lemon. Raphael smiled and took the empty cups.

"Deux autres s'ilt vous plait Raphael."

"Bien sur, Monsieur Marie" replied Raphael as he danced off towards the bar. Bob broke away from his crepe induced trance.

"You're the Mayor of this haven?"

The man nodded and gestured for Bob to eat his food. He didn't need a second invitation and tucked in.

"Yes, Bob, I am the Mayor of this piece of 'eaven and I ask you your business as I wish to keep it this way. I have seen places ruined by small articles in journals titled 'Secret France' or 'where the French want to live'. It would kill a place like this. We welcome the occasional visitor like yourself but we don't welcome Trip Advisor, well apart from my entries of course! You wouldn't come here if you read what I say about the place!"

The Mayor smiled with satisfaction remembering some of his comments about the place he loved. Bob listened as he consumed one of the top three crepes he had ever eaten.

He asked "Can Maisonvide survive without visitors or outsiders?"

The Mayor smiled at Bob's question.

"People 'ave sat where you and I sit now for centuries, I am sure that Maisonvide can survive. We have enough movement of souls to ensure that Raphael is kept busy. I 'ope you enjoy your time here in our village and everything it 'as to offer, but I ask one favour of you, I only ask that you don't tell your friends, be selfish, keep this treasure to yourself and that way it will be the same as you left it when you next return, which Monsieur I hope you do."

Raphael entered the space with crepe number two and more coffee.

"Now, sir I will leave you in the capable hands of Raphael, to enjoy your food."

He drank his coffee in one slug and got to his feet. Bob rose and offered his hand again.

"Mr Mayor, I will, if you agree, tell my wife of your village and I promise I will return for much longer next time. I might also be able to help in your quest to keep this place untouched for many years to come, an opportunity to achieve this will arrive quite soon, you need to be ready. I hope of course that you will remain in office for many years to come."

The Mayor took Bob's outstretched hand and shook it using both of his, he took a 10 Euro note from his pocket and placed it on the table, along with a small card.

"Bob, I 'ave been elected, unopposed for fifteen years on a ticket of NOT improving the road or mobile phone coverage. I am sure I will be 'ere to welcome you and your wife when you return to us and thank you for offering your assistance with my ideal. I do not quite understand what you mean, mais, I will be on my guard, au revoir mon ami."

He departed with a nod at Raphael and left Bob to his second crepe.

It was made of a stone flour and had been folded like an envelope around the contents, all of which had come from within a half a mile of where Bob was sat. It was a local variant of the Forestier, absolutely delicious.

Crepe number three was made of a sweetened flour and contained ice cream of a flavour he had never tasted before, a combination of wild flowers and honey.

Enough!

He pushed back his chair, a warm food glow enveloped him. Raphael cleared the table, leaving a short coffee, a mint, and a small bill. Bob was mulling over his meeting with the Mayor. It was perfect. Someone who would never encourage a Twinning visit or people like Peter was in charge. He was the guardian of the village and its way of life.

Bob checked his watch, it was time to amble back to the hotel, he beckoned to Raphael, who danced gracefully over.

"Thank you so much for feeding me, it was food fit for a king. Please could you inform the Mayor the next time you see him that his secret is safe with me?"

Bob leaned in towards the waiter and lowered his tone to add gravitas. Whilst back in Devon he and Pam had spoken at length about all the permutations that might happen when the Twinners actually arrived here in Maisonvide, it was an inevitability that at some stage someone from Whiterock, other than Pam or him, was going to discover that it had all been a massive crock of shit.

They both knew that they couldn't completely control that exact moment in time as it hadn't happened yet, however they could put the crock of shit into a precarious wheelbarrow and vaguely try to steer it in a direction that would be beneficial to them. Pam had come up with the best wheelbarrow and Bob was about to sell it to the Maître d'.

"Raphael, I must warn you that in a few weeks' time your village will receive a few visitors. I don't know how many, they won't stay for long and I promise you that when they leave they will never return. Maybe to help make sure they do not enjoy the visit too much the chef might be sick that day or the wine may be corked, perhaps you may have a story to tell about a bad person in your village who tells lies to get attention and thinks he is the Mayor? If you are able to convince these visitors of this, then I can offer you two things. One, you will never be selected to take part in a Jumelage again and two, with me and my wife, Pam, you will have two loyal and generous neighbours and customers for many years to come."

He pulled back from Raphael, who nodded in comprehension.

"Monsieur, merci, I will of course inform the Mayor and he will, I am, certain to be pleased. I don't pretend to understand why you know of these future visitors, mais, I have a good feeling about you, 'ow you say? You have bien vibes? I will remember your advice. Au revoir Monsieur, bon voyage et bon chance."

Raphael shook Bob's hand cordially, picked up the money that had been laced with a generous tip, turned and quick stepped back to the bar.

Bob walked away from his table and headed towards the other side of the square. He turned to take in his possible retirement abode, 'very nice', he thought, 'very nice indeed'. He took some pictures on his digital camera to share with Pam and slowly wandered off in the direction of the hotel.

He passed some well-kept gardens, teeming with produce, fowl everywhere, birds without borders. Where there were gaps between the houses, he was treated to breath-taking views out towards the Mediterranean Sea and the Spanish border.

A screech of brakes brought him back. A brightly coloured Unimog had come to an abrupt halt down the street. A stream of mismatched, chattering school children bought new life to the frame. Bob walked on towards the archway that he had been driven through earlier that morning by Robert. As he passed underneath the ancient portal he noticed a small homemade sign propped against one of the downstairs windows saying 'A Vendre', followed by some details of a name and number to contact. They looked familiar.

He took out the card that the Mayor had left on the table; it was a match. He touched the stone wall and said, probably out loud:

"My own castle, that will do very nicely."

There was a tangible change in the air as he left the archway and headed off along and down the track. It was as if he had left a dream, or a different world, and it wasn't down to the altitude, the coffee, or the crepes. He walked past beautiful mountain meadow-pastures that he had missed on his way up, and just before the track started to drop off the plateau that contained Maisonvide, he stopped and turned around.

He could now see that the village had been perfectly sited on a rounded hump that long ago was probably a volcano. The surrounding land was teeming with life, both with flora and fauna, a product of the fact that it had never been intensively farmed. Generations had only taken what they needed to survive; and in return nature had rewarded them with her best efforts.

Bob couldn't wait to be part of this Nirvana. If everything went half as well as he hoped it would then the very last place in the world that any member of The Whiterock Twinning Group would ever want to visit again would be here, this was heaven on Earth.

Bob actually waved at the village as he turned on his heel and headed off down the track. Thankfully no lift on this journey so he used this lone-time to focus and clarify the work ahead of him.

The plan was entering its most difficult stage, but now that he had seen and tasted the prize he knew it would be worth it. He enjoyed the rest of the walk knowing that he would be returning soon. As he neared the end of the track where some of the tarmac had remained where it was laid, his phone briefly came back to life, two texts and a missed call from Pam. Text one was from EE belatedly welcoming him to France, the other was from the book dealer; could he come a day earlier to view the collection? Bob mentally brought his organisational chart to the front of his mind. He could probably afford one day's difference. He made it to his car and leaned on the bonnet to return the call to his beloved. All was well, she just loved him and it was way too quiet at home without him.

Bob was booked in for one more night at the hotel, and as he passed through reception on the way to freshen up, he checked out the newly posted menu for that evening. It was a local delicacy. He ought to try it out as he hoped to be eating a lot more of it in the future. He stopped at the bar and asked for a large glass of the local red to take up to his room with the remainder of the bottle to be taken to his table for his evening meal. The multi-tasking employee asked if he had had an enjoyable day. "The best" he replied "the absolute best".

He took his red nectar up the stairs to his room. Once in he threw open the windows and took in a large lungful of the sweet evening low mountain air. He got his notebook out. It contained a concise version of the master plan. He had written it like it was a plot for a film or TV mini-series, all names had been changed in case it fell into enemy hands. He fell back into a comfortable chair by the window. He glanced through the pages, then took a long and large slug of the wine.

"Bugger me, this is serious stuff, life changing, happening to me, now!" He said out loud to the room.

He closed his eyes and tried to imagine what the day-to-day would be like, in simple terms. In six weeks' time he and Pam could be living in Maisonvide. Not just on a mini break but forever. They would never be able to use their passports again. Maybe in a few years' time they could venture out around Southern Europe. Maybe arrange to meet up with grandchildren.

His eyes remained shut. 'Here for the rest of my days, yes, why not.'

Maisonvide was a truly beautiful place, even on a winter's day, with driving snow and no chance of leaving. As long as he was with Pam, he didn't much care. It wasn't the end of anything; it was the start of everything. Of course they would get to see the grandchildren. I mean how much of a news story was it going to be? Headlines for a day or two? Demoted to the inside pages fairly quickly; then almost forgotten. Maybe the odd false sighting would raise occasional interest but it was hardly Madeleine McCann territory.

How pissed off would the Whiterock residents be? Yes, fuming to start with but, like the newspaper articles, their anger would diminish given time. He couldn't see any of them adopting a Charles Bronson type alter ego, arming themselves to the teeth and spending the rest of their days hunting Bob and Pam down to exact a terrible and bloody revenge. How many people near Maisonvide would even have heard of the crime? Maybe a journalist would venture here to the hotel for a comment about the failed Twinning trip, but could they even be arsed to make the trip up to Maisonvide itself for a comment about something no resident was aware had even happened?

The one outcome that Bob couldn't really get his head around was the reaction of the police. How tenacious would they be? No one, he hoped, would be physically hurt during this crime. It was simple theft and fraud; it wasn't even burglary.

He had the keys to the houses and the owners' permission to be in them; well sort of.

Yes, big fraud I grant you, but Mr Failed Canoe Man didn't get that long, about six years and he was out in two. Of course Bob had no intention of getting caught. How far would the police follow this theft? They would be sure to go to Roscoff at some stage or through Interpol alert the French police. His passport would be traceable to the port. Roscoff always seemed quite laid back but they were sure to have all the latest equipment and CCTV. However, for a good while no one would actually know that a crime had even been committed. He and Pam would have made a discreet vehicle swop and hopefully be long gone; lost somewhere on mainland Europe.

He made a mental note to plan the campervan exchange carefully. The Land Rover would be easy to spot on any subsequent garage forecourt security system. Would the police bother to travel down to Maisonvide? Maybe a young and over enthusiastic Devon and Cornwall Constabulary Detective might smell a free jolly to France.

Was the British perception of a relaxed, almost rural French police force warranted? Or would they be like little French terriers and not let up until justice was done? He just didn't know. No one did. It hadn't happened yet. Bob pulled himself back from his thoughts, opened his eyes and got out of the comfy chair; supper time.

Downstairs, the restaurant section of the hotel was quiet, three couples and two singles, Ted and Lyn were there; she smiled over at Bob. Ted nodded without looking up from the menu.

Bob made his way over to a corner table; best not to interact with anyone too much. He ordered the set menu from the chef/cleaner/receptionist who returned with his part-empty bottle of Chateau Juliette. He sent Pam a text, optimistic that it would make it to her sometime before he arrived home himself. He wanted a long and deep sleep in readiness for the long drive home in the morning. The meal came and went in four delicious courses.

He was the first to leave the dining room. He headed for the bar and picked up a double nightcap on his way up the stairs to Bedfordshire. It worked, and as soon as his head touched the pillow he was away to the land of nod and a dark, dreamless sleep.

He awoke before his alarm went off, he was deeply refreshed and energised from a night of sleeping with the window wide open. He quickly packed and went downstairs to check out. He ate a small breakfast of pain au chocolat and coffee. The car journey back to Brittany and the port might have been eventful but he wouldn't have known about it, he was in auto pilot mode. Only a small part of his brain was being used to navigate the car. The majority was being utilised to once again go through the plan with a fine-tooth comb. Even at this late stage he was finding flaws, making changes and exploring new avenues. He had settled on the crucial campervan swop event; happy now that no schoolboy errors would take place.

On arrival in Roscoff he bypassed the main drive to the ferry terminal and opted for a small road which approached the terminal building from the side. It appeared to lack any form of surveillance equipment. Half way along stood the Vasco De Gama pub. A non-descript semi industrial unit offering the desperate a last snifter before the ferry trip. He pulled into the car park and couldn't see any cameras so made for a corner and parked up. With his camera he left the car and walked to the edge of the parking area. From here he could see all the goings on at the port.

This would make the perfect venue for the campervan swop. He made a mental note to text Mon Champs-Blancs the address. Bob then watched as some of his fellow passengers arrived for check in. He had done it before himself lots of times but he wanted to observe it from outside of a car to see if he could glean anything that might help Pam in her effort not to leave the country.

The system, although relaxed in the French way of things, was still pretty rigid with very little room for an unobserved exit. He had faith in Pam's abilities but didn't underestimate the task she had ahead of her. He took a few images of a coach going through the security gates to show her later. They might stimulate an idea or at the very least help her to get prepared for the greatest escape ever.

He went back to his car, trying to put himself in Pam's position in a month's time. She would have to adapt to her given circumstances and he trusted she would come up with something. He left the carpark and joined the small queue of cars heading back to Britain. As he waited in the embarkation line he felt a pinch of nervousness.

The half full return ferry was spitting out its contents and Bob could make out the individual vehicles. He would stick out like a sore thumb in Terry's ultra-camper. There was a clear moment in this operation when only fate could decide if Bob and Pam were going to get away with it Scott-free. Yes, they could try to guide and help fate but at this juncture, in a months' time, they would be calling in all their favours from all of the spirits.

The return ferry was even quieter, but still had a few contenders for the

'I can't find my car' game. Bob had booked a cabin, and after buying Pam some new perfume (he was a sucker for gimmick marketing – the pretty little bottle sported a miniature fur coat and had a heart-shaped padlock) he retired to his bunk; texting Pam his undying love before he went to sleep.

He was awoken by the soft melodic Celtic music and treated to an early morning view of the Devon coast. Yes, he was going to miss his home shire but he was really excited and a huge smile enveloped him. Not long now and he would be back with Pam and the plan would enter its next phase.

Bob was so wrong about the competition. His nominated couple were sat in their car before he was. A complete rank outsider came from nowhere. The man had clearly overslept, was carrying too much, and despite having the information card in his mouth was trying to locate his car by using his key fob to activate the central locking, which wasn't really working because he was parked behind one of the only lorries on board; how did he not realise that? What a worthy winner, what a knob.

Whiterock was only about an hour from Plymouth and it was before the morning commute had got going so he made good time and entered the village before most people had left for work. As he rounded the last bend before his house he clocked that some eager beaver had erected the posts to support the new Twinning signs. 'What a shame' he thought and pulled the wriest of smiles. Pam was waiting for him, all hugs and smiles. She loved the perfume but most of all she loved him.

Bird Books ...

"Pinch punch lover!" giggled Pam from under the duvet.

"A slap on the thigh for being so sly!" made up Bob as a quick retort.

"Maybe we should have planned for all this to take place on April Fool's Day, for an added twist" he mused "... no the 10th is good. We still have lots to do. I am meeting with the bookman today to finalise the deal whilst Dr Roberts is away on church business. You need to finish off the packing. I can take any 'keep for the children' boxes to the storage unit later if you want?"

Pam plumped her pillow up and replied wistfully "I now have less than ten full days in this house, how exciting. You know love, I don't feel one bit sad. I just want to get on with it."

Bob got out of bed and jumped in the shower. He had the cats to feed at the Doctor's to coincide with the visit from the bookman. Pam stayed in bed, looking around their bedroom, thinking about the place that Bob had described to her in Maisonvide. She had seen his pictures and although they obviously didn't do the place justice, it looked heavenly and she would have all the time in the world to make it hers.

"I am off to Dr Roberts', see you dreckley!" Bob called. He could drop into broad Devonshire dialect at will.

He checked the key collection, he was still missing Terry's and as he went out through the front door he filed a mental note to get one soon.

Mary Braces had suddenly appeared by his side. "How is your Mum?"

"She died ..."

He started on auto reply before his brain had a chance to engage and now Mary was waiting for the conclusion of the sentence.

"She dyed her hair so she looks good for the surgeon" offered Bob, Mary bought it.

"Oh Bob, for a minute there I thought you had lost her early and you could have come on the French adventure, not that it would be worth your mum dying, I mean the trip would be brilliant but it can't be compared to the loss of a loved one."

Bob had thought about helping Mary out of her hole digging speech but he remembered all the times she had been rude and all the times he had cleaned out her fish tank, so he left her to carry on excavating her increasingly deep and painful pit. To try and end her trauma Mary enquired,

"What colour has she gone?"

"Blue" replied Bob "must rush Mary, I don't want to upset Dr Roberts' cats!"

He trotted off up the road.

There was an unusual shaped car in the driveway.

'Shit' thought Bob 'I told him to wait in the road and to be on time and not too early'. The book dealer was sat in the old car, and unsurprisingly, was reading a book.

Bob, slightly panicked, felt he needed to appear as though he was coming out of the house. He made for a gap in the hedge, bundled through, and commando rolled down a grass bank. He was aiming for the side door for which he had a key. One of the cats spotted his ungainly approach. He was late and it sauntered over to inform him of his error. The meowing appeared exceptionally loud to a tense Bob,

"Sod off you buggering fur ball!" He muttered under his breath.

The cat, needing to emphasise the tardiness, started to wind itself around Bobs legs. Bob reached the house wall and started to edge along towards the side door. The cat now viewed Bob with great suspicion and total contempt in equal measure.

Bob found the door key. Once opened he would have just 30 seconds to make it to the control panel to deactivate the alarm. He visualised his route and possible obstacles. Ok, go! He unlocked and opened the door, ducking through it in full-on stealth mode.

The cat, now properly pissed off as well as hungry, tried to trip Bob up so that he fell in the direction of where the food was located; lest he had forgotten. Bob swerved left to avoid the fur ball and to get to the kitchen door. It was locked. "Shit!" Key, fumble, locate. He opened it and sped through the kitchen, across the dining room and entered the hallway. He opened the downstairs loo door and got to the key pad just in time to discover that the old girl had forgotten to activate the alarm. "FFS!"

He exhaled rapidly and kicked the ever present cat. The doorbell rang. Bob jumped. The cat glared and sauntered off whilst Bob went to open the front door.

"Good morning, its Mr Mycock, isn't it?" Said the bookman on the door step and offered his hand to Bob enthusiastically.

"Please, call me Rob." Replied Bob jovially. He was quite pleased with his pseudonym. If anyone did think it strange they were unlikely to mention it and would want to move on to avoid embarrassment. The visitor didn't appear to have really thought much about it.

"Please come in, it is Mr Bird is it not?"

Mr Bird offered his card and smiled as he entered the hallway. The business card was yellow, ornately embossed, and smelt of musty book shelves. It proclaimed 'Bird Books'.

"Does the name affect your business much?" Bob asked – actually interested in the answer as opposed to just starting a conversation. Mr Bird had the look of a man who had spent rather a lot of money on his business cards and stationery.

"The internet hasn't really helped much but fortunately I was quite well established before search engines narrowed my target customer base."

The still unfed cat now decided to investigate whether the new visitor was going to open any pouches of food and its head butting of Mr Bird's legs was becoming increasingly violent.

"Mr Bird, please come on through, apologies for the behaviour of Mother's cat. I will feed it now, please go and take a seat in the dining room."

Bob grabbed the now quite deranged cat and made for the kitchen. Mr Bird followed until he was distracted by the contents of the shelves.

"Mr Mycock, sorry, Rob, may I take a look at the collection?"

"Please, knock yourself out." Bob immediately passed this sentiment on to the cat as he used the furry one's head to open the kitchen door.

"Would you like a cup of tea?" he called through.

No reply came.

Bob opened a pouch of food and placed it into a bowl. The cat took one look at the late offering, a second look at Bob, then proceeded to exit stage right through the cat flap. 'I hope you double up in pain with hunger pangs you twat cat' Bob communicated telepathically with the cat's arse as it disappeared outside.

Mr Bird looked about as excited as a book dealer could look. He had about him three pairs of glasses, one set on a chain around his neck, another high on his forehead, and the pair he was utilising on his eyes, to check out the first edition hardback copy of 'The Tale of Peter Rabbit'. He was a man of advanced years, perhaps 70 but had retained the long hair of his youth. Bob coughed at the door to the kitchen, Mr Bird didn't look up but muttered.

"Tea, yes, tea please, white with three."

Bob returned to the kitchen and carefully made two cups of tea, painstakingly memorising the layout of all the items so that nothing would be amiss when the Doctor returned later that evening.

He added an extra half a sugar into Mr Bird's cup and took it through to the dining room. He coughed again. He didn't want this to take too long, he didn't want to push his luck and although her return wasn't for many hours he hadn't got a watertight blag for this situation should the Dr return home early.

He had mentioned to Mr Bird in an earlier telephone conversation that his mother was suffering from a rare form of dementia that made her appear to all intents and purposes perfectly normal, but that this hid the true extent of the disease which made her forget major events; like the fact that Bob was her son and the selling of her entire book collection.

Bob had no idea what he would say to the Dr if she caught him with a strange man in her dining room, so he moved the situation on with another cough. Mr Bird brought a selection of books to the table. He was clearly impressed, and most refreshing to Bob was that he didn't attempt to hide this emotion to try for a better deal. He obviously drew more pleasure from the books than he did from money. Bob liked Mr Bird.

"I am so sorry you were not able to come down in February to view the items, you could have met mother."

"Mr Mycock, sorry Rob, the photographs you sent me were more than enough to whet my appetite and I am sorry to have missed the lady that had the foresight to amass such an excellent collection, won't she miss it?"

"I am afraid my mother does not really grasp the situation fully, she is visiting a potential residential care home today with my brother Paul."

Mr Bird's face made an involuntary twitch. Perhaps he had just considered the odd choice of forenames for the Mycock brothers, but he wasn't going to say anything.

Bob continued. "This is the main driver for the sale, we as brothers are unwilling to divide the collection and my mother will need all the money she can get to keep her comfortable in her dotage. The home she is looking at today, Castle Grove, charges in excess of £900 per week."

Mr Bird audibly inhaled. He had never until that moment really considered the true cost of long term care.

"My good Earthmother, is that legal? That is a fortune! Now that I have been able to carry out a proper assessment of the collection, I am happy to say I can improve on the guide price I offered you during our recent telephonic exchange."

Bob liked Mr Bird even more, and not because of the increased offer.

"I am willing to give you £95,000 for the collection now that I have confirmed the validity of the Biggles set. Now you did mention you required this transaction to be in cash, did you not?"

"Yes, Mr Bird, I do not wish to appear vulgar, but the less money that mum appears to have in her bank account the better it is in the long run. There is very little government support available until she practically runs out of funds, so yes please, cash on collection."

"Rob, this is not a problem, anything I can do to ease the pathway of an obvious book lover will be a pleasure, cash on collection it is. Now we are due to meet up on April 11th, is that correct?"

Bob nodded.

Mr Bird continued. "I will be here as arranged at 11 in the forenoon, may I ask one small favour? I would like to take one book away with me. I am happy, nay, insist on leaving you with substantial recompense to assure you of my intention to close this deal. £5,000 cash now and I leave here with Tintin and the Black Island to tide me over."

Bob had to think quickly. Would Dr Roberts miss one book? She would be at home for 9 days before the trip, did she count her collection every night like the giant in Jack and the Beanstalk? The £5,000 would be useful this week as a cash slush fund and most of all he didn't want to put Mr Bird off.

"Yes I am sure we can accommodate your request, would you like a bag?"

"Good, good, yes, yes, a bag, thank you Rob!"

Mr Bird started to return the books to the shelf except for the Tintin. Bob went to the kitchen to get a bag, he found a clean Waitrose carrier bag. Mr Bird was standing by the table, a thick bound pile of £20 notes stood by his undrunk tea.

Bob handed him the bag.

"You haven't drunk your tea ..."

"No, sorry, it was too sweet, maybe you have a different cane here in Devon."

Bob wished he had gone to school with Mr Bird and that they had remained close friends throughout their adult life. He started to show his new friend towards the door and stopped in the hall to admire a large family group photograph on the wall.

"I took this picture."

Offered Bob, very quickly hoping beyond all hope that the makeup of the party in the shot would allow his scenario to be true and it was; the Dr had a Niece who was a single parent.

"Yes, your mother has the look of a true lover of the printed word. Please pass on my sincere gratitude and inform her that I shall look after her collection."

Bob shook hands with Mr Bird and walked him to his car. From the front Bob could see it was a Jowett Javelin.

"My father used to have one of these beauties, swore by its flat four engine, balanced power, he used to say" said Bob.

"My goodness me Rob, your mother a fine collector of books and your Father a Jowetteer, I wish I had grown up in your household! Goodbye until the 11th."

Bob went back inside and passed the shelves. Mr Bird had left the books exactly as he had found them. He was sure she wouldn't miss one out of her huge collection.

He took the cups to the kitchen and poured the tea down the sink 'too sweet' he chuckled to himself. He checked the back door was locked and that everything was how it should be. He saw the cat skulking in the corner. It viewed Bob with a look that said 'you are up to something and it better not interfere with my food supply you bastard.'

Bob headed for the front door, entered his date of birth into the keypad, and headed home. He had some calls to make and needed to prepare for the shotgun licence officer who was visiting tomorrow afternoon – to check over the cabinet he had yet to install.

Pam was busy packing when he got back home. They had decided to keep the hallway and one room looking normal and lived in so as not to raise any suspicion from visitors. The pair kissed and carried on with their jobs – Pam packing and Bob fitting the gun cabinet into the hallway cupboard. It seemed a bit pointless as the guns would hardly ever see the inside of it, but it was a means to an end. He needed to get a license number to allow him to sell Terry's guns semi-legit. The shooting fraternity were notoriously 'by the book' when it came to procedures. The rest of the day passed in a quiet but productive manner without incident.

The work-like atmosphere was broken in the early evening by the phone ringing. Pam was closest and answered. The call seemed to start off alright but her voice changed as the conversation continued, she was putting in the odd phrase of 'I see' and 'oh I am sure it has a simple explanation'. Bob was becoming increasingly worried. Pam was giving him looks that no person on Earth could translate, but something wasn't right.

"I will go and get Bob from the shed, I am sure he will be able to sort this out" she covered the phone and pressed the mute button.

"It's Dr Roberts and she says that something is missing from the house!" she whispered urgently.

Bag for Life …

The very life and soul drained out of Bob as if someone had fitted a wine box tap to his knee and turned it on fully. As his entire being started to flow out of the tap and spread itself across the front room floor, it was being replaced with pins and needles, dryness and a very light head. He had completely forgotten about Mr Bird's request.

"Shit, what's missing love?" he loud whispered at Pam.

"How the hell should I know? She didn't say, only that she is concerned, Bob you need to speak with her, whatever it is we can't blow it now!"

Bob barely had any strength left to take the phone. He had no time or functioning cognitive ability to come up with an excuse. He hadn't planned for this, it wasn't on his flow chart, bloody hell, make a water tight plan and stick to it you idiot. He grasped the phone and unmuted it.

"Dr Roberts, sorry I was in the shed, how can I help you?" he tried to sound as normal as he could.

"Well, Bob, this is a bit awkward but on my return this evening from the conference, I noticed that something was missing from the house. I didn't want to jump to any conclusions, so I thought I would ring you first."

The line went silent. Bob steeled himself. He might be able to blag that he was borrowing the Tintin book to read, but she would want its return long before the Twinning trip set off.

"My Waitrose carrier bag is missing." The Dr continued.

Bob leapt in.

"I am so sorry; I was going to return it after I had read it!"

"You wanted to read my carrier bag? I didn't think it would be that interesting."

78

Bob froze, his fear emptied brain was trying to re-engage with the situation. The wine box tap on his knee had been turned off.

She was worried about a bloody Waitrose bag.

"Sorry, did I say read? I meant *clean*, yes I wanted to *clean* it. Your cat had an incident in the kitchen so I went for the nearest thing to hand to clear up the mess, and grabbed the bag, sorry."

The life juice was returning and filling Bob up. The relief of the situation was intense and he felt light headed again.

"Bob you should have left a note. Poor old Professor, being ill, now don't be daft about cleaning the bag, you can keep it. Just pick me up a new one sometime soon. I like to put my shopping in it when I go to Lidl, it keeps the neighbours guessing. Glad we cleared that up or glad *you* cleared it up I should say." Dr Roberts had a stifled uptight laugh, like it was rationed. She hung the phone up.

Bob sunk to the floor clutching the handset. "Silly cow, all that stress over a 10p bag for life, what a snob, packing Lidl items in a Waitrose bag in case a neighbour is looking. Get her a new bag, cat mess …"

Pam touched his shoulder and bought him back to reality. All this would be over soon; he would never have to talk to Dr Roberts or interact with Professor Cockwomble the cat again.

"Pam, love, whatever happens, we must never deviate from the plan, never again. Did you pack away that Welsh whisky? Please say you didn't." Pam went to a box in the kitchen and retrieved the Pendryn, she poured out two large glasses, full.

A Cabinet Meeting ...

"Must see Terry today and secure his keys" Bob lay in bed; he had been awake for a while. His late Father's voice had been going around in his head, 'Turn every mistake into a lesson'.

He spoke out loud. "Sorry Dad, it won't happen again. I will stick to the plan. Any changes or deviations from the path will be carefully thought through and checked before being adopted."

"Who are you talking to lover?" Pam asked drowsily from under the duvet.

"Sorry darling, I didn't mean to wake you. I was running a few things past Dad. That was a close one yesterday, never again."

He got up and turned on the coffee pot, went to the table and put a red cross through yesterday's entry on the flow chart. At least there was nothing to carry over from the task box.

Right, focus, shot gun officer due at 11 am. Pam was off to the solicitor's office in town to sign the contracts for Mary's house. Bob had placed £300 cash into an envelope for Pam to pay the firm for the massive and complex task of witnessing a signature, 'robbing bastards' thought Bob until he remembered he was currently situated in a very large greenhouse surround by piles of stones 'I suppose they are legally allowed to rob people' he smiled to himself, and took Pam her coffee.

The licencing officer arrived bang on time, Pam was just leaving and the two of them exchanged pleasantries at the front door. The lady was wearing a uniform that didn't really work, it was trying to be emergency service style, but failing. Part prison officer, part lollipop person.

She introduced herself as Carol and handed Bob a card. Her sleeve was covered in dog hair. He showed her through into the sitting room, offered her a chair, and said "We are having some decorating work done, please excuse the state of the place."

"As long as the integrity of the secure cabinet remains intact, sir, it is of no consequence to the office that I represent."

She spoke as if she were giving evidence at a murder trial. Bob had always had a pet hate of anyone trying to be too wordy to cover up the fact that they weren't really very important and had very little to offer society, but he needed to play the game. A drink was offered and brusquely declined.

"Thank you for the offer, sir, but I do not partake of any stimulants whilst on duty, lest it impair my judgement. A glass of Adams ale will suffice."

Bob got Carol a glass of water.

"Now, sir, before I check the suitability of said cabinet and the secureness of its fixings I need to confirm some details with yourself, being the mentioned applicant. Can you assure me, as a representative of one of Her Majesty's Law Enforcement Agencies that as yet, you do not, at this moment in time, actually possess a firearm or shotgun?"

"I can confirm that I do not currently own a shotgun."

Offered Bob in a solemn manner he hoped Carol would approve of.

"Thank you, sir, now I can confirm that you have never crossed paths with any other law enforcement agency, which is admirable, not even a speeding fine. Can I ask why you wish to own a shotgun?"

Bob was of course prepared for this question.

"My neighbour, Dr Roberts owns 18 acres of land and I have offered to control the rabbit population in exchange for the occasional clay pigeon shoot. The land is situated away from the highway or any place of habitation."

"Thank you, sir, that all seems to be in order. Please can you allow me access to your secure cabinet for its inspection?"

Bob showed her back through to the hallway and opened the cupboard, which was empty except for Terry's spare gun cabinet, now securely fixed to the wall on two sides. The moment Carol clocked it she directed Bob to move aside. She carried out a very thorough and over exaggerated visual inspection accompanied by sounds that Bob couldn't interpret as either positive or negative. Carol then stood back and reached into her back pocket to retrieve a pair of white gloves.

Bob suppressed every nerve ending in his body that was connected to his tongue that might bypass his brain and said nothing. He concentrated on trying to make his facial expressions convey a look of awe and wonder. Carol moved towards the cabinet as if it was full of a highly volatile exploding liquid. She ran her now gloved hand across the top as if she were checking for dust, she wasn't, she was just starting her strange relationship with the box. The keys were placed in the lock, she moved closer and knelt down like a safe cracker might approach the prize.

Carol, very carefully, in bomb disposal mode opened the door. Slowly at first, then, at the halfway stage, a quick reveal. Empty. Just as Bob had told her. She let out a long deep breath, what had she expected? A crazed dwarf armed to the teeth, with a hatred of annoying females in shit uniforms?

Carol then proceeded to check that all the fixings conformed to the British and European standards. The cabinet needed to be fixed on two planes; the floor and the rear. Bob had done his homework and everything was in order. Not even Carol could find fault.

She removed the keys and returned to her full height of 5 feet and 2 inches in heels. she de-gloved and directed Bob back into the sitting room. She sat at the table and opened her combination locked briefcase, shielding the dials from prying eyes as if the digits were also the launch code for a punitive first strike of thermonuclear warheads.

A brown envelope was opened with great ceremony and she proceeded to read through the contents, nodding at various stages, she took out a pen from the briefcase and made a great deal out of the fact is was a real ink version by blotting the nib. She then proceeded to sign the form with all the gravitas of someone signing the treaty of Versailles. She stood up, turned to Bob, and in a type of faux graduation ceremony, handed over his new shotgun certificate.

"Sir, I am pleased to be able to inform you that you are now free to purchase a shotgun. This certificate contains a section which is to be filled in by the retailer or the selling owner. You are legally obliged to inform me of any acquisitions so that I can update my records."

Bob nodded in agreement, with two hands he clutched his certificate with a gravity that he knew Carol would appreciate. She got all of her things together and reset the briefcase combination lock and made for the front door. Just before exiting she turned in what could only be described as a very theatrical manner, and, with an added slightly sinister demeanour, she spoke.

"Before I leave, I must warn you that as Her Majesty's representative in this district I am authorised by law that at my discretion I can carry out spot checks 24 hours a day, seven days a week. Woe betide if I visit you and find that your weapon is not in its proper place or find a weapon that I have not been made aware of, do I make myself clear, sir?"

"Crystal." Replied a slightly threatened Bob, who was thinking two things.

One was, 24 hours a day, really? You would turn up at 3.00 am unannounced to check the contents of my hall cupboard and two, in a week's time I will be gone forever, so good luck with all that. Carol stopped being sinister and became just annoying again.

"Sir, I bid you good day, be safe."

Carol made for her car which Bob was surprised to note didn't sport any form of flashing light on the roof indicating that she was very important and might have to speed through traffic in case someone had failed to dust the inside of their cabinet.

He went back inside and turned the kettle on. He got out the flow chart to update with a large positive tick. Pam arrived home all smiles. There had been no hitches, contracts had been signed, and all funds were to be transferred using BACs on April 11th at 12 noon. Another big tick on the chart.

The pair spent the rest of the day packing and not saying much; just enjoying each other's company.

The Unveiling ...

"I really think we should both go later darling" Pam suggested "we don't want to raise any suspicions."

"Why would anyone be suspicious love? And what about? I just feel a bit awkward looking at all of them." Replied Bob.

"Look lover, you are right they have nothing to be suspicious of, but remember they are the ones feeling awkward, they are off on holiday leaving you with an ill mother and their pets, let's just go for a bit."

The Twinning committee had organised a send-off party as a chance to get together and finalise arrangements, but above all to get into the French party mood. 7.30pm at the parish hall, bring a bottle and a French themed snack.

Maybe it was just Bob's conscience pricking at him, something he hadn't really counted on happening or planned for. He was about to ruin some of their lives, but they were going to raise a glass to him and break bread with him. Pam was right. He just had to smile and nod. He was already a bastard so it didn't really matter to what degree of bastard he was.

The house was really starting to thin down now, it had become an exercise in what did really matter. In the hall were four suitcases. They were to contain the only items that they both wanted to take with them into their new lives. In the spare bedroom were the boxes that needed to go to the storage lock up – for the children to sort out.

Some had sentimental value and some were items that could be sold. In one corner of the sitting room were the items that Bob was slowly filtering into the charity shop system. All the clothes, books, pictures etc that were once deemed important in life; but now actually weren't at all.

Without anyone noticing Bob did four car trips that day to distribute a lifetime's worth of accumulated junk. It felt quite liberating, and with every empty return trip home his soul felt a little lighter.

The Parish Hall lights glowed in the early Spring evening. Soft French accordion music filtered through the air as they approached the party.

Pam and Bob were still the heroes of the village; all this good feeling was down to them. The French 'four cheek kiss' greeting had now been adopted village wide.

Bob made a point of avoiding Peter who had obviously embraced the situation with gusto. He witnessed some very awkward man on man cheek action. Bob's back was repeatedly slapped and Pam was kissed so many times that everyone else ended wearing her foundation.

Terry bought everyone to order with a loud cough.

"Madame et Monsieur, je voudrais votre attention s'ilt vous plait!" He began.

People were suitably impressed by his attempt at pronunciation but he quickly returned to the vernacular.

"Thank you all so much for coming. The excitement is building isn't it? I don't really have much to add to Peter's already thorough itinerary leaflet, that I am sure you will all read avidly."

Bob detected an almost imperceptible eye roll from Terry.

"I just really wanted to impress on you the importance of being here promptly for departure on the 10th. The coach will leave here at 6.00pm, and it will not wait for anyone, not even Pam! Which leads me nicely on to the last matter. Now I am sure all of you have by now thanked Bob in your own way (they hadn't, not one single one of the buggers!) but I just wanted to officially thank Bob and Pam for everything. I am so glad that Pam is able to join us and I am sure that Bob will be travelling to our Twin village at some stage in the future."

'You'd better believe it' thought Bob.

The room erupted into enthusiastic applause. Maybe it was brought on by the guilt they all felt for not having thanked Bob personally, but actually it probably wasn't. They were all quite rude really. The applause died down and conversations started amongst the group about the arrangements and the trip.

"What is the weather forecast?"

"No, I couldn't find it on google street view either?"

"Wasn't there something about the French farmers planning some mass public sheep cull on the central reservation of every main motorway next weekend or is that just a normal festival event?"

Pam and Bob held hands as they scanned the room, they were picking up on bits of chat and looking at their neighbours, but unlike most times, they were really looking closely at them.

Having surveyed the scene and factoring in what they knew was about to happen to their cosy little village lives, do you know what? They didn't feel one bit guilty. I mean they didn't hate anyone here. This wasn't some glorious act of revenge. The police or press would never find the core nugget at the centre of this crime. The pair just saw it as a job. A retirement plan, yes. A major career change, I grant you, but it was just a different type of work. Without anyone noticing Whiterock's Bonnie and Clyde sidled out and went home.

Credit score ...

Bob had set aside the day to finish applying for as many credit cards and loans as he could. He had made a start last week, and the flexible friends had begun to trickle through.

Due to some annoying complexities, he had decided not to sell Peter's house, but just to clear out his bank accounts and cash in his pension pot.

He had recently read an article about a person who had opted to make himself bankrupt but just beforehand took out numerous loans and credit cards. He withdrew all the cash he could and then went under. The person had lived like a king for 3 years without working and it hadn't really affected his long term prospects. Throughout their working life Bob and Pam had built up an excellent credit score. They had always paid their debts and never defaulted on a loan or mortgage.

Bob sat at his laptop and checked the Maisonvide website. He answered another stupid question from Peter about charging up electric vehicles if he ever hired one.

He then navigated to the money pages. Basically all the top lenders would be happy to issue Pam and Bob with quite large unsecured amounts of cash. Bob's credit card company had increased his level of borrowing to a ridiculous level and Pam had been offered a large amount of easy money from her supermarket, despite only going in there for toothpaste. This in-depth financial arrangement had been authorised at the till by Mandy.

When leave day came, neither would be using any of these accounts again. They would only exist in the cash economy for some years to come. The pair would keep live the French account that had been opened in Pam's maiden name, however they were not stupid and realised that modern cyber detectives were very clever and it wouldn't take them much to follow BACS payments or transfers. It would only lead to one of them making a small cash withdrawal from a hole in the wall of a sleepy French village, that's the sort of thing a man in a canoe does; so cash only for a bit.

By 3 o'clock that afternoon, sadly, but not unbelievably, Bob had secured over £120k in unsecured funds. All he had to do now was start withdrawing it and converting it into Euros. They would be well clear of it by the time any patterns of erratic financial transactions rang alarm bells across the square mile. Companies were falling over themselves to offer money, but nonetheless he had to be cautious. These lenders all communicated with each other using algorithms, it was well known how much they valued and shared data. Bob's elderly Uncle Bill had once bought some draw tickets from some obscure charity that was raising money for Donkeys with ADHD and within two weeks he was getting up to three letters and four phone calls a day from animal welfare charities always with some flea bitten mistreated example of human cruelty on the front of the envelope or mentioned at the start of the call.

With his exit so close Bob didn't want to raise any awkward questions about excessive borrowing. They probably had about a week's grace before computers talked to computers and put a stop to any more transactions and cash withdrawals.

He flipped down to the town and withdrew the maximum daily amount from each of his existing cards. He would leave balance transfers until another time. He had stated on all the application forms that the reason for borrowing was for a house extension or home improvements, they love bricks and mortar, something tangible they could take off you if you ever defaulted.

On his return from the banks, Bob utilised the empty gun cabinet to store the start of his cash pile. Pam had packed a small overnight case as they were off to see the children. Not for the last time ever, but for the last time in a while; and just before the first grandchild was born they would be away for two nights.

Bob had put a not unsubstantial amount of cash into two envelopes. They both realised that if they asked the children not to open the letters until the following week, that they would be ripped open the moment the door was shut behind them. So instead they agreed not to ask. Rather, they had written a small note saying about a recent windfall of funds that was a gift to help them through the next few months and it was probably a good idea not to tell anyone about it and that was why it was in cash.

Bob also wrote down the location and number of the storage unit on the back of Andrew's letter, with the line:

I am sure you will know what to do when the occasion arises, love Mum and Dad.

Bank error ...

They got back quite early from seeing the children and both agreed that the visits had gone really well.

When it came to it, both siblings had opened the letters right there and then in front of them. The large quantities of cash had been received with lots of smiles and gratitude; fortunately, not too many questions followed.

On the drive home, Bob had shared his thoughts with Pam that maybe something genetic was going on. The children weren't daft; they had clicked that something bigger than a long holiday was happening but both seemed to trust their parents. This pleased Bob immensely and made Pam a little less heartbroken.

They could hardly open the front door upon their arrival as so much post, all of the new credit cards and loan cheques, had arrived. Letters from the mortgage company, the equity release sharks, and solicitors added to the pile.

Bob gathered up his hard day's work and took them off to sort out. He had set up a spreadsheet to keep a track on cash limits, loan amounts, and credit card withdrawal amounts. Pam unpacked the small case they had taken with them. She needed to get it ready for the Twinning trip. Only three more sleeps in Whiterock. She could hardly believe it.

Due to the distinct lack of household soft furnishings and pictures, when the front door was knocked on loudly it really was *very* loud and almost sounded pre-police forced-entry. They both jumped. Pam moved slowly towards the half frosted glazed front door. Quite a diminutive figure stood on the other side; not the imagined full force SWAT team. Pam opened the door gingerly and a very cross looking Mary was on the other side clutching, nay, waggling a letter in the air.

"Did you get one of these too?"

Pam had to think very quickly here, if she said no then Mary might turn and head off to find someone who had and Pam wouldn't find out what 'one of these' was. She swallowed hard and banked the other way.

"Yes! We did! Isn't it awful?! I was about to come around to yours!" Pam spoke assertively.

"They've got a bloody nerve these fisher people!" Mary ranted.

Pam was still none the wiser and so was unable to offer any support or guidance to the incensed Mary.

"Mary, come in. Bob put the kettle on. Mary has had one too!"

Bob had been eavesdropping, but like his wife didn't have a Scooby's what Mary was prattling on about. Pam was taking the best approach but he was more than a little concerned. He went to the kettle.

"Excuse the mess Mary, the decorators are due in soon for a total makeover, now come and sit down, you need to tell us what you think we should do about it."

Bob offered Mary a seat.

"Of course I have read about this sort of thing in my paper." She began. Bob hadn't realised that Mary owned the Times publishing company.

"They are called fishers. They send out bogus financial requests or made up bills, just hoping to get a response, but what they are really after is our data or bank details. They come from the East you know …" Mary pointed angrily in a northerly direction.

'What, they're from Dorset' thought Bob. Mary continued pontificating,

"You have to be clever! They can be really convincing, I mean look at this letter head, just like my bank, but I knew something was up when I saw the bogus account number, same sort code, different number!"

Mary tossed the letter onto the table, Bob casually exchanged it for the tea tray. He perused it with feigned interest. The letter was totally legitimate and from the solicitors' office confirming all the arrangements following on from Mary's i.e. Pam's meeting with them.

The transfer sum had been finalised with the equity release company and minus the expenses (robbing bastards!) and was ready to be transferred. Could she please confirm her bank details to ensure the BACS transfer was without issue on April 11th?

"They are good these people, they know where I live and that I don't have a mortgage, I mean the letter head is exactly right, it might even be an inside job. Well Pam, I was going to arrange a meeting to sort this scam out, I mean someone might actually fall for this and give over their details, now, you had one too, didn't you? Can I have a look at yours to compare it?"

Bob's brain was working about two seconds faster than Mary's mouth; he was already pretending to look for the letter that didn't actually exist. Pam, who's brain was working two seconds faster than Bob's jumped in with the hook.

"Bob love, I have already taken it down to them. Mary, I got ours yesterday and was so cross about the situation that I went straight down and demanded to meet with the manager to get an explanation. I am seeing her this afternoon. I am happy to take your letter with me as well if you want?"

Bob poured Mary her cup of tea whilst smiling weakly at Pam with a faint look of 'oh crap'.

"I could come with you Pam, two angry people are better than one. What time are you going?" Mary was getting really into this now.

With lightning speed, Pam flicked Mary's weekly calendar activities through her mind's eye, today was her foot day. The well turned out lady in the red Audi always arrives at 2.00pm.

"2.15pm Mary, you are most welcome to join me!"

Bob visibly winced. He lacked Pam's inside knowledge and courage.

"Oh dear, one of my ladies comes to me at about that time, I could cancel her, this is much more important …"

"Look Mary, I can handle this. I already have the branch on the back foot. I was going to push for some compensation. Now if I take your letter with me I will have extra clout. If you are not satisfied with the outcome you can always go down yourself another time."

Pam let it hang there, Mary hesitated but then relented and handed Pam the letter who studied it carefully, it was all correct and had her sort code and account number, Pam shook her head.

"What a bloody cheek and they only valued your house at £290,000, they put ours even less."

This peach from Pam allowed Mary to return to her normal indignant self.

"Well, I suppose I did have all that work done last year. Anyway, it doesn't matter Pam, it's all a scam anyway, neither of us is selling our houses, so we mustn't worry about the valuations they have stated. You and Bob have a lovely little house and with the new paint work I am sure it will go up in value. You give them hell and try to get some decent recompense, tell them I intend to go to the press if I am not satisfied!"

Not for the first time in his recent past, Bob felt weak again, he had briefly had the weight of two Marys on both his shoulders. That was no mean feat but now thanks to the brilliance of Pam the weight was lifting and he felt a bit light headed. This crime was getting stressful; it had better be worth it.

"Don't worry Mary, I will give them merry hell from the both of us!"

As Pam smiled, the great flow chart realigned and the exit plan was back on track.

Mary looked at her watch. She got up to leave with her beady eyes darting around the room.

"So what look are you going for in here?"

Bob felt calm enough now to re-join the game.

"We thought we would go European." He said proudly.

He knew this would go right over her head, already being European, although it wasn't lost on Pam who coughed to disguise the laugh.

"European, so apt, what with our little trip coming up, now, are you sure you don't mind looking after my little estate Bob? What with your mum's situation?"

Mary was actually going out of the door as she said these words. She had no interest in what Bob was going to say or the wellbeing of his long dead Mum. Pam closed the door behind Mary and slumped to the floor clutching the letter.

"Holy crap, that was close, in the unlikely event we ever do anything like this again we need to alter the predictive charts, turn every mistake into a lesson!"

She winked at her man, who joined her in slumping to the floor. He put his arm around her back.

"Right partner in crime, we will never be repeating this again, we won't need to as we will be set up for life. We had better fake up a letter head and write an apology, although a bit unorthodox, we could put some cash in the envelope to stop her taking it any further."

"I think" said Pam "we should get her some tokens for, say, Homebase. Or is that a bit cruel?"

"Homebase vouchers it is, I need to pop down and withdraw some money today anyway." Sighed Bob.

Later that evening Pam popped around to Mary's with a 'we're sorry' card. It contained £100 worth of Homebase vouchers. Mary made a big deal of lowering herself in accepting this offer, but she did, and the matter was closed.

With a drop more Welsh whiskey the pair of them slept very deeply that night.

Only two more sleeps to D-day.

The Nadder Arms ...

Pam's last two days in Devon for the foreseeable future were rammed. She had no time to dwell on anything. They both worked until they dropped packing away the last items, but trying to keep a semblance of occupation, in case anyone should call in.

Bob only just managed to fend off a visit from a very over-excited Peter. He saw him approach the house and ran to intercept him on the path.

"Ah Bob, hope you don't think this is too much but I have put together a checklist for everyone."

Bob scanned the list, it included some suggestions for appropriate gifts to give to your host.

"No, it's not too much Peter, it is very thoughtful. I will pass it on to Pam, thank you."

Peter hesitated a bit before he spoke again.

"Now Bob, I know you are not joining us and I don't want to rub salt or anything but have you or Pam ever checked out the Maisonvide website?"

Bob braced himself. Was this to be his undoing? He felt a couple of Peters starting to climb on to his shoulders.

Peter continued,

"Now it is a small place I know and maybe the web designer is not very IT literate but nothing has been added about our visit. The festival poster is on there and yes fair enough someone did answer a very important enquiry I made last week, however, don't you think it's a bit odd? Only two days until our visit and no mention anywhere."

Peter just had too much time on his hands. Bob relaxed a bit and felt the weight leave.

"Peter, I am sure everything is fine, maybe it is just the French way, you know how laid back they can be. Pam did say that our hosts are a little slow on the website side of things, but there is someone there and I don't think you need worry or contact anyone."

"Yes, yes, you are right Bob, just last minute nerves I guess. It is a lot to think about, sorry. Now there was one other thing I needed to run past you before I deliver the rest of these lists to the Twinners. Don't worry I added it to the sheet that I will leave on the worktop for you, just a little extra favour. I have managed to secure a spare skittle alley for the Parish Hall."

Bob felt himself die a little inside

"A nice gentleman is bringing it over next week on Wednesday, he insisted it should be cash on delivery, so I said you would meet him at the hall at about midday. I have put £200 cash in this re-cycled envelope, would you mind? With your Mum and all that?"

Bob was struggling to conceal his facial expression. It was a combination of contempt, anger and bewilderment. The three combined emotions together actually made him look almost normal, with maybe a touch of wind.

"Peter, I am sure that Mum can be ill around the delivery, which at least you have arranged to take place in the middle of the day so as not to interfere with a normal day's work. But above all I can't believe that the village didn't already have a spare skittle alley."

Bob felt the sarcasm building, he checked himself.

"£200 sounds like a real bargain, yes of course I will be there, Happy to help."

Peter handed him the cash.

"Now, Bob, that is a lot of village money, don't leave the country will you!"

The irony nearly knocked Bob over, he took the heavily selotaped letter.

"Don't you worry Peter, the village's money is safe in my hands."

Peter turned and skipped off to annoy the hell out of everyone else on the trip.

Bob had one other major jigsaw job to complete. He and Pam had talked about it at length and in the end had both decided that even though they were robbing people blind, they never wanted to be accused of being cruel to animals.

There would be a gap of nearly two days between Bob leaving for France and the Twinners' returning from the trip back to their houses; well some of them anyway!

They couldn't bear to leave the animals unfed or uncared for. When all this escapade came out into the open, soon, within the first two weeks, the press would have a field day, what a story and what a crime, but knowing the British public, uppermost in their thoughts would be the pets.

Not the fact that people had lost their homes, possessions and money but poor old Mary's chickens left to fend for themselves for two whole days. It would be an act that would turn them from folklore Robin Hoods to heartless bastards.

They both knew that it didn't really matter what anyone thought, but, heaven forbid, if they ever got caught they wanted to be portrayed as the loving couple who nearly got away with the most audacious multi-crime ever and not as the pet murdering bastards who should rot in hell.

The canoe couple were looked upon with pity and sympathy, not with hatred. No cat had been harmed in the canoe death life insurance crime. Bob and Pam had thought long and hard about the right candidate for the job. Most of the village was going to France so options were limited.

Bob had decided to ask Stacy, the landlady of the local pub. The main reason being that most of her customers would be away in France so she would have time to do the pet rounds. Bob had decided to call in on her on the way back from today's cash withdrawal run.

The Nadder Arms was less than a mile from the village on the main road into town. It was surrounded by a small cluster of cottages. The current incarnation of the pub had been built on land opposite the original thatched one.

For many years Stacy and her pub had been the cause for much speculation around the village as to how she ever stayed in business. The capacious car park never seemed to have that many cars in it. Folk had spread rumours of a low quality, vaguely agricultural prostitute ring, others said she housed numerous Eastern European workers, 8 to a room. Bob had even once heard that Stacy fronted a massive housing benefit scam with countless people claiming on room numbers that didn't exist.

If anyone had bothered to look closely they would have seen that actually Stacy was a shrewd little operator, making a bit here, a bit there; letting the pennies turn themselves into pounds.

Lots of wet sales during the day when no one was looking at the car park. Her establishment was the go-to venue for local wakes, again all happening during the day when most people were at work.

She had also started a good little camper van 'park, eat, drink, sleep' business. So, on the quiet, Stacy did alright; and not a low quality brothel to be found anywhere.

"Alright Bob?" Stacy looked up from her laptop at the bar. She was in the middle of launching a new offer called 'Lager, lasagne, lift'.

Bob wasn't what you would call a regular but neither was he a stranger.

"Alright Stacy, half a Devon Red please and a small favour?"

Stacy posted her latest tempting offer on to the Nadder Arms' Facebook page. She got an immediate 'Like' from her mother, who liked neither Lager nor Lasagne but might need a lift home sometime.

She poured Bob his half and gave him her undivided attention.

"Now what is this favour Bob, you off to France with the rest of 'em?"

"No Stacy, but it is connected to that. I have to stay back here, Pam's going but I need to be around to help my mother, she's having an operation you see."

"Fuck me! Who's carrying out the procedure Bob? Dr Frankenstein? Your mother died years ago!"

Bob didn't think he changed colour but a strange noise emanated from deep within him. What a total twat. They had held his Mum's wake in the pub, Stacy had put on a lovely spread. Shit!

"No Stacy, my real Mum! Not Josephine who you helped to send off on her final journey."

He was getting much better at reacting and credible yarn weaving, Pam's talents must be rubbing off.

"I was adopted when I was very young. Josephine bought me up as her own. I called her mum because she was to me. My actual mother came to me after Josephine had passed, she didn't want to step on anyone's toes."

"Oh Bob, I am sorry love, I didn't know. Still a bit of a bonus having two mums eh?!"

Stacy had the knack of defusing awkward situations. Always the sign of a good landlady.

"Well, real mum is having an operation and I said I would stay with her, it falls at the end of the Twinning trip, so I will be with her and the Twinners won't be back in time to see to the pets right. It's for two days and two nights, five houses with numerous animals, sorry it's a big ask I know."

Bob closed with a pleading look.

"Don't you worry yourself Bob, I would love to have a nose around some people's houses and see how the other half live. You let me know when and where, it won't be a problem."

"Thank you Stacy, that's a real life saver. Look, can I ask you to keep this quiet, I don't want to confuse or upset anyone. They are off tomorrow and some of them might get a bit funny if they thought that someone apart from me was in their houses. I will drop down a list and the keys one day next week if that's alright? Now how much do I owe you?"

"No worries, £1.40 please."

Bob drained his half.

"Do you know what, I will have another pint if that's alright Stace. I really have earned it today."

The landlady smiled and poured Bob a pint. She returned to her laptop. Four more 'Like's. Just as she thought, the as yet untapped lager, lasagne and lift fraternity was hers!

Bob sent Pam a text; ALL GOOD X STACEY WILL COVER PETS X STAYING FOR A PINT X

He sat on a bar stool and took a sip of his cider, big day tomorrow.

His phone beeped.

GOOD IDEA BABES X I DON'T THINK THEY SELL DEVON RED WHERE WE ARE GOING XX

Pam had a point, the French don't do pubs like the British. They, like most of Europe, do bars. Bob wouldn't miss it that much, the bar he sat in on his trip to Maisonvide was glorious. It was warm and they were bound to sell a local cider.

Three other people joined him at the bar, he knew one of them in passing. Stacy kept the four of them happy, dealing with and entertaining each at their required level.

Bob didn't stay long and even though The Nadder Arms was known as a 'five 'n' drive' establishment and it didn't really matter if he lost his licence; he did want a clear head for the coming week.

"Thanks Stacy, I will pop down soon with a list of instructions and keys, and don't forget, mum's the word." Bob raised a finger to his lips.

"Which one?"

"Which word?"

"No, which mum?!" Stacy smiled knowingly.

"Very funny." Bob smiled too, she even found the humour in having a dead mum.

When Bob arrived home he found that Pam had ground to a halt. All that she could do was done. This was her last night ever in the house. This time tomorrow she would be in a cabin, on the boat, leaving these shores; maybe for the last time.

She found the prospect of this extremely exciting and she was glowing.

Bob had come in clutching a bag of fish and chips. He had done a detour. He was a thoughtful man even after a couple of ciders.

"Fish and chips for a last supper. Britain's national dish, how apt." Pam quipped as she got the plates and some ketchup.

"We will still be able to get fish and chips in France darling. But I thought tonight you might enjoy some proper sized chips not the anorexic European ones." Bob began to empty the greasy paper bundles onto the plates.

They sat in silence as they ate. Both their minds were turning over events past and yet to come. After they had finished, Bob cleared up the things and Pam laid the flow chart (edition 7) on the table. The critical path had reached its goal in stage 1. A moment in time that deep down neither of them really ever thought would come. Their little adventure was coming to fruition. It was like a scene from a war film. The two protagonists from the escape committee, meeting in a Nissan hut before the off. Checking stories, carrying out final checks on equipment, clarifying rendezvous points. This was it, they couldn't plan anymore.

They were in the lap of the gods and so to bed. To ponder, to cuddle and to sleep.

Ready to rise on the day that the greatest journey they would ever take actually began.

D Day ...

D Day. Departure day.

The coach wasn't due to leave the Parish Hall car park until late afternoon, so they couldn't really start their new life of crime in earnest.

Bob didn't really want to do too much until he had got a text from Pam stating that the boat was free from its moorings and there was no chance of any last minute changes to the plan; like someone being taken ill and not going, or a mislaid passport, or even Peter returning home for an emergency compost turning session.

They still had things to do to keep themselves occupied. Bob withdrew some more cash and they took the very last items in the house to a charity shop. They called in and closed the lock up store for the last time. Bob wouldn't need much stuff for his remaining few days alone and of course he had the campervan if need be.

To be honest the day dragged a bit. The levels of adrenaline were high and the departure of the coach was the starting pistol so they were both feeling nervous and a bit on edge.

The buzz in the village started earlier than they thought it would. Terry had arranged for the hall to be opened early so that people could gather ahead of schedule. This was so that he could monitor any suspected lateness and frantically call around should the matter arise.

It didn't.

Everyone was early and everyone wanted to get off on holiday as quickly as possible. They had all been feeling like Bob and Pam but for very different reasons. To the trippers it would be preferable to be sat on a coach in a car park in Plymouth than to wait at home any longer.

Peter had actually had a clipboard made especially for the trip. Its back was a merger of the two nations' flags and the two villages' names. He couldn't understand why no one else was interested in owning one at only £6.00. Which was a worry to him as he had thirty to shift.

Bob kept to the shadows. Not through guilt; he just didn't want a bloody clipboard.

He gazed upon his fellow villagers for the last time, he wouldn't miss any of them.

Terry had really pushed the boat out. He had laid on a crate of champagne to get the party started and everyone except Peter was tucking in.

Pam approached Bob with two full glasses, her eyes never left his.

"To us my darling, to our big adventure and to the rest of our lives." She breathed excitedly.

They drank and kissed.

"Oi, you two! Get a chambre!" It was Terry. "Nice drop of bubbles eh Pam? Bob be a mate would you, when we've gone the glasses have got to go back to the shop in Cowick Street, you can keep the deposit pal for your trouble."

Bob was about to tell him where he could stick the glasses and the deposit but was saved by someone, unidentified, with a piss-poor grasp of the French language.

"Le voiture arrive!"

The throng started to exit the hall. Bob watched as the clipboard left the room to shouts of "No glasses on the bus, please!"

The coach was a monster, and Bob was confident that it would never make it up the road to Maisonvide. It had the requisite Northern Irish number plates, whose letters stood for no known initials of any person alive, but they beautifully hid the age of the coach.

It was old. It still had working ash trays on the back of each seat and the closest the driver ever got to a tacho was when he drove past a Mexican restaurant. None of the occupants cared, it was like being back on a school trip but this time champagne fuelled.

Everything was loaded and the climate change assisting engine sprang into life. Bob watched as Peter used his clipboard to count all the heads. Pam made her way to the rear and sat by a window.

"Right Bob, that's it we're off." Terry stubbed out his cigar. "You are in charge of the village, au revoir mon ami!" He shut the coach door.

Bob walked to the back of the bus slowly. Pam raised her palm to the glass. She had written 'I Love You' on it.

Bob placed his hand on hers on the other side of the coach window.

"I love you too" came from his mouth as the coach moved off.

Pam ...

Pam saw him mouth 'I love you too' and it filled her with hope; unlike the roadworthiness of the coach which filled her with dread.

As the wreck pulled out of the village hall car park she didn't look back to wave at Bob. She wanted to take in the village one last time. This had been her home for more years than she cared to remember. Her children had been raised here and yes, she had had some wonderful times, and some of the people she had met hadn't been that awful.

In the early years she had made some good friends at the mother and toddler group but these people had moved on to places new, a bit like she was doing now; only thirty years later. She allowed herself an internal wry smile.

The coach slowed down just outside her house to allow a car to pass. It had been a lovely little house, safe, warm, and theirs. Without this little haven and the fact that they had always been working she probably would have died of boredom. For the retired members of the village community time almost ground to a halt. If it wasn't for 'Cash in the Attic' and 'Homes Under the Hammer' you probably wouldn't be able to witness the passage of time actually taking place.

The coach moved on. 'Goodbye house' she mouthed as all other familiar houses and haunts started to pass by. My goodness it felt odd. She had travelled this road so many countless times; at least twice a day every day. Now she was probably doing it for the last time.

Despite what Bob said she had no inclination whatsoever to return here thirty years hence. I mean, why would you? To see Mary living in the bus shelter because her house had been sold under her? No, this was a chapter to close, a book to finish. A new exciting one was ready to be written and this bus journey was page one. As this final thought floated through her mind the sign for Whiterock serendipitously passed the window.

The feedback that emanated from the coach's intercom system actually removed one of only three bones that exist in the human ear. Although now partially deaf, Pam heard someone in the seat in front of her mutter "FFS please don't give Peter the microphone, please no!" Terry stood up followed by a cheer.

"Fellow Whiterockians, don't worry I won't be passing the mic to Peter for a metre by metre commentary on the hidden delights of the British hedgerow followed by a section on motorway signs I have loved ..."

Another much louder Champagne-fuelled cheer went up and Terry continued

"Only joking Pete (he wasn't), just a couple of notices then you will be left alone. Not long to the port as you know, I have all the tickets so when we get there please stay seated until we have gone through checkpoint Charlie, once on the old tub you are free to wander about. You will be given your cabin entry card by the lovely Jean."

Several wolf whistles went up.

"Calm down. I've got Jean's cabin card so back off!" Terry exclaimed with faux protest.

Moans and jeers.

"Our drivers on this little adventure are Bill and Sheila. Sheila is at the helm now and assures me that despite all outward appearances we are in a very good mode of transport. Everything works and we have all the mod-cons. When we get to the other side of the briny on the long French leg ..."

A single wolf whistle went up.

"Steady" warned Terry heartily, "on the longest part of our journey through France, a range of snacks and drinks will be available to buy from whoever isn't driving at the time, sorry everyone, what's that Bill?"

Terry covered the mic and the feedback was incredible. Full hearing was now restored to most passengers.

"Yes, thank you Bill, sorry about that folks. Bill has asked me to tell you not to use the on-board washroom facilities as that is where they keep the snacks. Right then, I will shut up now and leave you to watch the Devonshire countryside roll away, no Peter, not now!"

A loud cheer and some applause went up as Terry refused to let Peter steal the mic.

Everyone settled down, Pam returned to her window and her thoughts, but not for long. Someone coughed next to her. It was Dr Roberts.

"Hello Pam, thought you might like a bit of company. It must be strange without Bob. I'm used to being on my own but for you it must be different. Now I know it may seem a bit uncouth but do you fancy one of these?"

Dr Roberts produced a couple of cans of Gin and Tonic from her carpet bag.

"No ice I'm afraid and yes, we will be drinking straight from the can, just like the old days at the back of the school bus eh?!"

She winked at Pam and offered a can. Pam took it and smiled. They both opened up and chinked tins.

'Why now after all these years do you choose now to endear yourself to me?' Thought Pam 'you silly old moo!'

"Cheers." They said simultaneously and drank the contents together.

The hour-and-a-bit to Plymouth passed very quickly. The conversation wasn't deep, but flowed easily following the combined consumption of champagne and G&T. It was the most they had ever exchanged in all the years put together; until now. Everything up until then had revolved around pet food, setting alarms, and where Dr Roberts was going to go next on holiday.

Here on the coach, Pam was no longer in a subservient position; they were all equals. 'She's only going to lose a few books; it's not like were killing her' Pam thought this to reassure herself not to excuse it. Her and Bob were robbing the old girl blind after all. So yes, Pam wasn't trying to excuse anything. She had chosen a path of crime and much to her delight she was really embracing it, 'bollocks to boredom' she thought, nay, shouted to herself.

"Dr Rob ... sorry, Shirley, do you have another can of uncouthness? After all, neither of is driving are we?" Another can was produced from the carpet bag, that contained an Aldi carrier bag.

The tone of the coach engine changed. They were leaving the Devon expressway and entering Plymouth. The sign for the Ferryport flashed past.

Pam sent a text to Bob.

PLYMOUTH X

A reply wasn't far behind.

TEXT WHEN BOAT LEAVES LAND X

Dr Roberts peered over "Is that Bob? Tell him to feed my cats first won't you?!"

"Of course I will."

Pam pretended to send a text.

"It's been such a comfort over the years having you and Bob for neighbours. I have been blessed. I mean, you can't really trust anyone these days can you? I hope you don't think I ever take you for granted. If you have then I'm very sorry, you are truly the best neighbours in the world." Dr Roberts spoke with sincerity but Pam wondered if it was the alcohol talking.

Fortunately for Pam, the years of fridge magnets and tea towels had added many layers of epidermis. So although touching, this long overdue apology didn't wash. Too late. Much too late.

Plymouth's ferry docks were not very inspiring. The coach crawled through the red-light area. Not many girls were out tonight.

Pam had always felt sorry for the French arriving here. They left behind them incredibly artistic roundabouts full of flowers and tableaus. All the port could offer here was an old handcart with flaking paint filled with self-seeding weeds. A visiting tourist might interpret this offering as either a true reflection of the state of Britain's fishing industry or that most of the nation was 'as pissed as a handcart'.

The probably already disappointed visitor would leave this crap installation, drive 300 yards around the corner, stop to ask a local girl for directions and get arrested for curb-crawling.

The coach was directed to join lane one and came to a halt behind two other coaches. One had been converted into a mobile home of sorts, it seemed to be occupied by an extended family of yurt-dwellers; probably hailing from Totnes. From looking at the state of repair of their vehicle, Pam mused that the grand tour of Europe would probably end in tragedy in a layby half a mile outside of Roscoff.

The embarkation queues were filling up and Pam was able to have an early punt on who might be in the running for 'where's my car?' – Bob's favourite game.

A sharply dressed lady from Passport Control had got on to the coach. She spoke with Terry, who got up and turned to address the passengers. Everyone winced.

"Madames et Monsieurs, please may I have your attention?"

Terry had managed to control the mic feedback issue a bit. It was now down to a level equivalent to being inside an empty oil drum with four feral cats.

"Oh, sorry about that, damn mic, anyway please could you all pass down your passports to the front? The lovely Rachel from immigration services will collect and process them en-masse."

Rachel from Immigration Control tapped Terry on the shoulder, he covered the mic. Pam was ready for the feedback and had her fingers in her ears. She thought she saw a small trickle of blood coming from Dr Roberts' ear.

Rachel was having an animated conversation with Terry. It didn't last long and a sheepish Terry uncovered the mic.

"Ladies and Gentlemen, I would like to start again if I may. Rachel, sorry … sorry … Mrs Sterling is a professional Immigration Control Officer. She is part of the UK Border Force and she isn't lovely, I mean in her capacity as Her Majesty's Inspector, she doesn't need to be lovely. And being lovely didn't get her this difficult role, because she isn't lovely. I mean she is but …"

"Get Terry a spade!" Someone shouted. The very uncomfortable atmosphere was thankfully cleared.

Officer Sterling took the mic. No feedback – she was good.

"Thank you Sir, I think! Now please could you all pass your ID documents to the front. I will carry out a check as you exit the coach. My colleagues will be searching the luggage bays, so please don't be alarmed by any strange noises."

"With this engine we probably wouldn't notice anyway!" Offered the same joker of the spade quip.

Pam noticed that it was Mr Smartin who was thoroughly enjoying the situation, keeping Terry in his place -just in case he had delusions of grandeur and wanted to become the patriarch of the village. Not if Mr Smartin could help it!

Rachel handed the mic to Sheila at the wheel, they both rolled their eyes and Terry sat down suitably chastised.

The passports were taken away, checked, and brought back. The Officer stayed on board as the coach edged forwards and passed through the border control shed (it really was a shed).

The mobile Kibbutz had been stopped and several uniforms were enthusiastically searching for what they hoped would be the largest ever consignment of drugs to be smuggled *out* of the country.

Terry stood up. He had decided against using the mic; to protect what little hearing the village had left.

"Right all, please make your way to the front of the coach and only bring with you what is required tonight. Jean will issue a cabin pass card and the

Officer will return your passport. If any of you would care to join me, I will be in the Atrium Bar and the first round is on me!"

Hooray! The passengers cried in unison. Business as usual.

Bob …

Bob's phone vibrated. Although he had been doing odd jobs he couldn't really concentrate; so much was riding on Pam's text. He checked the screen, CAST OFF X ALL ON BOARD X I LOVE YOU X. Bob's imaginary egg timer was flipped to start in his head. His ferry was booked for the night crossing of the 16th. If all went to plan he would be driving the campervan off the ferry and past the terminal containing the coach – packed with the returning Twinners. You could spot the disembarking traffic as you waited to board at Roscoff, but only fleeting glimpses at a bit of a distance. It was a risk that Bob had to take.

He set off on his pet/house sitting rounds. 'Only five more times ever' he thought to himself.

The village of Whiterock was noticeably quiet with no lights or glows from outsized televisions. The odd resident had done the classic advert for would be burglars; they had the half-closed curtains that scream 'we are on holiday' to any opportunist crook who happened to be passing.

Peter had installed a light that came on with a timer and PIR. It was probably powered by his compost heap. Bob finished his rounds at Dr Roberts' place. The cat seemed to eye him up with greater suspicion than normal. If that were possible.

"It's a good job you can't talk puss." He said to the cat.

"I need to pack up your mistress's book collection, a nice man is coming tomorrow to pick them all up."

The cat watched on from his position sat in one of the boxes. As he carefully packed up the valuable volumes, Bob actually enjoyed the feline company and carried on conversing with The Professor.

"Bookman tomorrow, guns and Peter next day, the Chinese superfan is coming the day after, yes puss I agree that is the tricky one, too many unknowns and of course the language barrier. Mary's house money should be transferred tomorrow. I will need to exchange the cash from the book sale into Euros sometime and get money transferred into Pam's cash account. Bugger me I am going to be busy, now get out of that box you furry twat and let me finish."

Before he went home he popped down to various cash machines and withdrew the daily limit on each of his new collection of cards. On his way back he swung into the Nadder Arms to check that Stacy was still on for pet-watch at the end of the week. She greeted him with a wry smile as he entered the bar.

"Bob, you bastard! Arranging this foreign trip. I haven't had a sniff all day!"

"Sorry Stacy love, I'll have a pint of Devon Red while I am here to put a bit in the till. Look they will all be back here annoying you with their various ailments and border disputes before you know it. You could treat this as a small holiday yourself and close up early."

Stacy poured out a pint and placed it on the bar towel in front of Bob, who took a sip.

"Would it be alright to put a small poster up? Or do you know anyone looking for a car, Stacy? I am moving our one on. Could I put a card up for a couple of days? I need a quick sale."

"What sort of money are you after? I might be up for it meself."

Bob had quite a nice car, if a little old, but it was another loose end that needed tying up.

"Look Stacy, you know the car and its worth at least £6K, but as it's you and you're helping me out on Friday, you can have it for half that. I will even drop it down to you if you give me a lift home after."

Stacy eyed him up and down without moving her head, she knew he was up to something but was also well aware of a bargain when it presented itself.

"Cash alright Bob?"

"If it comes in Euros then yes. It is for holiday spending money."

The deal was done. He went home.

He didn't text his beloved as he knew she wouldn't have a signal on the boat. He had an early night. Busy day tomorrow.

Pam ...

The beautiful Breton music drifted through the cabin. It entered Pam's subconscious and helped her to finish off a dream. As the volume increased it roused her and it took her about five seconds to compute the situation. A huge smile developed across her face, 'what an exciting life I am leading', she thought.

Out through the porthole she saw her new home land. She sent a text to her man. MORNING LOVER X FRANCE AHOY X GOOD LUCK TODAY X. Pam got her possessions together and went down to meet the others for her free continental breakfast.

The Whiterock Twinners had taken over a cluster of tables in the on-board restaurant, some of the group were obviously jaded from the previous night's activities. Terry and Jean were nursing bad 'mixed colour wine' hangovers and Mr Smartin had yet to make an appearance.

"Morning Pam, don't bring that pain au chocolate near me please." Terry baulked at her.

"Blimey, you all had a good night by the look of it, ready for the long drive ahead today are we?" Pam took a bite from her pastry.

As Jean's complexion, under her formidable makeup changed colour, it made her skin look like one of those amazing Octopuses that blend into the coral reef to avoid detection.

Mr Smartin bumbled over towards them, his numerous duty free carrier bags doing their damnedest to trip him up, he could only muster one word.

"Coffee."

Pam offered over her cup, he took it without a word or hesitation and downed the lot. The boat's intercom crackled into life. French language first, Pam had always felt that these announcements were a good way to learn

French, you could hazard a guess first time then check your answers when the English came.

"Madam et Monsieur ..."

"Something to do with a delay with disembarkation, I think, an industrial accident or maybe industrial action?" Pam offered the group.

The English translation confirmed that Pam's second guess had been correct. The port authorities were staging a 'work to rule' in support of some goat farmers from the Alps whose cheese had been deemed not to smell bad enough for a new European classification, or something similar.

Peter and his clipboard, who were both unaffected by the previous night's excesses, headed off to annoy the poor person at the information desk. He returned quite quickly, shaking his head.

"Right folks, I am afraid that yes, there will be a delay in us leaving the port. This is due to a planned day of action in support of various workers from across the country. I can only hope that this won't affect our onward journey too much. We will be boarding the coach as normal but might spend some time on the harbour tarmac. I cannot believe that this wasn't considered at the time of booking. If it is an oversight of mine, then I can only apologise. Right, I will revisit our schedule and see if there are any gaps or some flexibility. We might have to cancel our stop at the accordion museum en-route."

A huge cheer went up. Peter looked crestfallen and sat down to look over his massively over engineered itinerary.

Pam smiled and thought, 'he's clever that man of mine, what other delights does he have in store for us?'

The group gathered up their things and headed for the exit as the announcement ended with some shallow thanks from the Captain and his crew who hoped that they would all be welcomed back on board again in the future.

"How else do you think we are getting home numb nuts?" muttered someone.

"Well Captain Pinot Noir can shove his bateau up his derriere for all I care," replied someone else.

A ripple of laughter hovered around the group with various compliments about Mr Smartin's grasp of the French tongue.

Pam held back a bit to check on her runners in the 'I can't find my car' championship hurdle. It was looking good for her as the couple she had chosen to win had fallen out somewhere between the gift shop and duty free and at present weren't talking to each other. This new lack of communication combined with an internal compass made of a cork tile boded well for Pam. She re-joined her group as they shuffled towards the coach.

Thankfully Peter had stopped counting people by tapping them on the head with his clip board, this was in part due to a threat not dissimilar to the one directed toward Captain Pinot Noir and the issue of where his bateau might end up. Pam was last to get on to the coach. She stopped by the driver and coughed to gain everyone's attention.

"Come on everyone, it is not that bad, we are on holiday after all, with an adventure to come. At least you are not Bob, stuck at home, mucking out pets!"

A cheer went up, with lots of muttering about "poor old Bob" and "Pam's right we are on holiday".

Pam sent a text DARLING X NICE DELAY X WILL BE HELD UP AT PORT X GOOD LUCK TODAY X.

The delay had made Pam's selection in the competition null and void. The couple Pam had chosen were the last able bodied passengers to reach their car, however a mobility scooter user did follow later. Pam made a mental note to check the rules with Bob with regard to wheelchair users, but it didn't really matter now. She wouldn't be on any ferry trips for some time to come, hopefully.

Despite some noisy protests from the depths of the coach's internal combustion engine, the beast reluctantly came to life, almost like it had been on a session itself; too much Castrol GTX maybe. Some dull daylight appeared in front of them.

Bill was now at the wheel; Pam couldn't see Sheila. Maybe she was inside the rest room, sorting out the shop. The vehicles in front started to move. Bill inched the coach forward through the bowels of the vessel into the full daylight. A heavy double 'clank' off the ramp announced their arrival on French soil and Pam's new home.

They were ushered into an overflow car park by some people who had been plucked from the administration office, given a high visibility waistcoat, and told to organise disembarkation. These people were a picture of enthusiasm. Bill bought the coach to a halt and killed the engine. Terry got up and took the mic.

"Well my friends, here we are in France!"

A muted and somewhat sarcastic ripple of a cheer went lamely around the coach's interior.

"I will endeavour to find out what is going on and see what time we can expect to leave Roscoff. I have asked Peter to stay on board the coach with his clipboard to avoid a full international diplomatic incident."

This remark was greeted with full laughter.

"Only joking Peter, you are in charge of the coach while I am away."

Terry handed the mic back to Bill and opened the door. An extremely unenthusiastic Hi Viz jacket made her way towards the coach. She lifted up her hand to stop Terry, who had not even gone two paces from the vehicle and was now backing up. Pam could see lots of gesticulation and sign language, she also witnessed Peter straining at the bit, clip board shaking with nervous anticipation. Terry returned on to the coach, followed by the official, who didn't need the mic. Her English was perfect which made Pam wonder what all the hand signals from Terry had been about.

"Madam et Monsieur, I would like to apologise for the delay in your departure from Roscoff. I expect the situation to resolve itself within two hours. Please remain on the vehicle as you have yet to pass through our control system. Thank you for your understanding and cooperation; Vive La France!"

She got off and shut the door behind her. Terry got to his feet and gave a fantastic Gaelic shrug and sat down again. And that was that. Two hours. It was no big deal really and it meant no accordion museum visit. Due to this fact, everyone on board, except Peter, felt total solidarity with their French goat-cheese-making brothers and were quite happy to sit in a car park to support the cause.

Bob ...

The mobile rang. Bugger. It was the other mobile; the 'Mayor's' phone. Bob reached it just in time and had his French persona engaged ready.

It was Terry explaining about the delay and that it shouldn't impact on the ETA, just in case anything was being organised in way of a welcome event. Bob, sorry, the Mayor, assured Terry that everything was fine, not to worry and that now he was in France he should relax and enjoy the journey.

Bob put the Mayor's phone down. He had received Pam's text and was already on his way to meet the bookman. He had completed his animal rounds early, to the surprise of lots of pets. He didn't want any slip ups now. It was bang on 11.00am.

Mr Bird was waiting outside in his immaculate Jowett Javelin. He had removed the back bench-seat to make room for the precious cargo. Bob decided to forego his previous SAS style entry and made for the front door. He opened the door, went in and deactivated the alarm. Mr Bird put the book down he was reading, took off one of his four pairs of glasses and got out of the car. Bob returned to the front door and offered a hand.

"Mr Bird, thank you for being so prompt. Tea with exactly three sugars wasn't it?"

"Rob, why thank you, yes tea, better make it two sugars, strong cane at this house I remember."

He followed Bob into the hall, past the empty shelves and into the dining room where all the books had been boxed with lids left open, and the spines exposed; ready for inspection. There was a tangible feel of mutual trust and respect in the air and, although Bob was robbing Dr Roberts blind, between him and Mr Bird it was different.

Bob left the bookman to gaze upon his prizes. When he returned from the kitchen, having fed the cat and made some tea, he was stopped in his tracks. There, fanned out on the table was the cash; presented in such a way that you could see a bit of each £50 note.

"The remaining £90,000 in cash, as agreed Rob. Excuse the theatricals but somebody once tried to con me out of a substantial sum of money. They had placed several real notes on each end of a large wedge of worthless paper and it looked very realistic. The person concerned was purchasing a signed first edition of 'The Wind in the Willows'. He was wearing white shoes. My father told me never to trust anyone wearing white shoes unless on a cricket pitch or tennis court! So bearing my dad's advice in mind I started to count the bundle. The white shod joker exited stage left, without the book or his real notes, and since then I have always been in the habit of total transparency. Thank you for the tea and for packing the collection up."

Bob handed over the tea and gazed at the table. Yes, this week he was in line to clear over 1.3 million pounds, but at this juncture in his life the £90k in front of him was the largest amount of cash he had ever seen and it looked wonderful. Mr Bird took a sip of tea; his pleasure was audible.

"Perfect, thank you Rob, now if everything is to your satisfaction I will load these treasures into the old jalopy."

"Yes, please do, everything is in perfect order, allow me to give you a hand."

Bob turned the £50 note fans into neat stacks and placed them into the large canvas money bag that Mr Bird had brought it in. He then fell in behind Mr Bird with one of the boxes and they made several journeys until all were loaded neatly into the surprisingly capacious vintage car. Mr Bird closed the boot and went to the passenger door, which he opened, and retrieved from the seat a beautiful bouquet of flowers.

"For your dear Mother as a small token of my respect. Please assure her that her collection will only go to people who really care about books and the characters they contain within their pages."

Bob felt a flush of guilt, half for Dr Roberts and the other half for Mr Bird who would no doubt soon read about this encounter and curse Bob from afar. Of course Dr Roberts would never know who now held her collection, and Bob would leave that for Mr Bird to decide if it remained like that. So, in the interests of transcendental meditation, Bob decided to enjoy the moment and embrace this brief bromance.

"Thank you, for both these flowers and for the professional and honest way you have handled this delicate transaction. I hope you have a safe onward journey and I also hope you have as much enjoyment from the books as will be had with the proceeds."

Bob signed this friendship off with a firm handshake. Mr Bird smiled and returned to the Jowett, which started on the button, and carefully drove the books off to start their next chapter.

Bob took the enormous bunch of flowers into the house, picked up his money bag and surveyed the empty shelves. He spoke directly to the cat who had made its way to Bobs side to investigate the nutritional value of the blooms.

"Look puss, they are only things. Your mistress couldn't take them with her and she had read them all, so I don't feel bad."

And guess what? He didn't.

Pam ...

Pam's phone vibrated just as the coach choked into life and stuttered forward.

BOOKMAN SORTED X CASH + BONUS X LOVE YOU X TAKE CARE X

Pam deleted the text and looked out of the window. The coach party having now been directed to make their way slowly through the car park towards passport control. When their turn came, Terry opened the coach door and went down the steps; he was carrying a large bag containing all the passports.

Pam could just make out all the goings on from her seat. Terry went over to the booth and started to unpack the little books, placing them carefully onto the shelf of the little window.

The official inside the booth took one look at the enormous amount of impending work and started to gesticulate in a very animated fashion. He was indicating and probably using some broken Breton/English vocabulary towards Terry. It looked like he didn't want to see anyone's passport. He had, after all, just returned to his seat following some intense industrial activity without a coffee, and was in no fit state to offer any homeland security.

Terry repacked his bag and returned to the coach. He gave another excellent rendition of a French shrug and sat back down. Bill drove the coach a short distance to the front of the terminal building and parked up. Terry stood up and everyone covered their ears. Terry put the mic down and simply spoke in a raised voice.

"Ladies and gentlemen, well that was easy enough. I wish I had been smuggling a bit more than a few tins of Ambrosia Cream Rice Pudding! Anyway, a short comfort break here, then a big push to try and make up some time. I have made contact with the Mayor of Maisonvide to explain our plight and with true French charm he told us not to worry and to enjoy our drive down, which I am sure we will. Shall we say 15 minutes?"

Pam got off to stretch her legs around the cavernous, sterile, and very empty ferry terminal building. She wanted to get a feel for the place ready for whatever might happen in a few days' time. She needed to seek out any possibilities or glitches there might be in the system, maybe a side door to get from the loading area back into the passenger building. There was a café/bar staffed by a lady who looked like she spent all day asking herself how she ended up working in this place and trying to pinpoint the exact moment it had all gone so wrong in her life.

There were some faded posters trying to convey the delights of the local area. Even the poster designer realised that the majority of people looking at his artwork were either just about to leave the area or going to speed through it to get further south and nearer the sun; so the posters weren't really working. To Pam they looked like an explosion in a tourist information centre, there were images of elderly ladies sporting incredible, gravity defying headgear surrounded by crepes, cheese, glasses of cider, and some lighthouses.

Pam popped into the café, bought herself a large coffee and positioned herself by the window. The last of the cars must have left the holding area as the gates were now up and the vehicles returning to Britain were moving forward. A tiny knot appeared inside Pam. In a few days' time, all being well, she would be in that queue executing a fantastic, fool proof exit strategy; but as yet she hadn't a clue what it was.

She watched the embarkation process unfold but nothing really jumped out at her. It was time she headed back to the coach. She finished her drink and left a large tip in the saucer, enough to prevent the café lady from self-harming after her shift finished.

As she got to the door she was forced to stop and allow a large human crocodile of Hi-Viz clad drones to pass by. They had just come from cleaning the boat, and like the café lady didn't look hugely satisfied with the cards they had been dealt. When the last of them had gone through a service exit, Pam made her way back outside to the coach.

Peter was standing by the door, he had been promoted to chief passport returner, a role he was taking very seriously and executing in a fashion that would put any real passport control officer to shame.

"Ah Pam, we are from the same decade I see."

"Yes Peter, but not from the same planet!" Replied Pam, just wanting her passport back.

Peter, as usual wasn't listening to a word that anyone else said, so didn't take offence to Pam's retort. He was just about to actually check Pam's photo against her face when she nigh-on snatched it out of his hand. He really was an incredibly annoying person.

She got back on the coach and returned to her seat at the back. The last four to embark were the smokers who had collectively chain-smoked three fags each to compensate their lungs for the lack of tar over the next few hours. Peter did an official looking, and over exaggerated, search around the perimeter of the coach.

"Get on you knob-jockey!" Shouted someone.

"No, quick, drive off without him Bill!" Said another.

Terry got to his feet and exchanged words with Bill as Peter climbed back on board to no cheers.

"Right folks, that's it we are now ready. Bill will endeavour to cover as much ground as he can, we will be stopping every few hours to change driver and allow us to stretch our legs. Maisonvide, here we come!"

Following an excellent briefing from her man, Pam was up to speed with the planned journey. It would take a good day and night with a few driver changes. The route would take them over the Monts D'Arree, drop down to the coast near Lorient, then south towards Nantes, and beyond to Maisonvide.

Bill started the coach, its engine turned over with reluctance; as if it knew a lot was about to be asked of it. Pam gazed thoughtfully out of the window, much to her relief, no-one had decided to sit with her. Yes, she was being very reflective, that was it for her now. She had little to do except keep Bob up to date with developments. He was doing all the leg work now.

Pam felt surprisingly calm about the whole situation and very excited. It was a shame that she didn't have any real close friends that she could share things with, but under the circumstances it was probably for the best. The police would have eventually tracked them down and put pressure on them to reveal the whereabouts of the Great Rogues of Whiterock. No, it was just her and Bob.

Pam was sure that Maisonvide would offer her some new opportunities for a close friendship in her dotage.

The coach was now into her stride, eating up the miles. The C roads had turned into Route Nationales. They passed through numerous picturesque villages and towns; most with a standard cluster of commercial outlets. A bar/Tabac, mini-super Marché, a Brocante, a small bakery/café, and of late some sort of artisan craftsperson specialising in the local delicacy.

The road they were on took them over the high Brittany hills and through lush agricultural land – not unlike Devon, but with fewer people.

They were approaching the first large conurbation on the West coast when Bill had to apply the brakes quite sharpish. They had been coming around a bend and came up fast behind a long queue of traffic. Several of the occupants of the cars in front had already alighted and were donning their Hi-Viz waistcoats.

Sheila got up from her slumber and put on her official looking yellow jacket.

Pam saw her exchange some words with Bill before he opened the door and she got off. It wasn't long before she returned having had a conversation with a driver from one of the cars in front.

"Ladies and Gentlemen, I am sorry to have to report that there will be another delay in our journey. It seems that the industrial action we saw earlier is happening all over the country. A large number of farm animals have been released onto the motorway ahead of us. We might be here for a while, sorry."

Pam smiled and sent Bob a text. It was now early afternoon and they were well behind schedule. The first cracks in the entente cordial were starting to show. It would probably be a cheap French roadside hotel for the bed tonight.

Bob ...

Pam's text came through and Bob smiled. He thought there would be further disruption to the journey but not that far North. The Twinners would probably be adding an extra night in some basic hotel.

After the book man had left that morning, Bob had spent the majority of the rest of the day changing the book cash into Euros.

Due to it being such a large amount, he had gone to three supermarkets, two banks, and two travel agents. All seven venues had wished him a pleasant holiday and offered him luck in his new venture.

The nights were drawing out now and so he spent a leisurely evening doing his pet rounds and made himself an interesting hotchpotch supper out of the various tins that were left in the kitchen cupboard. It seemed a shame to waste them. Tomorrow was a big day. Bob would meet the gun man for the first time and it was the moment to use Alexa to access all of Peter's accounts.

The group were far enough away now for any issues with the banks not to worry Bob. Peter would not have time to find out what was happening, or be able to get home to sort it out.

Bob did his rounds. Only three more times would he have to do this. He made a mental note not to offer his services to anyone in Maisonvide. Although on reflection he felt it probably didn't happen in the little French village. All the animals seemed to be loose and the care was distributed equally amongst the inhabitants.

He got home and poured himself a generous tot of Welsh whiskey. The very large bouquet of flowers was still wrapped and in a bucket on the worktop.

"I will pop these down to Dad and say good bye before I leave." Bob actually said this out loud. It was not a sign of madness. Most of us do it eventually when we are on our own for any length of time. His father had died some years before. It never got any better and he missed him as much that evening as he did on the day he passed away. His sleep that night was what you would call fitful; lots of dreams, short and at the front of the head. It felt as if the brain almost had too much to digest. He woke well before the alarm went off and had dressed and made coffee before his phone eventually told him it was time to wake up.

Rightly or wrongly, Bob had thought it would be better to hack into Peter's accounts before normal business hours. He of course realised that it was all done electronically, however there must be some human eye checking it over and any large transactions or total financial U-turns might send up an algorithmic red flag.

If it did, Bob mused, it would be better greeted by some half-asleep trainee bank clerk who would be more interested in checking their Facebook page to see what they had got up to the previous night and figure out how the hell they had even made it into work that morning, than by an overzealous IT guru fortified by lunch, wanting to spoil someone's day.

Deep down Bob realised it wasn't like this, but it gave him a reason and a target.

His phone vibrated two inches to the left. Would all phones eventually vibrate themselves back to their place of manufacture given enough missed calls and battery life? Like the long shore drift of product recall.

It was a text from Pam. They were walking from the Formule Motel back to the coach. She had slept well, most of the others hadn't. The coach party would make it to the hotel at the bottom of the mountain road near Maisonvide, where he had stayed, by tonight.

Bob had three major transactions to navigate over the next two days. Then sort out the campervan, the Stacey car-swap, visit Dad, then hop over the channel and he would be home dry.

It sounded do-able when he said it in his head. His other phone vibrated towards China, it was the Mayor's phone. Bob let it ring this time. He would call the Twinners later after he had been to Peter's which was where he set off to now.

It was going to be a glorious spring morning in that part of Devon. The birds were going nuts and the sap was rising. Oak before Ash this year – in for a splash. Bob would miss the smell of rain on an English summer's day. He nodded in passing to one of the lesser known inhabitants of the village who had opted not to interact with anyone and had stayed at home to mind his dog, and his own business.

Bob arrived at Peter's place bang on 7.30am. He dealt with the animals first, made a large cafetiere of fair-trade, organic coffee and then sat down at the breakfast bar. The kitchen looked messier than he remembered and he was surprised that Peter had left it like this. Bob stared at Alexa. It felt a bit like the weigh-in just before a fight. Bob got his note pad out, he had listed Peter's assets from the last time he had spoken with Alexa. He probably didn't need to but he coughed to get Alexa's attention.

"Good morning Alexa, I wish to complete some financial transactions. Please can you list my current monetary situation?"

"Good morning Peter. As of close of business last night, you had £4,280.40 in your current account, you have £86,802.00 in your savings account, £22,200.00 in your NS&I Premium Bonds, and your Share Portfolio was worth £44,410.00, up 1.26% on the day with a dividend due from your Pennon Group holding today."

Bob was writing this all down. He had decided not to wipe Peter out and now that he had so many credit cards lending him money he didn't need all of it.

"Alexa? I wish to change my nominated bank account to sort code 40-20-29 account number 91406567, can you confirm this?"

Fortunately for Bob, current technology hadn't advanced enough to give mobile devices suspicion. They worked on cold, hard instructions and systems.

"Confirmed change of nominated account."

Bob thought he would start with the current account – not clean it out; but leave enough for Peter to draw on in France so as not to early warn him.

"Alexa, transfer £3,800 from my current to my nominated account and confirm."

It felt longer than the 10 seconds that it actually took.

"Confirmed, these funds will take 24 hours to clear."

"Alexa, please transfer £86,000 from my savings account to my nominated account and confirm."

Even though he was interacting with an inanimate object, he still thought he should use please and thank you.

"Confirmed. These funds will take 24 hours to clear. Please note your enhanced savers interest rate of 0.35%APR has been voided."

"Whoopee fucking Doo." Bob let out on an involuntary basis, reflecting the not very attractive interest rate.

"I'm sorry I do not understand this request," came the monotone reply.

"Oh sorry Alexa, I am mumbling."

Bob had forgotten that Alexa would pick up on everything.

"Alexa, please cash in £21,000 of premium bonds and transfer the funds to my nominated account and confirm."

There was a decidedly longer pause after this request, a small bead of sweat exited Bobs temple.

"Do you wish to cash in 21,000 bonds immediately or wait until the next monthly draw?"

"Alexa cash in immediately and confirm."

Not so long this time as Alexa already knew her way around the NS and I algorithms.

"£21,000 has been realised and will take 3 working days to clear."

Bob made a note that he would have to move this money on the day he was due to leave the country, he continued with the electronic burglary.

"Alexa I wish to sell some of my shares, how should I do this?"

She had to think about the request, Bob had done some research on the internet and thought it would probably be by stock name rather than monetary amount.

"I can provide a list of your current holdings and the value as of yesterday. You can state sell or hold as required. HSBC bank holdings remind you that each transaction will be charged at £10.85 plus 0.5% of the realised value."

Bob decided that this would probably take some time, so he poured out a large cup of coffee and pulled up a stool.

"Thank you Alexa, I wish to sell some of my holdings, please list my stocks."

Alexa, if able, would have cleared her electronic throat.

"Beowolf, 45,000 shares, £456.20."

Bob gave it a second.

"Sell."

Alexa replied "sell 45,000 shares in Beowolf – confirmed"

"The proceeds of this transaction will be cleared in your nominated bank account within 2 working days. Cadence minerals – 400,000 shares – £526.00 ..."

Fortunately for Bob, Peter did have some substantial holdings in Lloyds bank, The Harworth Group, Oxford Biomedica, Sirius Minerals and Solomon Gold; these realised the greater part of the £44k. He left some of the smaller dodgy mining companies in the portfolio so as not to raise a flag at head office indicating a total account clear out. Eventually Alexa reached the end of Peter's portfolio.

"Alexa can you please confirm the details of my most recent transactions?"

Bob was waiting for the machine to answer when he became aware of some movement upstairs. Probably just the cat. He glanced around the room and caught sight of said cat curled up on a coat by the front door. Still, Bob didn't panic. 'Well it can't be the bloody rabbit, just the old house creaking as it wakes up' he thought.

Alexa sprang into life.

"Your most recent transactions are as follows. Yesterday cash withdrawal from ATM converted to Euros £86.20. Debit card transfer to Formule Hotel Group, Euros 72.50. Today £3800 transferred from current account to nominated account."

As Alexa continued with listing Bob's fraudulent deeds, the door at the bottom of the stairs suddenly opened.

Bob froze.

Rose, Peter's somewhat haphazard daughter stepped down into the kitchen; tying up her dressing gown cord as she walked passed a petrified Bob.

She nodded at him and made her way towards the cafetiere that had been made earlier. It had to be said that she didn't look brilliant at the best of times but with absolutely no makeup on or any attempt at taming her hair, she did look very odd. All her main features, eyes, nose, ears etc looked like they had over developed by about a month in the womb. The stop-growing development gene had broken and as a result she bore more than a passing resemblance to Mrs Potato Head.

Bob still hadn't moved.

Alexa continued to drone on about the morning's events.

His normal cognitive abilities had left his body and he couldn't even function enough to reach over and turn her off. Seconds passed ... felt like hours. Alexa came to an abrupt halt after sharing the total amount of Bob's fraud. £150,800 was to be transferred to the nominated bank account. This last statement hung in the now silent kitchen.

Thoughts inside Bob's deeply disturbed mind turned to murder and body disposal. He had time to dispatch her. He was already going to be doing a long stretch for theft and fraud so what would manslaughter on the grounds of diminished responsibility add?

"Morning Bob." Offered Rose. Her mouth remained open after she had finished speaking. Bob opened his mouth in the vain hope that something would come out.

"Rabbit." Was all he could muster.

"Yes, look I am sorry, I would have done it myself but I knew Dad had made arrangements for you to do it and I didn't want to upset Flopsy's routine, he doesn't even know I am back" her mouth remained open. She looked incredibly vacant.

"How was Wales?" Bob asked. He was on the verge of a nervous breakdown and he was somewhat perplexed as to why she hadn't asked anything about him engaging in large financial transactions using Peter's Alexa, before eight in the morning, in their kitchen.

"Look Bob, promise you won't ever tell Dad, but I haven't been to Wales on a retreat. I've been in Weymouth staying with my new man. I am only back here to get some more of my things. Dad wouldn't approve of Kirk, he's not his type."

An early sunbeam suddenly streamed into the dull kitchen. It reflected what was happening in Bob's core. Yes, Rose was really that vacant and so absorbed in her tiny little world that nothing else entered into her low level consciousness.

"Rose, I won't say a word, do you want me to feed Flopsy tonight?" he said carefully.

"Bob, to be honest I hate that rabbit. Dad thinks I am still a little girl. I am a woman now; a woman who is being ravished in Weymouth by an unsuitable dropout and Dad's paying for it."

Poor old Peter, being screwed by everyone except a gorgeous female.

"Sorry to ask but could you give me a lift to town? I just can't be arsed to walk and could you sub me a few quid? Kirk's money doesn't come through until next week."

Bob got up and felt in his pocket. Plenty of ill-gotten gains were to hand. He reached around and pulled out five £20 notes which he passed to Rose.

"I can drop you down in about an hour if you want. I need to be back in Whiterock for 11.00am."

"£100 squid! Wow nice one Bob! Dad will be good for it and see you right."

Bob knew he would never see Peter, the gormless Rose or the £100 ever again and he didn't care one jot.

"No worries Rose, you and Kirk have a ball. I will see you in an hour. Listen out for my honk out front."

Bob picked up his bits of paper from the table and turned off Alexa. Rose didn't take any notice of Bob as she was deciding what to spend her cash on. Her mouth remained open.

Bob went home, still in a strange sort of daze, he couldn't really compute what had just happened, but there it was. He had cleared out Peter in front of his own Daughter; unbelievable. He had time to collect himself, sort out some more cash to turn into Euros, give Rose a lift into town and be back in time to meet the gunman.

He made a mental note that he must sit down later and do a stocktake, funds and cash were building up all over the place and he needed to keep a better track on it all.

He made a cup of coffee and sent a text to Pam warning her to keep an eye on Peter for any changes in character or watch for any irate phone calls. He didn't think the bank would react too quickly but in this technological age you could never be too careful. He only had to survive three more days at this level of stress and he would be gone.

Pam ...

Pam's phone made a noise. She was back on the coach, and under the circumstances it hadn't been too bad a night. Not that she cared as she was enjoying every single minute of this adventure.

Late last evening a group decision was made to abandon transport and make for the nearest hotel that had a bar. The coach had stop-started for a few more kilometres but they were not really getting anywhere. Terry had been trying to contact the Mayor but without success. The arrival would have to be delayed yet again.

Due to the nearest roadside hotel having a decent bar and chef, spirits remained surprisingly high amongst the Twinning party. Pam also knew that this meant one less day at the final destination and with that, one less day to do any digging around. So she joined in with the group and allowed lots of people to buy her a drink.

"Good old Bob, he probably had the right idea staying at home." Someone had said before they remembered about his mum's risky operation.

"Sorry Pam, how unthoughtful, let me get you a drink."

The staff at the Formule hotel had never experienced anything like it. In that location they rarely got above 30% occupancy. It was only the bar being frequented by some locals that kept the place profitable and last night they had made more behind the bar than they would normally take in a month.

The breakfast had been the best yet, with fresh pastries, still warm from a local artisan baker's oven. Bill had reported that all industrial action had been suspended due to an offer from the government to reduce the tax on all goat produce, plus the fact there was a big football fixture on that evening.

In various states of hungoverness the party made its way back to the vehicle. Terry had tried again several times to make contact with the Mayor but to no avail. Peter was corralling the tail enders with his clipboard. Pam read her text and made a note to watch Peter more closely. She sent a reply text to Bob suggesting he made contact with Terry so as not to raise an early alarm. It was Terry who now got to his feet following an over exaggerated nod from Peter.

"Fellow Twinners. I hope you all had as good a night's sleep as you deserved to. I would like to apologise to everyone about my attempt at Karaoke especially as Jean now informs me that the hotel didn't even have a Karaoke machine! So really sorry about that. Bill has told us that the strike has been called off so no more delays. We will push on as fast as we can with only a couple of short comfort breaks. Sheila would like to remind you all of the extensive range of items stocked in the loo, sorry, shop."

He was interrupted by his phone ringing, he looked at the screen to see if it was some twat wanting to help him put in a claim for the accident he hadn't had whilst on his way to post his PPI refund letter. It wasn't. It was the Mayor of Maisonvide; although the code looked different.

"Sorry everyone, I better take this, it is our host."

Terry got off the coach and started to have a conversation. Peter seized this rare opportunity to promote himself and stood up. He then proceeded to say almost everything that Terry had just said about the shop, the route and plans but in a different order to make it sound like new important information was being disseminated. But nobody was listening to him except Pam, who didn't detect any signs of distress due to bizarre financial irregularities. He was still a total tool. Terry got back on and Peter sat down.

"Right folks, I have smoothed everything over with our Twins. The Mayor suggests we just get to and settle in our hotel tonight, and we can make all the detailed arrangements in the morning. So Bill and Sheila, if I can hand over to you, let's get this show back on the road."

Bill nodded and fired up the charabanc. It was a long drive ahead and they had the expected nightmare around Bordeaux, but it was early, dry and neither driver had gone near the bar last night. So with a bit of luck they would make the hotel in good time for a meal and a glass or two of the local grape.

Pam sent a text to Bob to say that the phone call had gone down well and they should make it to the hotel that evening. Bob replied.

MAYORS PHONE NOW DESTROYED X CONTACT NO LONGER NEEDED X HANG IN THERE LOVELY X

Pam responded.

WHATEVER YOU THINK DARLING X YOUR PLANS ARE WORKING WELL X I
LOVE YOU X

The atmosphere on board was quite upbeat which surprised Pam
somewhat, seeing as how they were a day late and had wasted so much time
looking at the hard shoulder plus spent a night in a non-descript cheap hotel.
She was acutely aware that the mood would quickly change once they tried
to reach Maisonvide tomorrow sometime.

She and Bob had spoken at length about this situation and tried to second
guess people's reaction. Sadly, they lived in a blame culture so the journey
back to Roscoff would be very uncomfortable for Pam. It had, after all, been
Bob's idea to set up this link in the first place; he had made contact with the
Mayor and arranged for the trip to take place.

The pair had toyed with the idea of Pam going to ground and disappearing
at Maisonvide but this would lead to early alarm bells and a high probability
of the Police getting involved – suspicions would be raised too close to their
new home. So no, not an idea they ran with.

Pam had made a suggestion that might just work. It would rely a lot on
luck and on the reaction of the people of Maisonvide. What if Bob had quite
innocently been in contact with a complete and known fantasist? Some nut-
job resident of the area with delusions of grandeur. Bob and Pam would be in
the clear for those vital last couple of days. 'Poor old Bob, he fell for that one,
hook, line and sinker' yes everyone would be disappointed and proper pissed
off, but importantly, frustrations would be directed at the faux Mayor and
not at the real perpetrators.

It might get Pam back to the ferry in a cloak of sympathy and not at the
end of daggers. She didn't really mind anyway – it was only for two days and
she would never have to see any of these people again. The only thing they
didn't want to happen was for a large blimp balloon to go up at home and
stop Bob from getting to the port.

So this was the ruse they had settled on. A rogue Mayor.

It would need a lot of input from the village of Maisonvide but as Bob
had gathered from his fact finding mission the main residents did not want
too much contact with the outside world. Bob had tipped off Raphael with
the suggestion of a fake Mayor, along with other ideas that would put off the
visitors ever wanting a partnership.

The best thing in Bob and Pam's weaponry was that the Maisonviders had
shunned all previous French government attempts at getting them to enter
into the spirit of Entente Cordiale. If Pam could position herself in the midst

of it maybe she could plant a seed of doubt, set a scene about a disgruntled former member of the community. This could help to explain the total lack of comprehension when the party arrived for the supposed grand welcome ceremony.

Bob had spoken with Raphael the waiter, and the Mayor. He had warned of a future invasion and suggested the serving of cooking wine to the party. They were both confident in the intelligence of the inhabitants and that they would go along with the yarn.

The coach had now left the hotel and was heading South through the French countryside.

Next stop Maisonvide.

Bob ...

Bob read the messages from his girl. He had now totally destroyed the Mayor's phone and, having read numerous articles on the subject, he felt the best way in which to do this was by placing it in his workbench vice and gently applying pressure. He got a surprising amount of pleasure by doing this. He knew of course that it didn't really matter about the traceability of this phone. It would be too late for the Police to do anything with it. Pam and Bob would have been unmasked as the daring duo well before the phone was traced, but Bob still enjoyed gently squeezing the life out of it.

The gunman was coming to the house at 11.00am. Bob had already been to Terry's that morning to feed the cat and retrieve the guns; which now resided in his newly approved cabinet. He had not met the buyer and all the dealings had taken place over the phone. Bob hadn't minded paying a small finder's fee to the agent. The buyer had also paid a generous contribution to prove his commitment to the purchase. The agent had confirmed that both parties held a legal certificate and that the serial numbers matched the records. Bob gave the guns a quick wipe down and locked them away. He wanted to appear professional and to do everything correctly. No mistakes needed this late in the day.

Just as the kettle switched itself off Bob heard a low engine hum coming from the front of the house. Its decibel level and pitch was such that he felt his very soul vibrate to its rhythm. He went to the window and spied a beautiful Range Rover Vogue V8 in midnight blue with the registration number GUN 1 ticking over in his driveway.

The driver was using the in-car phone and his voice could just be made out, even over the purr of the engine and through Bob's front window. The occupants voice had an abrupt military twang. The conversation seemed to comprise of short incomplete sentences mostly pointing out the shortcomings of whatever poor soul was at the other end of this telephonic exchange; which was now coming to an end.

A very tall and elegant man exited the Range Rover. He was in full shooting regalia taken straight from the Edwardian era. He approached the front door, as did Bob who wanted to open it before this character probably knocked it off its hinges. A deeply tanned hand was thrust in Bobs direction.

"Major Tom Thompson, RM retired. Bob I take it?"

Bob took the outstretched hand.

"Yes, sir, please come through" he took the retired Major through the hall, past the cabinet, and into the now quite sparse sitting room.

"Moving?" Came the abrupt question.

"Downsizing."

"Local?"

"Abroad."

"Children?"

"Left."

"Wife?"

"Away."

"Guns?"

"Yes."

"Thank you."

Inside Bob, somewhere, a small fist punch happened as he beat the Major in a one worded conversation competition. He went into the hall and unlocked the cabinet. Bob returned to the sitting room where the Major was still licking his wounds after being defeated. 'Why had he said thank you instead of thanks?'

This would haunt him for years to come, surmised Bob, who now laid out the weapons on the table. The Major turned and actually bought himself to attention as if a more senior officer had entered the room.

"Would you like a cup of tea whilst you look over the items and then if you are happy I will get the paperwork and we can do the deal."

"Tea? Yes, please. English Breakfast if you have it. Now let's have a look at this lovely pair."

Bob bought the kettle back to the boil, he found an English Breakfast tea bag amongst the collection half-inched from various hotel stays over the years.

He looked at the package: 'Twinings'. The trigger for all this adventure had started with a simple cup of tea and now look. Only a few months on and he was standing in a nearly empty house about to sell his neighbour's antique shotguns to a verbally constipated retired army Major. Incredible or what?

Not wanting to start another round of one-worded conversations, he asked the Major "Would you like some sugar?"

"Yes please Bob. These are real beauties. Won't you be sorry to see them go?"

"Too many memories I'm afraid Major. And also nowhere to shoot at the new place."

Major Tom had donned white gloves and was engrossed in the guns, caressing them carefully, like they were the female form.

"Yes, always a problem, having no-one to shoot."

Bob didn't think that this was a Freudian slip. He left the Major to his erotic fumblings. He felt a bit of a gooseberry and thought about leaving the room.

"Right, excellent, yes must get on. Cash wasn't it? Good to get rid of some of the old paper money, builds up, don't always know what to do with it you know."

He reached inside his jacket to retrieve a large brown envelope, from the poacher's pocket, which he placed on the table. "I should count it if I were you. Got one of my people to do it. Not always up to it. You know – don't really trust them myself."

"Right, ok, I will." Bob opened the package. It looked exactly what £130k should look like. Big, fat, lovely wads of money.

The Major looked on and reminisced aloud. "I have never trusted anyone since the incident at Ali's Bazaar, Serbia, 1983. Paid for it with dollars and received the change in dried animal droppings or whatever the locals used. Damn them. God, what I wouldn't give for another crack at the Balkans."

Bob quickly counted the wads before the conversation became too right wing.

"All there, thank you Major. I expect you would like all the paperwork that goes with your new guns?"

The Major was still handling the guns. He had lifted one of them up to the shooting position. No doubt pretending to keep the empire alive by taking out a few innocent inhabitants of a former Soviet Republic state.

He lowered the sights.

"Yes, bloody forms, right, I think I have to sign something and then you send it off."

'Yes, that's going to happen,' thought Bob. He just didn't care now. He only had to last two more days. It was the disc sale tomorrow. The collector from China was flying in personally to pick up his prize. After that, Bob was nearly home dry.

He got the forms and placed them in front of what remained of the British empire.

"Right, jolly good." The Major signed the forms and Bob made a point of checking the serial numbers against the two shotguns. But this was just for show. The Major wasn't interested and neither was Bob.

"Right sir, that's everything in order. I will complete my side and send the forms in next week. Our transaction is finished. Can I get you some more refreshment? Or do you need to get on?"

Thankfully The Major did need to get on. "No. I simply must be going, I need to get these ladies to safety and then get down the woods."

He left that hanging in the air as if Bob knew exactly what he meant. It could have been for firewood or for dogging. Bob left it there forever in the ether. Major Tom disappeared out of the front door – minus the guns. He then returned moments later with two new soft gun cases which had retrieved from his vehicle. They were midnight blue to match the car, with monograms of initials picked out in gold. He placed the new acquisitions into the cases with the same care shown as that of a new mother placing her baby into the Moses basket for the first time.

He carried them to his vehicle and returned to the front door where Bob met him.

"Well Sir, excellent fuss free transaction. Just how it should be done."

He made it sound like he was filling in the feedback section on ebay. His hand came forward, still gloved. Bob took it, and shook it vigorously.

"Thank you Major, have a safe trip and don't forget, I won't be processing the forms until next week so don't panic if you don't hear anything for a while."

"I haven't got to where I am today by panicking sir. Anyway I know where to find you in case I need to and of course I have the guns now. Over and out."

The Major marched back to his car, got in, started the engine and before pulling away, barked some orders at the dashboard. Getting it to dial the next poor person he was going to give a dressing down to.

Bob watched him drive up through the village. He checked his watch, it was still early afternoon. The clipped transaction had bought him some time. He decided to go on a mission to Taunton and visit the banks and supermarkets to swap his sterling to Euros. He reached for his phone and sent Pam a text.

ALL GOOD HERE X ONLY DISCS TO DO X OFF TO GET MONEY CHANGED X HOW GOES IT AT YOUR END? X MISS YOU X NOT LONG NOW X

Pam ...

Her phone vibrated and woke her from a trance like state. Her eyes had been taking in the changing French countryside but none of this information had been passed directly to the brain. It was being held in a frontal lobe post-room, waiting to be picked up if ever needed. Her actual brain had been processing events that were about to happen over the next few days.

The mood on the coach was lifting in line with the steadily climbing temperature. Good time had been made by both drivers and the on-board shop had done good business. The scenery had started to change, slowly. They were following the coastal motorway, heading towards Bordeaux. Pam was being reassured by the size of her new homeland. Surely just the two of them could hideaway here and not be found.

Outside of the large conurbations, the population was sparse. She had read in numerous articles about the shift in demographics in France; large numbers of the young were being enticed to the bright lights of the city for work and for pleasure. Some rural communities were dying. Whole villages were being abandoned – even sold. Only last year Bob had shown her a small piece on a tiny hamlet near the Spanish border, being offered with a starting bid of 10,000 Euros. You could become Mayor of your own village for the cost of less than a garage in England.

It was getting late into the afternoon and they were due one more comfort break before the final push to Maisonvide. Terry was having a chat with the resting driver, he stood up, thankfully without the mic, and addressed the Twinners.

"Madames et Monsieurs, soon we will be stopping for our last scheduled break before we finally make it to the hotel. I have called ahead and they are happy to accommodate our evening meal requirements, so you don't need to fill yourselves up here. Shall we say 30 minutes? Lovely. Then arrival at our hotel will be about 8pm."

A small, polite, and relieved ripple moved back through the coach. It awoke a small kaleidoscope of butterflies inside Pam. They were getting close. Her new home and her new life.

The coach pulled into a rest area. Quite a good one, with a variety of shops and outlets. The assistants were wearing the local costumes and looking really self-conscious. Pam bought herself some local artisan biscuits and treated herself to a small bottle of wine; something she would rarely do at home. She sat down alone at one of the outdoor tables, the late spring sun warming her skin.

'I could get used to this' she thought to herself, before she corrected this out loud with "I need to get used to this."

A clipboard appeared in her peripheral vision. "Sorry Pam were you talking to someone?"

"Oh, Peter, no. I do talk to myself and I was missing Bob."

"Actually it's Bob I want to talk to you about, can I grab a pew next to you?"

This caught Pam out. She made room for Peter and put her logic-function brain into gear, ready for action.

Peter sat down. "Have you been in contact with Bob at all?"

"Well, yes we have texted and spoken a bit. Why do you ask?"

"I was wondering if you might ask him something next time you speak? I have been having trouble accessing the internet and communicating with my bank accounts. When you next speak, could you ask if there have been any problems at home? Sorry … at my home? The cat might have unplugged my hard drive or something. Maybe it's an issue with Whiterock but I was trying to do some internet banking and move some funds around. Anyway, it can probably wait until I return, but if you could give me the heads up then I won't need to ring the bank."

Pam's logical brain had already worked out all the permutations without her really having to think about what she did next. She and her brain both knew they had to stop Peter from contacting the bank.

"Peter, that is strange, look let's call Bob now and see if he can shed any light on the situation."

She had her phone to hand and instructed it to call Bob, it did.

"Oh, hello love, yes, no, all good thanks, look I won't keep you as the coach is leaving here in a bit, yes, very close now, only about three hours to go to the hotel. Now I have Peter with me, yes, right here next to me, he was wondering if there have been any problems with the internet back in Whiterock, or maybe an issue with his home connection, he wants to do some online banking. Oh, there has been, yes, right, I see, ok, scheduled repairs to the poles, intermittent service, yes I will tell him. Thank you darling. I know, not long now, you too, bye, no you go first." He did!

"Did you get that Peter? Yes, there have been some issues in general and he said not to worry too much. It would be sorted out over the weekend, he also said that if money was an issue then I can lend you some until our return."

Peter started to become quite animated with his clipboard. Pam thought he might actually be sleeping with it.

"Oh dear me no, Pam, completely the wrong end of the stick. Money is no problem; I have pots of it."

'Oh no you don't', thought Pam.

"I was just seeing if it was me, or everyone. No, don't need money, thank you for the update. I will contact the bank on my return if at all. I will leave you to finish up and embark. I need to try and round up the smokers before they light up another one. Thanks again Pam, and thanks to Bob for clearing that up."

"Clearing you out more like." whispered Pam to herself.

Peter and clipboard went off to herd up the nicotine addicts. She finished her wine, which for a service station tasted lovely, and headed back to the coach.

At the start of the journey she had the foresight to sit on the right hand side of the coach, just so she could fully benefit from this last leg of the journey. Their route ran parallel with the Pyrenees. This majestic mountain range was nature's border wall, separating the French from the Spanish.

As it was spring, the tops of the peaks all still sported white hats. If like Pam, you hailed from England, this range epitomised everything from The Lord of the Rings. She now knew what it felt like to be a Hobbit approaching Mordor; albeit in a coach.

The sun was getting lower in the sky, setting fire to the horizon. The Twinning party had now left the main arterial road and were motoring along various Route Nationales. Just as Bob had described it, the settlements became smaller and less populated. The quality of the roads, although superior to Devon, had lowered in standard.

Pam noticed that most of the idle chatter on board had ceased as everyone drank in the delights that rural France had to offer.

The light was now fading as the coach climbed and wound its way upwards towards the hotel. Excitement was building. Pam was keeping an eye on the altitude signs, she saw the 880 one and 967, and at last the 1080. The one Bob had said was close to the hotel. Sure enough the typical village sign appeared. The coach slowed to a snail's pace as both drivers scanned for the destination. The phone signal was intermittent at best so the sat-nav was accurate to about ten miles behind them.

The hotel was beautifully lit up. Spring flowers had been placed into the troughs outside. A few local customers were sitting on the terrace, enjoying a drink and the feel of the warmth that emanated from the stone walls. A lasting gift from the sun to keep off the evening chill.

The air-brakes of the coach sent the local pigeons to an early roost.

Peter got to his feet, this time Terry didn't stop him. Clipboard at the ready, he spoke. "Well here we are at the hotel."

"Non merde!" someone offered.

"Yes, sorry, bit obvious, right, our base for a few days. I suggest we all take our bags later, let's go eat and drink. We can sort out the rooms this evening. Big thanks to our drivers for getting us here ... Maisonvide tomorrow!"

They all started to clamber off the vehicle. It seemed like all the staff had come out of the hotel to greet them; as if a Victorian master had returned after a year of absence looking for the lost city of Z.

Pam bought up the rear, taking it all in. Her man had been here, laying the trail, and it was just as he had said, 70's kitsch. The party thronged passed reception and straight to the bar.

All the tables had been laid ready. Terry and Jean stayed at the front desk speaking, albeit in broken Franglais, with the hotel manager. Pam hovered close by, she didn't want to attract too much attention to herself just in case she needed to get a job here sometime in the future but she did want to make sure everything was ok and if not, pre-empt any problems.

She was feigning interest in a leaflet advertising a hat festival that had taken place 50 miles away, 2 years ago, when Terry and Jean turned away from the reception desk looking somewhat perplexed.

"Everything ok you two?" piped up Pam.

Terry was shaking his head.

"I don't know Pam, to be honest, it may be that my French is worse than I thought, or something is amiss. The manager welcomed us and has everything ready for our stay. I think she asked us if we were here for the castles. I said we had come to visit and link with Maisonvide and she looked really puzzled. Probably is my French. Anyway, I explained that I was having difficulties contacting the Mayor to inform him of our arrival and she laughed at me."

Jean joined in, her make-up was looking travel sick. "Yes Pammy."

Pam hated that name, but remembered what her and Bob were doing to the village and let it pass.

"All a bit odd" continued Jean "we thought the Mayor might like to join us for a welcome drink. I gave her the phone number to call from her landline but she just shook her head and repeated 'pas de Mairie!' that means no Mayor doesn't it? Your French is pretty good Pam; it does mean no Mayor doesn't it?!"

"Well yes Jeannie, it does. Maybe Terry is right and something has been lost in translation. I am sure everything will become clear in the morning. We are all going to our Twin village after breakfast. So let's not fret, and enjoy the moment. They have laid the tables and the bar is open. Come on let me buy you two a drink."

"Thanks Pam. The steadfast voice of reason as ever. And with those wise words of 'let me buy you a drink' how can I refuse? Lead on neighbour, lead on." Terry stood aside to let the ladies walk in.

Pam took them through and found a gap in the bar. She smiled at the girl, who had just been stood behind the reception desk, and ordered a bottle of the best local red and three glasses.

She then joined Terry and Jean at one of the prepared tables. The same girl who had just served at the bar now came to the table as a waitress. Her English was good.

"Madames et Monsieurs, for your delight we have prepared local dishes. If food is served in a green dish it is suitable for vegetarians, if in a red dish it is normal food, we hope you enjoy it."

She bowed her head and went off to get the food. She returned accompanied by more staff and lots of red and green bowls.

The food was excellent and the wine was very quaffable. Pam thought that this was the moment in time you would freeze if you could. Everyone was happy and content but it would all go downhill from here.

As the night went on, people left the proceedings in dribs and drabs. The coach hold had been left open so that people could retrieve their bags and check in when they wanted. By midnight Pam had had enough. She gave her excuses to the remaining group and made her way via the coach and the reception to her single room. She wondered if it was the same one that Bob had stayed in. Her head was still full of travel so she sat at the open window gazing up at the hills and mountains.

A small cluster of lights shimmered in the distance. They came from high up on a hillside. She wondered if it was her new home sending her a welcome message in twinkling Morse code. She took in a large lungful of fresh French mountain air and it tasted good. 'This will do very nicely.'

With a combination of full-bodied wine, rich local fare and a long coach journey, Pam had slept like the dead. Her internal clock had automatically adjusted to French time and she awoke to the still open window at 8am.

Down at breakfast she joined a few of the party. Bill the driver looked like he had either slept in the coach hold or not gone to bed at all.

The barmaid/waitress/receptionist/cleaner was serving fresh coffee, pastries, and of course a selection of cold meats just in case any of the guests had some German blood crawling through their furred-up veins.

By 9am everyone was up and about, Terry stood up and brought the proceedings to order.

"Right folks, hope you all had a good night's sleep. Yet another thing we are in debt to Bob for. Such a lovely choice of hotel. We owe him so much we just as well give him all of our possessions upon our return, eh Pam?!"

Pam thought and hoped that she put out a smile but it probably looked like she was having a mild stroke.

Terry continued. "Can I suggest we rendezvous on the coach at 10am, god these French words really do get everywhere don't they? Rendezvous at 10am so that Bill can take us the last few miles to our friends in the hills."

As he sat down to finish his pain au chocolate wrapped in luncheon meat, the young waitress approached him and spoke with characteristic French mannerisms.

Terry called over to Bill who joined them. Pam kept her distance this time. She couldn't keep trying to change things. It was inevitable that the merde was going to hit the fan. It was just a matter of when and how much merde would be produced. Pam assumed it would be of industrial quantities.

She let the three of them have their conversation before heading in that direction. The girl left the group and busied herself collating any untouched food that could be reassembled and relaunched as some other local delicacy later that week. "Everything alright boys?"

Bill looked up at Pam. "Yes, thanks love."

Pam hated that.

"Little French Maid said we would not be able to drive up to the village, I explained that I have been driving the lanes of Devonshire for forty years and a poxy French track was no match for Bill the Bus."

Pam thought 'Twat' but smiled nicely and made her way outside to join the others loitering by the coach.

Following a large amount of feedback, Peter had dispensed with his clipboard and was struggling to come to terms with his loss. He now just half-heartedly ushered people on board, who took absolutely no notice of him at all now that they were no longer under threat of having a clipboard inserted into them. Bill got into position behind the wheel, he gave off the aura of one who was about to compete in an extreme sport. Pam wondered whether she should remind him that he was driving a coach and not a quad bike but then thought better of it and sat down. Jean was the last to join the party. She appeared to have applied all of her duty free purchases in one sitting and resembled the floor of the ferry boutique in the aftermath of a Force 12 in the channel.

The coach seemed surprised that it was being awoken after such a long drive the previous day. It eventually got everything working but it did all sound out of sync. Some of the hotel staff had gathered on the terrace, their collective expressions hovered somewhere between horror and disbelief, with the odd look of pity thrown in for good measure.

The coach finally got its cylinders firing in the right order and pulled away. Some local inhabitants had joined the staff and, upon hearing about the intended destination, half-heartedly waved the Twinning party off; most never expecting to see any of the occupants alive again.

Pam's phone vibrated. A signal must have appeared. She checked the screen. Two different providers were offering her a service and there was a text from Bob; sent the previous evening. It was sending her his love and thoughts. She quickly sent a reply despite knowing that the cost would probably be the equivalent of Albania's national debt.

ON COACH TO MAISONVIDE X LOVELY HOTEL X MISS AND LOVE YOU LOADS X

The coach crawled along the quiet main street, and passed the obscure fountain. Pam disagreed with Bob and thought it was a relief map of the area. They continued on by the abandoned shops and empty houses. The signpost to Maisonvide appeared ahead and this seemed to reassure everyone on board that the place did really exist. Dr Roberts made her way to the front of the coach and spoke to Bill who brought them to a halt. The Doctor alighted and crossed the road to take a photograph of the vehicle next to the sign. Having taken far too many images she got back on.

"One for the website."

She smiled as she retook her seat. Bill checked his mirrors and indicated left, changed into a low gear and headed up the road signed to Maisonvide. Pam swopped sides remembering what Bob had told her about the road and the drop down to the river and also that the crash barriers were probably made from recycled pasta. It started off okay, and the coach and all the occupants seemed blissfully unaware of the impending threat to their lives.

Before long the surface changed. Bill veered them all to the left, then hard to the right, trying to avoid the early potholes and precipices. The road fairly quickly turned into not more than a track. Pam became aware that people had stopped remarking about plants and the odd goat, and instead they were becoming silent except for the occasional stifled scream or sharp intake of breath.

To give Bill his dues, he had already made it farther than Bob had predicted. He was now in first gear and crawling so slowly; it was like a scene from "Ice Cold in Alex". At several points Bill, who was now sweating profusely, had asked Sheila to get off and visually guide him under

overhanging rock features. Sheila looked ashen faced and although she was waving him onwards, her head was constantly shaking. Pam estimated that over half the passengers had their eyes shut, several were rocking back and forth, and one person was even visibly praying.

Bob had walked this route so was unaware of the real peril involved. At one bend in the track, the middle section of the coach was actually suspended over thin air. As they neared the old shepherd's hut, the coach started to spin on the loose gravel and stones that made up what remained of any recognisable road surface. It suddenly lost all purchase and dropped back sharply, it was only about a metre but felt like a mile. Mr Smartin called out with a high pitched holler.

"Driver, stop this bloody contraption, I am getting off. Sod this for a game of soldiers!"

Bill the Bus(t) …

Bill gingerly applied the brakes and the coach came to a halt; thanks, mostly, to a massive pothole acting as natures handbrake. Terry raised his hand.

"Right folks, those who are still able to, I suggest get off for a breather. I am just going back down the track to retrieve part of my arse from the ditch it fell into."

Nobody laughed. They had all come face to face with death and were still unsure if they had come back. Everyone got off, and after a minor medical procedure was carried out on Bill to peel his fingers from the steering wheel, so did he. Some non-smokers took up the habit. Some just sat and caressed the ground like the Pope. Others discovered new religions and baptised themselves.

It remained like the climax of a Francis Ford Coppola film for some time. Mr Smartin was the one to take charge. It was only he and Pam who would not go on to suffer the long term effects of PTSD.

"As I said earlier, sod this for a lark, now how far is it to the damn place?"

Nobody really knew.

Sheila spoke.

"When the company planned the route we couldn't find this last stretch on any current map. It isn't on Google Earth so just guess work really. I didn't catch the sign at the main road, but it probably wouldn't be correct anyway. I mean who is ever going to get a vehicle up here to measure the distance?"

"Well I suggest we change tact." Mr Smartin offered "The coach could just about turn around here I think, what say you Sheila?"

She nodded. There was a wide flattish area in front of the shepherd's hut.

"Right" said Mr Smartin decisively "we have no idea how far it is, so let's split up. Peter, Terry, Pam and I will carry on up the track to find this blessed Maisonvide, Pam you up for it?"

Pam nodded and he continued,

"Come on then. The four of us will leave here now and the rest of you can help Bill to turn around. Then I suggest you all walk behind the coach and head back to the hotel bar. We, the advanced party can have a good recce and report back to the group. How does that sound? I have to say, and no offence to anyone, but this isn't looking very suitable."

He did make an involuntary glance in the direction of Pam. She would just have to put up with this uncomfortable feeling for maybe two or three more days. The pathfinder-four got their things together and started off on the onward journey.

The rest of the group waited for Bill to very slowly turn the coach around. Bill looked very deflated. For the first time in his long driving career the road had won the day. He would go on to never fully recover from this.

Initially the splinter group walked in silence. They were all still in a state of shock following the earlier near death experience. About half a mile up the track they stopped and turned to check on the rest of the group. Bill had successfully about-turned the coach and was proceeding very slowly to retrace his skid marks (literally).

It appeared that some of the returners had got back on board; maybe to offer some moral support to the driver. The majority opted to walk behind at a safe distance; some leaning on each other like the walking wounded from a scene straight out of a horror film.

As Pam turned back to face her direction of travel, she spotted a yellow vehicle up ahead in the distance. She saw its shimmering lights. It was reversing at speed having just spotted the visitors and was probably off to raise the alarm. This was a big moment for Pam, she was nearing the place she was likely to spend the next few years living in. It felt a bit like an arranged marriage, she hadn't really had too much choice in the matter. Bob had really carefully selected the place but neither knew how it was going to work out, she trusted her man, and that it would be fine.

Bob, of course, had been driven up to the village in what he described as a lunch box on wheels, but Pam had time to take it all in. The sounds of the river below the track, some unfamiliar bird calls in the scrub and, way off, the haunting melody of neck bells on grazing animals. The wind was warm, early butterflies were sampling the flowers, it was bloody idyllic. She broke the fairly strained atmosphere.

"This track makes our roads look first class. I don't think I will ever moan about another pothole again."

"You're right Pam, I wouldn't want to commute along this route every day. There is no way the coach would have made it up here." Terry agreed solemnly, and then with a brighter tone "Look team, I think we're nearly there."

They had made it to the plateaux with the beautiful meadows that had enchanted Bob. Terry pointed ahead towards the distant cluster of buildings. The ancient stone archway was just as Bob had described it to Pam; but the pictures, like all pictures, didn't do it justice. There were people milling about by the entrance to the village. A few of the houses that were built into the old walls had their washing out. No need for fabric conditioner here; it would all smell of meadow flowers and warm breeze. The group came to a stop next to the old style French road sign that informed them they had arrived at Maisonvide.

The space normally used to display the road number was empty. No wonder Bill couldn't find it on the map – the road didn't exist.

Terry and Peter both felt a bit nervous; they were both feeling unprepared for the next stage. They had had visions of arriving here on the coach to an official welcome with bunting, speeches and gifts. This wasn't anything like that.

Peter went first. "Well from what I could glean from the village website, most of the activity is centred around the old square. I suggest we make our way there and ask to speak with the Mayor. I left the speech and the Twinning signs on the coach so he will just have to take us as he finds us."

"Good idea Pete, lead on." Encouraged Terry.

The small, nervous group passed under the archway. Pam was looking out for the property Bob had mentioned as a possible home. The archway house itself looked inviting; but she couldn't see a 'For Sale' sign. Only one that read 'Vendu'.

Paradise Lost . . .

They moved along the narrow street heading toward the centre where they experienced a happy, busy little village. People chatting, steps being washed, paths being swept.

Terry had stopped to talk to some of the inhabitants and was beginning to wonder if 'Mairie" was French for Mayor because he was ever greeted with Gallic shrugs or wry smiles. The street they were on soon spilled out into the village square. A small market was taking place, perhaps five stalls, but they all seemed to be run by one man who was flitting between the tables. They made their way over to the café.

Pam of course knew the name of the waiter who was dancing his way towards them.

"Bonjour Madame et Monsieurs!"

It was Raphael.

Terry responded,

"Oui, bonjour, je suis la representent pour la village de Whiterock. Je voudrais une rendezvous avec le Mairie de Maisonvide."

The other three were very impressed by this from Terry, he couldn't have prepared it because this wasn't supposed to have happened.

"Vous etes Anglais? Please sit down and I will get you some drinks." Raphael pulled the seats back and elaborately dusted them off with his serviette. "Café?"

"Yes please."

Raphael disappeared into the café and the group took their seats and surveyed the situation. Everyone was just getting on with their business and there were no outward signs of any welcome event. No bunting or any

151

real interest in the arrival of four English visitors. The waiter returned with four coffees. He over-complicated the serving.

"Mais, Monsieur you asked to meet with the Mairie of our village. I cannot help you; we do not have a Mayor." He looked quite bemused.

Perplexed looks were exchanged around the table. Pam joined in as best she could. Peter was the first to talk.

"Excuse Moi, I didn't get your name?"

"Raphael, Monsieur."

"Well Raphael this is all very strange. We four are part of a group of 'Twinners' I think you say 'Jumeaux'. We have been in touch with your Mayor for many months arranging this visit. My friend here, Terry, has spoken with your Mayor many times. We have all been communicating with your website, the rest of our group have returned to the hotel at the bottom of your road as our coach failed to make it here."

Pam had noticed a slight change in the expression on Raphael's face as Peter had been talking. Like a one-cent had dropped somewhere in his brain. He nodded at Peter but wasn't really listening.

"This is very curieux et estrange, 'ow you say, strange. I am at the heart of this village and I have heard nothing of this and we absolutement do not have a Mayor, mais, I will call someone who may understand the problem, please wait. I will get you some more coffee."

"Thank you Raphael, um, do you have a menu?" Terry asked.

With excellent timing, the one-cent coin in Raphael's brain had dropped onto the neuron tip that was linked to the final conversation he had had with Bob.

"Monsieur, je suis desolate, we have no chef, we cannot make any food."

"Why is that man eating crepes?" Mr Smartin asked while pointing at an adjacent table.

"He bring his own food of course!" Came the obvious reply from Raphael who now left the table and headed for the telephone. He didn't need to make a phone call as the old Lada had pulled into the square and Bob's dinner guest stepped out into the sunlight. He made his way towards the café and was greeted with a coffee by the waiter who now sat down with him.

The conversation was accompanied by graves facial expressions and Gauloises. It ended with the Lada driver approaching the table. He gesticulated towards the empty chair.

"Bonjour, may I sit down? C'est possible I have an answer to this situation."

He took the seat, sat down and offered around his packet of Gauloises. No-one took one, although Pam was tempted.

"Raphael tells me of this story you have, he is correct, we do not have a Mairie, we are too small a village. I am however a Councillor. Is this the correct word?"

Terry nodded and their guest continued.

"I have never heard of this 'jumeaux' situation because of many things, but mostly the road. We are not a Twinning village, une moment s'il vous plais."

He gestured towards Raphael who came over. The Councillor spoke to him at speed. Some of the English group picked up a hint of the conversation. Something about a problem, similar to previous events, or along those lines. The Councillor drew deeply on his Gauloises.

"My English friends, excuse me and my friend Rapahel talking. Mais, we might be able to shed a light on the situation. Peut etre, Raphael is better at your tongue, so please Raphael ..."

The Councillor signalled towards the waiter who pulled up a chair.

"Madames et Monsieurs, some years ago we in this village had une probleme, une resident was very unhappy with the Councillor and the politiques of the area. He wanted power, too much power to change our community et not for good. A big hotel, a resort, we opposed him and he vacated the area. Malheureusement he has been trouble. Two years ago he had a rally divert through here, he has taken Maisonvide from the map and he oppose the road, pas de Google. The Councillor suggest maybe this man has been fooling with you to make trouble. We do not wish to Twin with anyone."

The four Twinners, well three of them, were in a state of shock. The whole trip, all the preparation, all the build-up and all the excitement had been smashed. They had been taken for a very uncomfortable, and as it happened dangerous ride. What were the others going to say?

This was hopeless, a lost cause.

For Pam and Bob this was the best news ever!

Pam's soul was fistbumping, she really wanted to share it with someone but it would have to wait. No Bob, and no signal.

The Councillor had given them time to digest the news.

"Je suis desolate, please accept my sincere apologies. I will inform the local Gendarme of this incident. Please let me buy you a drink. Raphael – une bois s'il vous plais."

The waiter stood up and left the stunned party. Pam got up shortly afterwards to follow Raphael.

"Just visiting the bathroom." She said in passing to the table.

She caught up with Raphael at the bar and reached for her purse.

"Non madame! Please, after all your troubles, this is sur la maison."

"Raphael, it is not about la facture, I have something for you." Pam whispered.

She opened her purse and pulled out an old bar receipt. It was the one Bob had been given after his crepe-fest. He had written a note on the reverse. Pam handed it over to the bemused barman.

"Ou est la toilettes s'il vous plait?" She asked; slightly too loudly.

Raphael motioned towards the corner of the bar area and looked at the till receipt, He turned it over and read the neatly scribed note.

"My friend, when they leave, they will not return, unlike me! My wife and I will see you soon for crepes. Kind regards, Bob."

He read it again and a smile crept across his face, he had his suspicions but this confirmed it.

Pam returned from the washroom and came to the bar to help with the drinks. The waiter clicked his heels.

"Enchante Madame Bob, Enchante!"

He smiled as he tore up the receipt into small pieces. Pam reciprocated the smile and helped carry out the large carafe of house red to the table. She returned to her seat. The mood had not lifted. They were all still trying to come to terms with the news.

Raphael, having poured out five large glasses of wine, beckoned to the Councillor who lent his ear to receive the update about one of the guests. A small wry smile could just be made out.

"If I ever find out who this twat is, who has led us this merry dance, I will bloody swing for him so help me god!" Spat Mr Smartin.

"Do you think there is any chance of salvaging anything here?" Asked Terry who already knew the answer.

"Look, this place wouldn't be suitable by any stretch. It is beautiful but it will always be tainted. What do you think Pam?" asked Peter.

"I have to say, selfishly, I am so relieved that it isn't Bob's fault. Whoever did this scam wants locking up! I think we should finish our drinks and return to the hotel. I don't mean to be Pollyanna about this but we are still on holiday in France. We should enjoy the hotel tonight and maybe return via somewhere interesting to visit. I know everyone will be disappointed but at least we will have something to moan about at the next social evening."

"Wise words Pam, wise words indeed" said Terry "I don't think we can do anymore here. It is truly a beautiful place but I can safely say I am never coming back here again. Let's get back to the others and see what they think."

The Councillor and waiter made their way over to the table of disillusioned travellers.

"Madame et Monsieur, we are tres desolate about this situation, please. I invite you all to be our guests here this evening. We have no chef but am sure the village can do something."

Peter got to his feet and held out his hand.

"Monsieur, you are very kind and your village is very beautiful, but we must turn down your invitation. We intend to return to our hotel in the village at the bottom of your road and tell our friends the sad news that we are not to be Twinned with Maisonvide."

"Can we offer you a lift down the valley?" Offered Raphael. All four members of the Twinning splinter group took a step back.

"Non merci, we will be using shank's pony, sorry, we will be walking, la facture please" asked Terry.

"Monsieur, I would not dream of charging you for these drinks, we wish you bonne chance et bonne voyage"

Hands were shaken and the group turned and started to head out of the square. Pam turned around and without being noticed by her party, gave and received a generous wave. If waves could be interpreted, this one would have said 'you can relax now and I will see you soon'.

The three men walked in silence through the narrow streets. Pam however had her head up, busily taking in as much as she could of her new home. The neat gardens, the well-kept houses, a glimpsed breath-taking view between buildings. She smiled at passers-by. This felt so right. They exited by the same gate that they had entered by. Pam lingered her gaze at the old gatehouse, briefly closed her eyes, and made a wish which she left hanging in the air by the old front door.

Bob ...

He wasn't worried. Pam would be out of signal; probably at the hotel. It was all in the lap of the gods now. He would have enough warning to get out of it had it gone wrong. At worst the Twinning party was at least two days away from him and Pam would be able to get hold of him if she needed to. He just had to focus on the day ahead; the sale of the discs.

The last big cash injection of £120,000 into his retirement fund. He had taken a risk and turned down a deposit in exchange for cash on collection. The buyer had wanted to collect in person, to get a feel of the artist's house.

Bob had been feeding the cat these last few days and as per usual had not seen the pet in question. The bowl was always empty, so feline presumed alive.

He had decided to leave all of the disc collection hanging on the walls for two reasons; authenticity and just in case it had all gone wrong. They had agreed 11 o'clock. This gave Bob time to do his rounds of animal husbandry and to get a bit of a hold on the money situation. He had cash all over the place in sterling and Euros. He had been transferring large sums to Pam's maiden-named account from his multiple credit card and loan applications.

He was looking at carrying a large amount of Euros with him, stashed in the campervan, this would be enough to actually survive on for a couple of years. Maybe he and Pam would be able to visit towns nearby to Maisonvide to exchange sterling, but it couldn't be large amounts if they were to remain undetected. So the majority of his working slush fund was in large denomination Euro notes.

The account in Pam's maiden name would be safe for a bit but not that long; his French accounts would be the same; okay short term. but quite high risk. If all went well, Bob planned to open a new account with a local bank in the region of Maisonvide. Pam could move her money or cash it in, and then deposit it as Euros.

Yes, there was a lot of 'what-ifs' and high risks but Bob had ensured he had ample funds in cash for the next few years. He had asked for today's transaction to be in cash *and* in Euros, which had been agreed.

Bob has told the buyer it was for some 'charitable causes' in Greater Europe that the band wanted to support. No questions had been raised.

He had finished his rounds, gone home, and had a coffee whilst updating his cash flow chart. He set off at 10am for the big house. He didn't want the buyer to be caught sniffing around by one of the remaining villagers or for any questions to be asked. As he entered the long gravel drive he thought he spotted a cat's tail disappearing through a rhododendron bush; a rare sighting indeed. He was early and the house was empty. Bob fed the absent cat and opened up the big old front doors.

He had put the picture of himself and the band, taken at the Christmas party, onto the hallway table in clear view to add to the authenticity of the deal. He heard two set of tyres making their way along the gravel towards the house, so he went to the front door looking relaxed and welcoming.

The super-fan collector and his entourage had arrived in two new BMW X5's. They had blacked-out windows. The front car stopped and four people got out, two were in a sort of military uniform. The others in very sharp suits. One of these suits approached Bob. His English was very good and delivered in a quiet but menacing manner.

"Mr Bob, my name is Chox. I am security and translate, associates are all ex-Ghurkha regiment. They will check property, yes?"

"Yes, Mr Chocks, please feel free to let your Ghurkhas clear the house. They will only find me and the cat. Is Mr Wang not coming?"

Chox, standing to attention, nodded towards the direction of the other blacked-out 4x4. He then shouted some very fast instructions at the Ghurkhas who disappeared; one into the shrubbery and one into the house.

The remaining occupant of the first car had positioned himself in the middle of the driveway, he ominously had his hand inside his jacket. It didn't matter if he was holding his phone or a gun. It looked cool if not threatening.

Both of the ex-Ghurkhas reappeared, the one who had had disappeared into the bush emerged from the house and the other got out of the first BMW; they were brilliant.

Bob did think about asking how much it would cost to have a pet Ghurkha but thought better of it.

Mr Chox bowed and approached the second vehicle. The driver got out, booted and suited. He went around the car and opened the back door.

A small and immaculately turned out man stepped onto the path. He slowly surveyed his surroundings. This was where his musical idol had been brought up, he had been inspired by this place to write beautiful music. Mr Wang took a deep lungful of air, hoping it would inspire him to make yet more daring business decisions that would allow him to spend £120,000 without even thinking about it.

He walked towards Bob. Chox quickly fell into line next to Mr Wang, who stopped very close to Bob and bowed low. Bob returned the gesture and bowed. Mr Wang appreciated this and bowed again. Bob didn't this time as he felt this could go on indefinitely. Mr Wang spoke with a gentle voice, to Bob, via Mr Chox.

"My Master ..."

Bob had never actually heard this term uttered outside of the village pantomime, staging Aladdin.

"Is very honoured to meet you, 'The Manager', he is also eternally grateful that you have allowed him to make this purchase."

Bob did bow this time and spoke to Mr Wang.

"Mr Wang, the band thank you for your support and your discretion. If you would like to follow me into the Music Room I can show you the items you are purchasing."

Mr Wang bowed again and gestured to Bob to lead on, which he did. They passed the two Ghurkhas who had positioned themselves next to the front door pillars. They resembled a pair of ornate garden statues that would not look out of place next to The Hidden Palace.

The strange group strode purposefully along the hallway and across to the Music Room. Bob stepped to one side to allow Mr Wang to enter the room first, and on his own.

The discs were still all up on the wall, Bob had checked the hanging situation and it would be a simple operation to remove them. He had thought it would look better if they were on display.

Mr Wang paused, in reverence, at the threshold of the door. He took a sharp intake of breath as he surveyed his prize. Then as if in an art gallery, he walked up to the frames and with his hands clenched behind his back, viewing each disc carefully; one by perfect one.

After a few minutes, Bob entered the room quietly. Mr Wang had completed his task and clapped his hands together twice. Mr Chox appeared.

He was followed by the driver who was holding a small case. He handed the case to Mr Chox who placed it on the table in the corner of the room.

Mr Wang approached the case and opened it to reveal a large number of mixed denomination Euro notes. He then spoke with his servant who addressed Bob.

"My Master thanks you for your honesty in the description of these items. The case contains your agreed sum plus an additional gift for you to reward your efforts and time in this matter. Please to count the money."

Bob didn't move. He smiled and with gravity spoke.

"Please thank Mr Wang for his generosity. I have no need to count the money as I have total respect and trust in him and will not dirty the moment. You may proceed to load up the discs and I will help you."

"Mr Bob, there is no need, everything has been taken care of, I shall convey your sentiments to Mr Wang."

He turned and spoke to his master who smiled at Bob. Hands were clapped again. The driver and one Ghurkha appeared with several packing cases. These were carefully placed on the table. Mr Chox had put on a pair of white cotton gloves and proceeded to take down each frame and place it into a case. The driver then laid a piece of foam between each disc and when the first box was full, a Ghurkha took it out of the room and off to the car.

This sequence continued like clockwork until the walls were bare. Dust halos showed where the discs had once hung.

Over the last few days Bob had grown an extra layer of skin. He had become hardened to his crimes and never once felt remorse. These discs could be replaced and no-one ever really looked at them anyway. At least now they would be appreciated.

The last of the packing crates left the room followed by Mr Wang and his staff.

Bob was the last out, with his case, flicking the light switch with his elbow as he went.

Outside, all the boxes had been loaded into the cars. Mr Chox was giving some instructions to the drivers; one of whom got in and turned his vehicle around and started heading off up the drive. It disappeared from sight but Bob could still hear its engine and it seemed to be getting louder. What the hell was going on?

It was one of the Ghurkhas who spotted the source of the growing sound. It was a helicopter approaching from the near distance. It was approaching very rapidly and getting lower. It looked like it might be trying to land.

Bob had come so far along the crime road; he was just too close to let it all go to crap now. He needed to take control of the situation and react quickly to whatever this sidewinder was. He breathed deeply and took instant and clear stock of the situation. The helicopter was definitely going to land next to the old tennis court in front of the house. He grabbed Mr Chox by the arm and, over the increasingly loud noise of the descending chopper, addressed him.

"They are a bit early, I wonder if I could ask you to move back to your vehicles, there is nothing to worry about and Mr Wang is perfectly safe. The Ghurkhas need to stand down and retire to the cars please."

Mr Chox became quite animated as he spoke with his master, the entourage stepped back, not only to comply with Bobs request but to avoid the incredible down-draught.

Chox turned to Bob and asked. "Who is in the helicopter?"

Bob didn't have a bloody Scooby's.

"All in good time my friend, all in good time." He stated confidently.

Bob ushered them back towards the vehicles and made for the front door. It was still open and the blades were getting closer to the ground; the air could cause havoc. He pulled the doors to and turned to see who the surprise visitors were. He could clearly see the pilot now, the craft was barely three metres from the earth, in the rear seats he could make out a man and a woman. The girl he did not recognise, but he knew the man very well.

A Rush of Blood to the Head ...

It was young Smartin, the lead singer of the band. This was completely unexpected and would require commercial quantities of luck and charm. It would need a tale so convincing that not even the Pope operating a lie detector machine would raise so much as an eyebrow.

Touchdown! The engines were immediately shut to tick over and the rotor blades quickly reduced their speed of rotation. Bob waved at the occupants who all returned the gesture. The pilot cut the engine and within ten seconds the helicopter fell silent as all moving parts stopped. The still plotting Bob stuck his thumb up in the direction of the pilot who again returned the gesture. He took this as the go ahead to approach the craft; which he now did. At this point he was genuinely still making it up as he walked the thirty metres to the door. He got there, took a massive intake of air, and as he opened the rear door pitched his tale.

"Hi Tris, what a pleasure, you are going to make someone very happy but also ruin a massive surprise!"

"Hey Bob, good to see you too, what have I ruined? Wait up, I must let the girl out and introduce you to each other."

He leapt out; looking and smelling every inch the international super star. He slapped Bob on the back, made his way around to the other side of the aircraft, and let his companion out before returning to the highly strung master criminal.

"This is Maisie, she is from New York."

Bob did vaguely recognise her, although she was not the one who had been hanging on to the rock star's arm at the Christmas party.

"Hello Maisie, welcome to Devonshire, did you have a good trip?" He offered weakly.

"Yes thank you Rob, your fields are so small and cute!"

"Um, thank you Maisie, no one has ever said that to me before. Look shall we go up to the house? I am afraid there isn't anything in, no one was expecting you."

Tris flicked his long bleached hair back.

"Don't worry about that Bob, we picked up a couple of hampers from Fortnum's on the way down. Only staying one night while the old man is away in France. Who are the suits?"

Tris was looking towards the bemused party standing by the cars.

"I hate to be the one to ruin a big surprise, but it's something your Dad has arranged for you and the boys."

"Oh go on Bob, Father isn't here and I can keep a secret if you can …"

He winked and nodded sideways towards Maisie, who was undeniably beautiful but not his current girlfriend. Bob nodded his comprehension.

"Your secret is in safe hands Tris. I have never let you or your family down, despite knowing many a juicy morsel. Remember the tree house incident?"

A thin smile flashed across Tris' face as he fondly recalled the tree house affair.

"Bob, you have always been trusted, now get on with it, what's the old man been up to?"

"Ok, look its nothing too major but Mr Smartin has arranged for the total re-decoration of your old music room, he has also decided that it would be the perfect time to get all the band's discs cleaned and reframed. The gentlemen you see over there are here from the specialist framing company, they are based in China. The owner, Mr Wang, yes his real name, is such a huge fan of your work that he insisted on overseeing the project himself."

There. Bob had baited the hook with the old 'blow smoke up your arse' worm, launched a huge cast of the rod, and now waited to see if the float started to dip.

"Good old Pops, such a sentimental fool, so Mr Wang is a big fan is he? Look mate, Maisie and I would like to be left alone to explore the old haunt but if you can ensure his total discretion then I am happy to have a couple of pictures taken with him, say in the hallway, if it moves the workers on."

"The hallway, yes, lovely, wow, Mr Wang will be made up, I will …"

Shit! The picture of Bob and the band was in the hallway, shit again, think man think.

"How about in front of the helicopter, it would add some stardust to the picture, Maisie can stay here out of the lens. I will go and get the hampers and take them through."

"Nice one Bob. Always thinking ahead. You would have made a brilliant band manager. Yes, let's keep Maisie out of this, you go and get him. I will off-load our things and then the pilot can leave after the photo shoot."

Tris rubbed Maisie's incredibly gorgeous backside. "You stay close to Bob, babe, I won't be long then I can show you the trophy."

"I thought they were loaded in the cars" Said the quite vacant Maisie, while a small dull coin dropped somewhere in the background "Oh, naughty, don't be long."

Tris turned back towards the helicopter. Maisie didn't move. Bob legged it into the hallway, picked up the offending image, threw it in to the money case which he then deposited into a cupboard on his way out. He didn't have the time or nerve endings to stress or have any fear, he just had to keep running with it and think about the delicious crepes waiting for him in Maisonvide. He leapt back out of the front door and over to the still perplexed Mr Wang who was being shielded by Chox.

"Mr Wang as a surprise for you, I have arranged a very special visitor, he has agreed to meet and have some pictures taken with you. He has asked for your total discretion in this matter. You are not to mention the money or the purchase of the disc collection. Tris is finding this very emotional and tells himself that you are just taking away his awards for cleaning. Can we rely on your total respect?"

Mr Wang's command of the English tongue had not improved within the last hour so he turned to his PA for the translation; which was delivered and greeted with utter rapture. Mr Wang issued several quick instructions. Mr Chox turned to Bob just as a Ghurkha appeared brandishing a very expensive looking camera.

"Sir, Mr Wang is very grateful to you for your thoughtfulness in arranging this incredible meeting. You have his word that none of this ever happened, your gesture will not go unrewarded, please, lead on."

Bob, Mr Chox, and Mr Wang walked towards the helicopter in what must have been a contender for the most incredulous meeting ever to take place in Whiterock. As they drew near, Tris handed Bob a Fortnum hamper. Bob took it and spoke.

"Tris Smartin, please can I introduce your second biggest fan, Mr Wang."

Tris put his hand out. "Who is my number one fan then?"

"Well, you are of course".

The band leader didn't have time to decide how to take this as Mr Wang had seized his hand with intense enthusiasm and shook it in the style of some long lost martial art. Bob walked the hamper towards the house and picked up Maisie on his way in. The conversation now taking place around the helicopter was in the lap of the gods.

"Maisie, they won't be long, shall I show you what an English kitchen looks like? It is probably much smaller than yours back home, do you get up too much in it?"

Maisie giggled awkwardly. She didn't understand what was meant, by much, ever. She followed Bob and they unpacked the hamper, which was mostly Champagne. He was conscious of the time and not leaving them too long outside.

"You stay here Maisie and get the Bollinger into the fridge. It's that big white thing in the corner, I will get Tris away from his fans. It was lovely to meet you and I hope your stay is comfortable."

He left her heading for the washing machine and slowly walked back to the front porch. He was half expecting to be greeted by some angry people who had got to the truth of the matter, but to his great relief he wasn't. Tris and Mr Wang were just parting company. Mr Chox was rapidly taking another memory card's worth of images and behind them the helicopter was coming back to life. Mr Wang made a final low bow at his idol and then retired in the direction of the cars.

Bob waited for Tris. "Thanks for that, you have made him a very happy man. I have unpacked the hamper and left Maisie in the kitchen; an area of the home I don't think she is very familiar with. Look Tris, I am not prying but how long are you intending to stay? It's just that the decorators are starting tomorrow."

"As long as the decorators aren't in tonight I will be fine mate!"

'Oh, that's a bit coarse' thought Bob, belatedly, and Tris must have thought so too.

"Sorry, she's a lovely girl, anyway we aren't hanging around. Maisie is working with Victoria's Secret tomorrow and I am back in the studio with the boys, we will be gone by 10."

"Nice one Master Smartin, I will contact the painters and get them to delay starting until 11am, could you remember to feed the cat later please?"

Bob left that hanging there, Tris shredded every nerve end resisting the obvious bloke reply.

"God, is that thing still alive? I haven't seen it in years!"

"Neither have I and I've been feeding it for over a decade! Look Tris you won't say anything to your Father will you? It would break his heart."

"Bob, none of this ever happened. I won't say a word. Now if you don't mind I have a glass of Bolly with my name on it." Tris winked.

"No worries. I just need to pick up something from inside and I will get out of your hair and never see you again!"

Tris laughed and entered the house. Bob left him to head off to the kitchen then he went to retrieve his ill-gotten gains before shutting the front door and letting the love birds get on with it. The helicopter was up to full tilt. Bob checked around and gave a double thumbs up to the pilot, who nodded his appreciation and then proceeded to leave the garden, upwards.

Mr Wang and his large entourage were now back in their cars and ready to depart. As Bob approached the rear BMW, a blacked out window was lowered, and a very thick brown envelope was thrust out.

"Mr Wang is a very happy man and he thanks you for it. May your path through life be without obstacle, goodbye."

Bob took the bonus and said nothing in return; which was just as well because the window had been shut again. Now it wasn't that he was getting all blasé about money, far from it, he knew he would need all he could get to last him for the rest of his days; but this envelope was a real bonus so he decided not to open or count it until he was with Pam safely in France.

He let the two cars pass him and watched as they left the driveway and disappear off down the road. 'I wonder how that will work out when all this unravels?' he mused to himself. 'Tris has no idea who Mr Wang is. Will Mr Wang come clean and get in touch? Or will he keep schtum and the collection stay hidden?'

He made a mental note to avoid any contact with anyone Ghurkha-like in the future; just in case.

All these thought threads had brought him, without any sense of time or space, to his front door. He would only cross this threshold a few more times ever. He touched the doorframe and sent his thanks through it to the rest of the house for the shelter and safety it had afforded him over the years.

He felt he had earned a beer or two. His pulse and stress levels after the Tris Smartin event were only just returning to normal. He was well chuffed with his handling of the situation and couldn't wait to tell Pam.

If this part of the saga did ever become public knowledge, people would probably not believe it had ever happened. The ultimate blag. It would become folklore.

One day Bob's autobiography would be worth a fortune. He took a Hop House beer from the depleted fridge and referred to his spreadsheet. To be honest, at this late stage, it had morphed into a checklist, he was now able to put a line through the disc-sale task. Not much left now, just the campervan tracker swap, Stacey car-sale, visit Dad, lock-up keys for the children, and of course a cash-up which he started now with his second beer.

Au Revoir Maisonvide ...

At the same time that Bob was totalling up his ill-gotten gains, Pam was making her way back towards the hotel. Optimism was the wrong word but there was an air of 'clean break' about the group.

The discussion down the track was around how to break the news to the rest of the party. There was no guilt attached and they had someone to blame for the situation. Having a person to blame for a poor state of affairs was always a good thing.

Terry bought the Twinning advance party to a halt close to where the coach had had to halt in its attempt to reach Maisonvide.

"Look Pam, we three understand how hard this is going to be for you. Poor old Bob will be absolutely devastated about this turn of events, but rest assured, we know he is not to blame. Now if you want me to tell him about this crackpot rogue Mayor then just give me the wink.

Pam felt no guilt, she had added several layers of skin this past few weeks. "Thanks Terry, but I will be fine. Yes, Bob will be gutted; but cross more than anything. He will also be very embarrassed that he was so taken in by this crook. It's the others I'm worried about – they will be so disappointed – the French dream is over."

"Damn and blast the bloody French!" Piped up Mr Smartin "It's Spain or Italy for me. I'm sure they would appreciate us. Pam don't you worry about the others. A few glasses of the local plonk and they will forget that Maisonvide even exists!"

'I hope so' thought Pam 'I really hope so.'

The band of four made their way down the rest of the track; reminiscing about the near death experience that they had had on the coach. At the bottom of the track, where it met the road, they all stopped and turned around. Three of them thought 'never again' and one thought 'see you soon'.

Terry said he would gather up the troops in the bar and break the bad news. He also agreed with Pam that they needed to turn the situation around and make the best of it. They pushed on along the road towards the hotel; slightly more upbeat.

Two of the smokers were outside. The rest were ensconced in the bar, except for Mary who had gone off to her room with one of her headaches.

Peter, without the aid of his clipboard, got everyone including Mary, together in the bar. He called everyone to order, and Terry spoke.

"My fellow Whiterockians. We bring news from Maisonvide. Alas we are not to be Twinned."

The noise that emulated from the gathered throng was one of shock, tinged with 'thank fuck I don't have to go up that track again'.

"An individual with possible criminal intent has set us up. There has been no Twinning request from Maisonvide. The officials knew nothing of us. The village itself is beautiful and the people, although isolated, are kind and were very apologetic. This is not the first time that they have had trouble from this idiot and will be seeking advice from the relevant authorities."

He drew breath and gently assured Pam with a light touch on her arm. An unexpected twinge of guilt coursed through her veins.

"Bob and the rest of the steering committee were completely fooled. It is no-one's fault except this one person. I am truly sorry but this little Twinning adventure ends here. I feel that we must draw a line under it and head for home; a little wiser, yes, but resolve to get it right next time. Maybe Spain? Who knows?"

Pam looked around at her neighbours' faces and to be honest they didn't give much away, especially Jean's, but then her face never gave anything away. No-one really spoke. There wasn't much to be said. Mary Braces was the first to break the silence in the muted room. She opened her tight-lipped mouth and to no-one's real surprise, in full female Private Frazer style said "I thought there was something a bit odd about all of this."

Pam wasn't going to let the old mood-hoover get away with this. She filled up her chest and let rip in a shrill and cutting tone.

"Oh, did you Mary? You thought there was something odd about it all? Well I'm so glad you warned us about this feeling you had, because then we wouldn't all be in this terrible situation. I am so sorry that Bob and I ever even suggested this trip, really I am. To try and make amends in a very small way please let me buy everyone a drink."

Now, although Mary was absolutely right on this point, Pam felt really good about sticking it to her. Yes, sure enough in a few days' time from the comfort of her bus stop, Mary could start saying "I told you so" to all and sundry but for now Pam had taken the high ground.

Hard stares and glares were fixed on Mary. One of the party, Mike, broke the spell. "Pam, I think I speak for nearly everyone here."

He glowered at Mary.

"Under no circumstances can this be laid at your door, or Bob's. There is no way I will let you buy anyone's drink. In fact, I would like to buy *you* a drink to thank you for bringing the village together and for setting up this little adventure. Now, what would you like?"

Shouts of "Hear, hear!" went up.

Pam blushed. Mary flushed.

The doors at the back of the hotel bar suddenly flew open and in walked the Councillor and Raphael from Maisonvide. The two of them made their way through the gob-smacked group to the front; and stood near Pam.

Raphael spoke softly with Terry whilst everyone else watched with baited breath.

Before too long, Terry spoke. "Ladies and gentlemen of Whiterock, pray silence for Raphael, a businessman from Maisonvide."

Raphael stepped forward.

"My English friends, the Councillor and I wish to offer the sincerest apologies for all the trouble. I can assure you that we will make this person pay and that it never happens to any other people. Mais, we do not wish you to think the French bad and so the Councillor has instructed the hotel manager to charge all drinks to the village of Maisonvide, and he hopes that he never sees any of you ever again! Merci."

The coach party erupted into cheers and whoops. Even Mary cracked and joined in. People quickly made their way over to the bar.

The drinks started flowing. A brilliant move from the Councillor. All the questions and all the anger would be lost in a drunken haze.

Mike dodged through the throng and pushed a large house white at Pam.

Raphael and the Councillor mixed with the coach party; offering sympathy and listening to tales of the track. After an hour or so, when all were well-oiled, the deputation from the village started to make their excuses. Backs were slapped and hands shaken. Raphael caught Pam's eye, and his eyes seemed to say 'follow me outside I need to speak with you'.

The final farewells were said and the villagers made for the door. Pam turned to Terry. "I will see them off and thank them for their generosity. On that note please can I have another large house white?"

Terry winked and made for the bar whilst Pam made for the door.

Outside, the Councillor and Raphael stood by the yellow car; Gauloises in mouths.

"Madame Bob."

"It's Pam, je m'appelle Pam."

"Aaahh! Madame Pam. I hope all this has been satisfactory. The Councillor and I think maybe we won't have any more visitors to our village, except peut etre two?"

Pam smiled and the Councillor threw down his cigarette.

"Pam, je suis une Councillor, aussi I am the village agent for houses, comprende? Oui, please will you pass on a message for Monsieur Bob? His offer has been accepted on the old gatehouse, thank him for the money and I will give you the keys when I next see you."

Pam was overcome with emotion; the wish she had left in the doorway had come true. She leapt forward and held Raphael. The Councillor then received a kiss on both cheeks.

"Merci, thank you, Bob and I will return soon. After today I don't think your village will ever be asked to Twin again. It will be left in peace.

The Councillor pulled himself up to his full height. "Madame, au contraire, Maisonvide will always be Twinned with Whiterock, I shall inform the tourist association and I will even have a sign made. And then no-one will ever ask again. Parfait Madame, parfait."

"Une moment, Councillor, Une moment!" Pam walked to the rear of the coach and, as she suspected, the lock didn't work. She opened the boot and there just inside was the sign that Terry had had produced. She picked it up and returned to her new friends. She handed it to Raphael who peeled back the bubble wrap.

"Parfait, Pam, c'est Parfait."

He placed the sign on the back seat of the car. Raphael and the Councillor both got in and the mobile bag of spanners sprang into life.

"Au revoir, bon chance and see you soon!" The occupants both waved as the car sped off in the direction of her future home.

Pam got out her phone, she knew she had to tell Bob not to worry. She sent him a brief message.

GOING WELL X BETTER THAN PLANNED X WILL CALL YOU TMW X.

She made her way back to the bar which was in full party swing. Although far from forgotten, the road to hell was becoming a numbed and distant memory. The free alcohol was healing wounds. Pam sidled up to Peter and Terry. "So gentlemen, what is the plan of action?"

Terry replied "Ah Pam, didn't see you there, did you see our friends off ok? Yes, good, well we thought we would start heading for home tomorrow, when all the alcohol has left Bill's system. We will stop a couple of times on route and take in a taste of France to make up for today's revelations. Peter has found a couple of possible destinations, one even looks like it may be fun! Now, what's your poison?

Pam didn't know what time it was when she went up to her room, until she checked her phone in bed. It was 2.30am. Bob had replied and somehow the message had made its way through the winding valleys.

TOO MUCH TO TEXT X ALL GOOD HERE TOO X TALK TMW PM X I LOVE YOU X.

Pam went out like a light and slept like a buche.

Pam had no idea how much wine she had consumed the night before but she was still woozy when she awoke around 10am.

She packed her small suitcase and made her way downstairs to join the others for breakfast. There were not many that had made it down as yet. Before she sat down she needed to try something out. Something she had always wanted to do ever since childhood. She carried her bag through reception, across the carpark, and onto the coach.

Bill, probably shouldn't have been, but was at the wheel adjusting the tachograph to match that day's expected driving. Pam made her way to the back seat and placed the case on the overhead rack. She then sat down next to the rear emergency exit.

This was it. A dream come true. Her eyes fixed on Bill; her ears ready for an alarm. She pulled the door handle back. The door coughed open like an ancient tombstone in the valley of the Kings. No alarm, no reaction, and no £50 fine. She pulled the door shut again. It was pleasingly quiet.

Pam smiled to herself as she got up, climbed down from the coach, and went back in for breakfast. She picked her way through the previous night's excesses and found fresh coffee and croissants. For some unknown reason she sat down with Mary; who looked up sheepishly and spoke.

"I am sorry about last night dear, I didn't mean anything by it."

'Yes you did you wizened old crone' thought Pam 'but I don't care because I have sold your house from under you.'

What she actually said was "That's all right Mary, it has been a bit odd for all of us."

Others started to join the breakfast club. Terry looked like he had been involved in a very serious road traffic accident and Jean had a face like a blind cobbler's thumb. Eventually all the group had gathered and it was Peter who got to his feet first. This time, no one seemed to object.

"Right folks. I think we can all agree that there is nothing here for us. I suggest that after we have had our fill of life-giving coffee we all get back on the coach and start heading for home. Don't worry I won't arrange a French Morris dancing experience in a yurt. I have found a world class cave complex on the way which might be interesting and if it's not, it does at least have a bar and restaurant."

A small but grateful ripple of appreciation drifted about the room. That was it. They were homeward bound.

Many empty cups of coffee and pastries later everyone gathered on the coach; ready for the off.

Pam made her way to the back seat. She spread herself out and everyone got the message that she probably wanted solitude to be able to think about how she was going to break the bad news to Bob. She actually needed the space for what would probably be the most difficult part of this whole adventure for her; the not going home!

The Last Day ...

This was set to be Bob's last full day in England for what he hoped would be quite some time. He was booked on the late-night ferry crossing; leaving Plymouth at 11.00 pm the following day.

He was now aware that the coach was heading back in his direction, as of today, but it didn't panic him. Time was running out, but his to do list was shrinking and today was operation campervan.

He realised that it didn't really matter about the tracking device as it wouldn't take people long to discover that Pam had actually stayed in France, unless of course she had been really clever. Anyone would be able to put two and two together and assume that Bob had joined her with the stolen van and the crooks were living it up somewhere in Europe.

But you never know, if he planted the tracker in another van that was heading in the opposite direction to where Pam was thought to be, and if Terry and his insurance company insisted that the police track down his pride and joy, it would buy them some more time. It would also keep any suspicion away from the dealer in Brittany; well for a while at least.

The evening before, Bob had carefully gone through his criminal activity accounts. Peter's funds had been cleared and transferred. Mary's house money was deposited and the legal sale of their own house had been settled. The rest was in cash, mostly now in Euros. He had a bonus from the book man and hadn't even checked to see what the fat envelope from Mr Wang contained. He now set off on his morning pet-feeding rounds for the penultimate time. He would hand over to Stacy tomorrow afternoon.

Wow! He was finding this very exciting and had to pinch himself that it was really happening. Instead of him and Pam drifting into a retirement coma of just-about-existing, he was embarking on the adventure of his life.

He had never felt so alive as he did now and, despite the odd bit of stress, this was taking years off him. He whistled as he walked about the village doing his chores. As he neared Dr Roberts' house he heard the helicopter approaching on its way to pick up Tris and his floozy. Bob smiled. He still couldn't believe that he had swung that one.

A large motorbike slowed down and pulled alongside him. It was Andy, one of the few villagers who had remained. He stopped and took his helmet off. "Alright Bob, what's on?"

"It's the golden boy being picked up, you alright Andy?"

"Can't complain mate, can't complain." Which he then did for a full 10 minutes; but not in a bad way. Mostly about workload and unfulfilled dreams. He had lots of ideas and talents but never enough time to bring them to fruition.

Andy was the agricultural equivalent of a developing James Dyson. He was a very useful bloke to know and one of only a handful Bob could have relied on to help him and ask no questions. Thankfully he hadn't needed to.

Bob hoped there would be a French Andy in Maisonvide. The conversation was only ended by the roar of the helicopter flying low over the village, probably to allow Maisie a last look at all the 'cute little fields'.

When the hum subsided Andy spoke. "They must all be back soon mate, when is it? You must have missed Pam."

"Yep, most of them are due back the morning after tomorrow, to be honest I have been too busy to have missed my girl."

"Up to no good I 'spect eh Bob? Right on, I'd better do one, see you dreckley!"

He put his lid back on and spun off; leaving Bob to complete his rounds at Dr Roberts. He gave the cat a double portion. Not for old times' sake but more in the hope it got severe stomach ache.

He skipped the big house in the vain hope that Tris had left out some food for the invisible cat.

Back at home, Bob had sorted out the last of the house contents. He and Pam had been ruthless in what they were going to take with them. When all was said and done they had very little that really meant anything; a few pictures, a small collection of Quimper pottery, some rare Exeter hallmarked silver and some old family photographs. It just went to show how much commercial shit was in their lives. He loaded the boxes into the car and drove down to Terry's.

It only took two trips, and included some ancient carpets he had inherited from his Dad. Supposedly crafted by prisoners in Amritsar; but more likely from a sale at Trago Mills.

He carefully packed all the items into the capacious camper, then set about disconnecting the Advanced Satellite Security device. This task actually proved to be quite easy and, as the manual attested to, it continued under its own power, to produce a signal.

Hog and Hedge …

He could of course have just left the box there when he left the next day – but where would be the fun in that? Any delay in detection or red herring would give them more of a chance to get clean away in France. He removed the box from the van and placed it on the front seat of the car.

He set off for the 'Hog and Hedge' rest area on the A30; a site renowned for campervan conversion flexing. The moment he moved, it should trigger a message to Terry's phone; when it got a signal that was!

It was only a few miles to the service area and on arrival he wasn't disappointed; at least eight T4 and T5 owners were to be found eyeing up each other's pimped vehicles and reading all the surf shop bumper stickers. Once on a trip to Mid-Wales in 1984, Bob had seen a bumper sticker that read *'Warning no hand signals, driver convicted Arabian alcoholic'* and since then nothing had ever come close.

He parked up between two vans; both had their tailgates up displaying the well equipped kitchens and sleeping accommodation. Bob feigned interest and started to massage some egos. "Wow, what an amazing fit out, are you travelling far?"

"Nah mate, we are nearly there, off to the North coast to catch some tubes." Replied the fake-tanned twat. Bob immediately lost interest and moved on to the next van; who were also nearing their destination. He continued and hit the jackpot with campervan number four.

It was being driven by a lady called Sara who spoke with a Middle-England, silver-spoon accent. She was acting as a support vehicle for her partner Steve. Steve was driving a large dumper truck from Land's End to John O'Groats in an effort to raise money for a little known charity that Sara had recently set up called "Cats with PTSD".

After Bob had confirmed that they were heading for Scotland, he allowed Sara to bore him some more.

"People don't realise how badly affected cats can be after near-misses on the road or if their owners divorce or move house. I just wanted to do my bit to get more research done".

To try and gain more attention in this noble quest, Steve had decided to fill the dumper bucket with water, and place in it a wet-suited friend called Stuart; who, in a strange reality, was going to swim all the way.

Bob hailed this idea as brilliant and that he was moved to write a cheque out, here and now, to support Sara's charity. Would it be ok if he got into the van to fill out the cheque?

Sara beamed "Yes of course! Thank you for caring!"

To date there had been lots of interest in Stuart and the dumper-truck but this had not been converted into funds to help the traumatised pussies.

Bob went to the car to get his cheque book and satellite security box. He returned and got into the back of the T4. It was full of potential hiding places.

"Sara, I'm so sorry, do you have a pen?"

Sara disappeared around to the front and started rifling through her handbag and the glove box. Bob opened a low level cupboard which was part filled with Vaseline and Kendall Mint Cake. He made some room and secreted the small tracking device at the back just in time. Sara reappeared brandishing a pen.

"Hang on a minute, would cash be ok?" ventured Bob.

"Yes of course it would, anything will help!" smiled Sara appreciatively.

Bob wasn't going to use a traceable cheque. He reached into his cash pocket and pulled out a wodge. He counted out £200 and handed it to Sara who broke down into floods of tears. "You are such a saint! I was beginning to think no-one else cared about cats with PTSD!"

"Well I do, Sara, good luck and I hope you make it to Scotland!"

With that, Bob got out, and left Sara to share the good fortune with Steve and the still somewhat bemused Stuart; who thought Steve had been joking when he had asked him to don a wetsuit and swim to the other end of the country.

Bob got back into his car and drove home thinking how dull the world would be without people like Sara, Steve, and Stuart.

He was handing the car over tomorrow, so needed to see one of the children and visit his Dad before then.

Andrea and David had left for Belgium a few weeks back but Andrew and

Emma were about. Bob sent Andrew a text asking to meet up for the lock-up key handover. He wanted to see him one last time.

The text came back KINGS ARMS AT 7 X?

Bob replied and confirmed the meeting. He would visit his Dad tomorrow before he handed over the car to Stacy.

The house was nearly empty now; he only had one more night in it. He had thought about sleeping in the campervan – but wanted to be at home just in case he needed to react to any situation.

Bob put together the last of the items for the lock-up. Little things like the kettle and the television. He drove these down and put them into the large metal box. Before locking up he stopped momentarily and looked wistfully at his worldly possessions for probably the last time before setting off to meet Andrew at the King's.

At the pub, Bob ordered himself a pint of Yellowhammer and took a menu outside to peruse before his son turned up; which he did ten minutes later on the Enfield. Emma was on the back.

"Alright Dad? Why all the cloak and dagger? And why not at home?"

Bob got up and hugged his son, and gave Emma a kiss.

"Well son, your mother's away so I thought I would treat you both to an edible feast!"

"Nice one old man, I won't tell mum what you said, mine's a pint please."

The three of them sat outside and passed the time; happy in each other's company. Although in recent years they had drifted apart from each other, the bond between a father and a son was too great ever to cast asunder. Bob was under no illusion that it wouldn't be that long before his son went on a European motorbike holiday and told no-one.

The chill of the spring evening started to descend. Bob spoke. "Right you two, time you were off – the heaters are crap on the Enfields. Now, a while ago your mother and I spoke to you and Andrea about our plans. Well nothing has changed, it is happening and it starts tomorrow, son can you remember what we asked of you?"

His son smiled as he pulled on his leather jacket. "Number one: don't ask any questions, and number two: trust us that all will be ok in time."

A glow enveloped Bob. His son had remembered.

"Exactly my boy. Well, as promised, here are some keys and a note. I know I can trust you not to open it until tomorrow night. Your mother and I love you both more than you can ever imagine. Now sod off and be careful on that bike."

Hugs all round. Emma took the keys and the note. The bike roared into life and the pair sped off into the night.

Bob went back into the pub and settled up. 'Home James and don't spare the horses' he thought.

In his empty house he called Pam. It was good to hear her voice. She was on the coach. They agreed there was too much to say and that the bus was full of ears; so they kept it short as they had many years to fill in the details. Bob warned Pam that Terry might get twitchy about the movement of his van.

"Too late" said Pam.

Bob updated her on Andrew, and that all funds were in place. Pam couldn't say much because Dr Roberts was in the seat in front of her so she was mostly "yes" and "no". She mocked a speech about the revelations at Maisonvide and how no-one on the coach blamed him.

At this point the Doctor turned around and offered a sympathetic smile; she had been earwigging after all.

Bob signed off with the fact that he would be with her the day after tomorrow, and that after that they would never be apart again. Pam said she loved him. But he already knew that.

Bob downed the last of his Pendryn and went to sleep in his house for the last time.

Going underground …

The atmosphere on the coach was noticeably odd. Yes, granted, the after effects of last night's excesses were having an influence; but the air was flat. They were going home with nothing. They had all been on a fool's errand and like it or not Pam was at fault. She shut herself away on the back seat of the coach, she was ok, she knew inside that it was only for another day.

Peter had phoned ahead and booked a visit at a spectacular cave complex half way home. It did sound amazing and Pam hoped it would take people's minds off the current situation. Everyone just wanted to get home, except Pam, who didn't. Terry had booked a hotel near Nantes for that night. Sheila and Bill would share the driving so the 480 miles was do-able.

The coach seemed to be pleased to be re-tracing its treads, all its con-rods were in sync and it lapped up the miles. Pam stayed safely ensconced at the back, on her own. She would speak with Bob later that day but until then she had to front it out.

It wasn't long before her fellow passengers' phones started to come to life; one person had twenty-four new messages. Pam kept an eye on Peter but fortunately he was more focused on the visit to the cave complex than on his phone.

It was mid-afternoon when they pulled into the visitors' centre at the caves. Much to Peter's delight, the majority of the coach opted to take the tour. Terry didn't; he approached Pam in her domain at the rear of the vehicle.

"Hey Pam, the caves not for you?"

"Not really Terry. I have a lot on my mind. Bob is beside himself and not looking forward to everyone returning home."

"Now you listen here Pam, no one blames you or Bob for this debacle. We will put this down to experience. I mean how was he to know that there was some weirdo behind all this? So don't you worry about a thing, Pam. Now, can I ask you for a favour? It is only that I think my phone is playing tricks on me. My Advanced Satellite Security is telling me that my campervan is heading North on the A38 at about 15 mph. Please can you get Bob to confirm that it isn't?"

Pam thought that Terry's security thingy probably *was* heading North along the A38 at about 15mph, but she obviously needed to reassure Terry that it was safely in its garage.

"How strange! I will text Bob and ask him – he will be feeding your cat about now. Look, tell you what, I will call him now if you want and put your mind at rest" she offered.

"You don't have to do that Pam, anytime will do. Now let's get off and let me buy you a drink in the café whilst the others try and lose Peter in the network of underground passages!"

"Thanks Terry, that would be lovely. You get them in and I will give Bob a call."

They got off the coach leaving Bill to fiddle with his Tachograph in peace. Terry made his way inside the café whilst Pam pretended to call Bob. They had agreed to keep contact as limited as possible. Each had the intelligence and resourcefulness to deal with the hour to hour issues. End of day texts were ok and it kept the stress levels down not waiting for the phone signals to kick in. Terry returned with a tray of goodies.

"Bob says not to worry; your van is safe. He was stood next to it when I called. He also said that there have been lots of problems with the internet and phone lines around the area, but rest assured that your camper is not heading anywhere at any average speed. Thanks for the drink."

"No worries Pam, I thought there would be a simple explanation. I will let the others know when they re-emerge from the depths. Peter was having problems with his online banking earlier. We will be home the morning after tomorrow. I am sure we can survive a bit longer without modern technology."

The two of them sat down together. Jean had chosen to take the tour when she heard that water from the drip of a stalactite had incredible rejuvenating properties. The conversation between the two of them sat at the picnic table actually flowed effortlessly as they found they had a lot in common. Terry said they must get together more on their return. Pam replied that it was probably the holiday spirit talking so Terry took out his diary and looked to book a date for her and Bob to come for a meal. Pam said to see what happened when they got back. He might change his mind.

Some of the party started to drift out of the cave exit door. Jean didn't look any younger. Peter was the last to emerge, smiling, a brilliant tour coupled with a successful headcount and all without the aid of a clip board.

Bill and Sheila approached the café from the coach. Bill had a satisfied grin on his face as this time he had excelled himself. He had covered 420 miles with less than an hour behind the wheel.

"Right folks, we had better be off as it is still an hour to our hotel stop. At least it is only a short drive tomorrow to get back to the port." Bill started to usher people towards the door.

There had been quite a lot of debate about what to do at Roscoff. With all the issues at Maisonvide, the trip timetable had completely gone out the window. Instead of driving through the night and straight onto the ferry they were now almost killing time. Half of the group said they were happy to get some sleep on the coach in the port carpark, but, in the end Mary's harridan approach to negotiations won through and a cheap non-descript hotel had been booked for the last half night.

Peter had reminded everyone that Roscoff was actually a lovely town; sadly, overlooked by many who just passed through. He added that of course it was also home to the Johnny Onion museum; a must on everyone's bucket list.

Sheila did the final round up. Jean had bought out the gift shop's whole supply of cave-sourced miracle-water. Everyone then got back on board for the last hour to Nantes.

The hotel that night seemed to have been recently converted from a light industrial unit. Pam half expected her bed to have a vice fitted. There was a small bar that doubled up as the breakfast area and the changing rooms for the bleak pool that resembled a settlement tank at a sewerage treatment plant.

Pam stayed at the bar for a while and then made her excuses and returned to her room. She really wanted to talk with her man. She was missing him and needed his reassurances. Despite Bob having finished the Pendryn, he too was happy to talk. No one could hear them so the conversation flowed. Pam went into lots of detail about Maisonvide and the incredible message about the old gate house.

Bob told of his run in with Tris and Mr Wang. Pam said it would make a really good book one day – but no one would believe it could really have happened. The hour long phone call was cathartic for both of them; the last two days in particular had been very difficult. They signed off with undying love and wished each other skill and luck with the last few pieces of the jigsaw.

Pam ended the call and a text came through. It was from Emma. Everything was fine, the last scan had gone well, and the baby was on track to being perfect in every way. Buoyed up by Bob and the baby, Pam went back down to the bar/workshop/changing room for a nightcap. She only had to endure one last day then her life could really start.

Bob. D Day …

Although the ferry wasn't until 11.00 pm that night, Bob needed to leave in plenty of time. To date he hadn't driven the campervan further than to the end of Terry's lane for a practice, as he didn't want to attract any attention by driving it through the village. Not that any of the remainers would have batted an eyelid but he wanted belt and braces on this; the last day.

In the hallway stood the last of his things. Two suitcases, a box of food and the flowers from the bookman. He was going to give the flowers to his Dad. This was it. The last ever round of animal minding, Stacy would cover this evening and tomorrow morning.

The coach party was due back tomorrow afternoon. A small knot of Painted Lady Butterflies stretched out their wings deep inside Bob. He hoped that he would be anonymously driving South with his love as their ex-neighbours all returned to the scene of the crimes.

He whistled as he did this last round of chores.

He was kind and generous to all his animal charges as he always was but this time he included Mary's cat. He even left the eggs for Mary. The fact that she didn't own the house to cook them in wasn't really an issue to Bob. Dr Roberts' cat knew something was up but didn't say anything as it received its double helping of food without any mental anxiety.

Bob was hoping he might see the cat at the big house for old time's sake, but he didn't. He did however retrieve the photograph of him and the band – one to leave the Grandchildren, or sell to pay for a good solicitor. In the fridge he found a couple of bottles of Bollinger that Tris had left. He didn't think anyone would notice under the circumstances, and if all went well over the next 24 hours, then he and Pam would need something to toast their success.

Bob said goodbye to the compost heap at Peter's house and told Alexa that he loved her. She said she didn't understand him. Typical woman he thought. He returned home, put the last of the items into the car, and dropped them off at Terry's place. Then, just he and the flowers headed off to Bickleigh to say goodbye to his Dad.

The Salt of the Earth ...

The wet salt started flowing from the moment his hand alighted on the old lych-gate. By the time he reached the graveside he was always in floods of tears. Whoever said that time was a great healer, didn't have a Dad like Bob's. It didn't matter how many days flowed under the bridge, it never got any easier. He busied himself tidying up the plot and telling his Father what was going on, to be honest he didn't know what his Dad would have made of it all. He wouldn't have liked the dishonesty but he did love a trip to France.

Bob stood back to admire his work. He would not be back here for a very long time. He knelt down and picked up a decent handful of the red Devon earth and placed it in a sandwich bag. A little bit of his Dad was coming on the trip to help with the roses in his new garden. He got up to go and turning to the rude wooded cross he whispered ... "As I've always said Dad, it's not the hole you're in, it's the hole you've left. Now come on we have a ferry to catch."

With that he picked up the soil and started chatting to it on his way to the car.

It was nearly lunchtime so he stopped at the Fisherman's Cot for something to eat. He left his Dad on the front seat as he didn't want anyone to think him mad as he ate his last English meal. What would it be? He settled on a large Ploughman's with a pint of "Devon Red" cider.

He sat at a table on the banks of the river Exe and ate his meal alone. He knew that he would miss moments like this, but he was sure that Raphael could muster up something similar – and of course he would have to put up with all that balmy warm weather; what a bummer!

He arrived at The Nadder Arms just after the lunchtime rush, which today had consisted of Tony having half a lager and a pickled egg.

"Alright my lover, you've got my car 'ave Ee?" Stacy greeted Bob cheerfuly.

"Alright Stacy, yep and all the paperwork, plus the keys for the neighbourhood, still ok for a lift home?"

Stacy nodded and produced a brown envelope from under the bar. Bob exchanged this for all the car documents. He then laid out a selection of keys. On each fob he had tied on a brown parcel label with details of address, pet name, and any dietary requirements.

"I gave them all a good clean out this morning so there shouldn't be too much for you to do; the coach is due back sometime tomorrow afternoon. I daresay folk will pop in and pick up their keys as and when. You can keep any crap tea towels and fridge magnets as a bonus."

Stacy smiled and picked up all the keys, thought for a moment and said …

"Cor, with all these keys and enough time you could clear up and bugger off to pastures new! Maybe not, you'd never get away with it! Right Bob show me 'ow my lovely new car works. Tony, you are in charge, and I know exactly 'ow many pickled eggs are in that jar!"

Stacy drove. It gave Bob a chance to look at the village one last time. Just like Pam a week ago, he had mixed emotions but no regrets. The future was looking so bright he would have to buy some new shades from duty free on the boat. Stacy pulled up to the front of the house. Bob picked up his bag of earth and turned to her.

"I would ask you in Stace, but the house is literally bare."

"No worries Bob, I better get back and save Tony from 'imself. You take care of yourself, give my love to Pam and I really 'ope everything works out for you and your Mum."

With that she winked and let Bob shut the door before turning around in the road and rushing back to wrestle the pickled egg jar from Tony's shaking fingers.

Bob didn't know what to make of Stacy. She probably didn't know anything but always erred on the side of conspiracy theory to stay at the top of the gossip tree. He let himself in for the last ever time. The postie had been and there was quite a lot – mostly first demands from all the loans and credit cards he had taken out.

"Good luck with that" he said out loud to the empty house. He did a final check of all the windows and switches. The new owners were due to move in the day after tomorrow and he had left them a card and a bottle of wine. Inside the card he had written them some sage advice.

'Don't offer to look after any of the neighbours' pets, it will only lead to trouble!'

He took a last look at the hallway, placed his keys on the mat alongside the card, and pulled the door shut behind him.

Bob walked the short distance to Terry's place; he saw no-one on the way. He unlocked his new temporary home and stowed part of his Dad in the glove box. He then sat at the steering wheel and fired up the mobile palace. It purred into life. Good old Terry – he had even left her with a full tank of fuel. He let the van tick over to warm up and wrote Pam a text.

LEAVING WHITEROCK X ALL GOOD X SEE YOU TMW X I LOVE YOU X

Bob saw it leave his phone. Pam would be in Roscoff soon, where he would be by tomorrow morning. Unbelievable.

He took a deep breath and engaged first gear. Next stop Plymouth.

As Terry had mentioned on one or fifteen occasions in the past, the campervan was something special and became the source of much van envy on the road down to the port. Bob knew that the timing of his arrival at the terminal was critical. He mustn't be too early as that would afford more time for scrutiny from tyre kicking van aficionados and the port security services.

Pam ...

The atmosphere at breakfast resembled that of an enforced corporate staff development event rather than that of a jovial Twinning trip. It was way past Pam delivering another short Henry V speech about making the best out of a bad situation. She just sat there and quietly ate her rehydrated continental breakfast whilst an overly large child got changed for the pool at the table next to her.

No one needed rounding up this time. The whole party got on to the coach without the aid of a clipboard or even the threat of Peter. This last part was going to be a feat of endurance for Pam – everyone except her just wanted to go home. Even Bill could sense the bad vibe, so he turned on the cassette player to try and raise the mood. Unfortunately, he had Talking Heads in the machine playing 'Road to Nowhere'.

Sheila, also sensing the gloom, quickly turned it off.

Nantes to Roscoff only ate half of the last day and in the afternoon Bill squeezed the coach through the narrow streets to the hotel. It was on the outskirts of the town and had absolutely no endearing features; it really only served to hold people before they got on to the ferry.

Terry got up. "Ladies and gentlemen, here we are for the last night together, it is a very basic hotel so I suggest we use the afternoon and evening to explore the town – maybe stock up on those little French bits and pieces. Jean and I will be eating by the harbour in a lovely little creperie and would welcome any of you to join us from about 6.00pm. Now if I don't see you later I must remind you of our early start. The ferry is due to dock at around 6.30, so we all need to be on board the coach ready to leave for check in by 5.45am. Same as before, I will take all the passports on board and return them once we get back to Blighty. Right, any questions?"

No one spoke. Everyone got up and filed off the coach, except Pam who stayed at the back; watching, waiting, learning. It was the same now as it was at yesterday's stop. Doctor Roberts and Mary Braces were in the next two rows. The couple from the old post office were next. None of them looked back or checked. They were all up and out.

Pam stayed in the back seat for ten minutes before she got off. As she left she arranged her bag and coat on the seat to resemble a person asleep, it looked okay if the glance was passing.

She let herself out of the rear fire exit door, no alarms, no drama. She made her way to reception then her room. She left her small travel bag there and set off for the town. Peter was actually right – Roscoff was a lovely place. Beautiful houses with neat fragrant gardens; enjoying the frost-free environment. The church was majestic and the streets very Harry Potteresque.

Pam read with interest the many plaques. Mary Queen of Scots had to hunker down here over winter, avoiding the storms. 'There are worse places' thought Pam 'she probably should have stayed here and got a job in a little gift shop'. She did see a few of the coach party at various stages; some in a bar, a few in and out of gift shops. She saw one of the smokers leaving a Tabac with two carrier bags. But she herself was looking for a hardware shop or a garage.

Eventually, on her way towards the ferry terminal, she came across just such a small establishment. Inside she found what she was looking for – a Hi-Viz waistcoat. Her French was pretty good so the transaction and subsequent conversation were pretty painless. She left the garage and walked the last few hundred yards to the brow of the hill above the ferry terminal.

Bob . . .

Bob navigated his way through the city of Plymouth; following a one-way system too complex for even the most advanced sat-nav. Just after the Hoe, ironically the start of the red-light district, he pulled into the capacious car park of a harbour side bar called The Dock Café. This was in sight of the ferry terminal and from where he could judge the best time to enter the fray.

He got out, went into the bar and ordered a coffee. He didn't want to reek of alcohol at customs. He had a window of two hours before they shut the ticket barriers. He picked a table on the edge of a balcony from where he could see both the van and the booths. He sat down to bide his time.

Even at this early stage of the proceedings and from this distance he had already shortlisted two contenders for the upcoming 'where the hell is my car' event to be held in the early hours of tomorrow morning. He was watching the approach road to see if a suitable vehicle came along that he could tuck in behind, either a larger campervan than he was driving or a strange hippy conversion that would stretch port authority resources to the limit.

Almost on cue the perfect foil ambled around the corner, from this distance it looked like a cut and shut project made out of a cattle truck and a sun damaged conservatory. Bob quickly finished his drink and ran back to the van. He fired it up and drove back to the terminal entrance just in time to neatly slot in behind the mobile skunk lab.

Bob watched in awe as the incredible unit in front of him made its stately progress towards the ticket booth. He could have sworn the wood burner was still alight as a wisp of smoke emitted from one of the drain pipe chimneys. The mobile concoction ground to a halt just short of ticket booth number seven. One of the front seat passengers had to get out as either the driver's window wasn't functioning or the actual driver wasn't functioning.

A young lady, who had got dressed in the dark, approached the ticket window and handed over a large amount of paperwork. An exchange of words took place between the walking jumble sale and a bemused official – probably about the validity of the contents of the conservatory. Sure enough the girl turned around and banged on the side of beast.

It was the signal required to get the contents to reveal themselves. Bob counted four different ways in which the occupants vacated the vehicle and come the end seven types of humanoid lined up to be checked.

When, eventually and unbelievably, everything seemed to be in order, the rag tag group re-entered the catacombs and the truck slowly moved forward. Bob could have sworn that a small belch of smoke was emitted from one of the other chimneys, maybe it was powered by an on-board wood burning stove.

Bob pulled up to the ticket booth. He had completely forgotten that he was driving a stolen van and had recently embezzled over £1 Million of his neighbours' assets.

The lady from Brittany Ferries was also in some sort of parallel universe and would probably be phoning in sick tomorrow. Bob could have been sat there naked playing a xylophone made out of children's bones and she wouldn't have batted an eyelid. She processed Bob on autopilot and murmured a lane number at him, which he was going to ignore so that he could tuck in behind The Arkansas Chugabug.

Only customs to negotiate.

The Armorique had already berthed following its crossing from Roscoff and was spewing its contents out. Bob was aware of the feelings expressed by the majority of the occupants within the disembarking vehicles; their holidays were over and it was back to the grindstone. When he had been in their position, he had always looked on with envy at the queues waiting to embark but not now. This time was different. He would never feel like them again as he wasn't coming back.

Despite probably only being thirty minutes before they were loaded on board the giant vessel, the occupants of the amazing shanty town in front deemed there was just enough time to knock up a three course meal and carry out a civil wedding. Bob actually admired their complete contempt for time and order. They weren't hurting anyone, 'so let them be' he thought.

Before long, someone in authority directed them to pack up the ensuing country fayre, and enter into the covered custom bay shed. Bob, without being asked, gently moved forward so that he could experience this moment in time.

Sadly, it never happened. The Devon based customs staff looked on in abject terror at what had pulled up in front of them.

One of the occupants waved at them from an upstairs window. It was all too much for them; there wasn't enough ink in Plymouth to process this administrative nightmare. Where would they start? When, if ever, would it end?

With the power of uniformed telepathy, the customs officials communicated to each other that their French counterparts could deal with this situation. One of the uniforms made a half-hearted circulation of the wheeled Favelas, pretending to check that it was all legal; but all the time worried that one of the first floor extensions might collapse and injure them.

After this pitiful display of a customs search, the lead official, almost embarrassingly, waved the group forward. Neither Bob or anyone connected to the UK border force could believe what had just happened, but it had, and Bob was up next.

He was ushered forward. He could sense a new purpose about the customs team. They weren't in an enforced medical coma like the ticket girl. They all knew that they had slipped well below the professional standards expected by the British public. With fresh zeal they asked Bob to vacate his van. Two stern officials clambered on in his place. Bob, from the side lines then watched as a dog was told to wee on the wheels and a large wardrobe door mirror was pulled around under the camper.

"Is this your vehicle Sir, and did anyone else help you pack it?"

Bob, for the first time during this adventure, felt properly nervous. A bead of sweat gained speed as it trickled down his back.

"No, Sir I packed it myself." He didn't answer the first question. A finger tapped on the window next to them and the officer dealing with Bob was beckoned on board. In what seemed like an age he returned clutching a sandwich bag.

"What is this Sir? We found it hidden in your glove box."

"It's my Dad" replied Bob simply.

"I'm sorry Sir, you will need to expand."

Bob shook off his fear and summoned every last spirit who owed him one.

"It is some of the earth from my Dad's grave, I am taking him to France for one last trip. I am truly sorry if I needed to declare him but I have had other things on my mind."

This could have gone many ways, but the spirits came good.

"No need to declare it Sir, I lost my dear old Dad recently. I wish I had taken him to France too." The official smiled and gently rested his hand on Bob's shoulder. He then whistled; the wardrobe door mirror was taken away and the dog stopped urinating.

"I hope the trip works out for you Sir, please be on your way."

Bob got back into the driver's seat and placed the bag on the dash board. "Nice one Dad, even in death you helped me. I love you."

Bob turned the key and moved forward to re-join his hillbilly friends who had opened a pop-up corn dolly shop and were currently staging a harvest festival. They had barely had enough time to erect the skittle alley before they were being ushered onto the boat. Bob, counting his blessings, followed. The clunk of the axle as he left English soil resonated through his entire body, oh my god, he was nearly there.

Pam ...

The late afternoon crossing was boarding and Pam watched the proceedings with interest. Some of the people she saw in the distance might well see Bob as they disembarked in Plymouth, if all went to plan that is. The coaches and lorries passed through the Brittany Ferries ticket offices and then they were held before the customs part of the procedure. During this period a large security presence made its way from vehicle to vehicle issuing a yellow sticker when any search was carried out.

Slowly, and in no particular order, the traffic then passed by the customs booths and more checks were made. Pam moved closer to the activity to get a better view of what would be the most critical part of the trip for her.

Once ticketed and custom checked, the coaches pulled forwards and lined up in the embarkation car park; engines off, waiting for their turn. The last of the disembarking vehicles drove off of the ferry. They passed barely one hundred metres from the lines of vehicles waiting to get on. Bob, driving Terry's van, would be at his most exposed at this point.

The turnaround time was incredible. Barely ten minutes after the last car touched French soil, the loading started. This was to be Pam's window of opportunity. The lorries and coaches were first. A signal came from a Hi-Viz jacket. Engines started. She would need that to mask the sound of the door opening and she would hope that she was going to be followed by a French lorry or coach as a left-seated driver wouldn't see the emergency door opening.

The queue jolted forwards. This was it – the moment she was waiting for; her exit. What happened to her after that would be in the lap of the gods. She couldn't know how the dice would roll. Would anyone see her? Would any of the Twinners miss her before they got on the ferry? How many other Hi-Viz jackets would be around to lose herself amongst? And would that be enough to allow her to exit the secure area? Oh my god, so many things could go wrong. She needed a drink, a proper drink. She stood up and headed back towards the town.

Two ideas, small ones, came to her on the way back. She walked along the quay to join Terry and Jean at the creperie. Quite a lot of the coach party had come together in a last gasp of camaraderie. Pam saw this as a chance to help her in the morning. It would be very early anyway, and still dark. Everyone would be tired and grumpy. If she could add a thick head to the proceedings it might improve her chances of a clean break.

"Now everyone, I am sure I don't need to tell you that this region is famous for its cider. Nowhere near as good as Devon Red I grant you, but very tasty all the same. As it is our last evening together please permit me to get you all, my neighbours, a bowl or two of the good stuff."

A round of applause went up. Pam went to the bar and ordered several large jugs of strong Breton cider. These duly arrived with lovely drinking bowls to add to the experience, and ensured that everyone had a go.

Peter and several of the others joined the crowd in dribs and drabs as the evening wore on. He relived frame by frame, the Johnny Onions museum visit; much to everyone's delight. More jugs of cider magically appeared throughout the evening, to accompany the savoury crepes, and spirits were high once again. They were going home tomorrow; back to their safe zones. Well, most of them were!

Pam's phone vibrated and she got up and went outside to read the text. Bob had left the village and was on his way to Plymouth. A lump appeared in her throat. Half the lump was her old empty house and the other half was her man drawing closer to her. They cancelled each other out and the lump went away. She put away her phone and re-joined the throng. Her last ever night with this bunch of wombles.

It was Mary that burst the cider balloon.

"Come on folks, we have to be up early, we don't want to miss the boat. Haven't you all got homes to go to?"

Pam giggled. The irony was not lost on her even though she could not share it with anyone. The party must have agreed with Mary as they all started to finish their drinks and settle the accounts before heading back to the boarding house.

Pam kept to the back so that no one became attached to her. She didn't need a new close friend at this late stage. The group gingerly made their way back to the hotel with no loss of life or significant damage to the town's infrastructure. They said their goodnights and dispersed to their rooms for all of five hours' sleep.

Bob ...

Just as his partner in crime was heading for bed Bob was safely stowed inside Amorique. He had shortlisted his contenders for the last ever game of 'where the hell did I park the car' down to three. An elderly couple who probably shouldn't really have gone on holiday unescorted let alone contemplate driving on the continent, a young couple from the extreme wing of born again Christianity – their car had at least six jesus related stickers including the slightly worrying 'I don't need insurance – the lord has me covered'. They got out carrying a guitar and tambourine.

The last group in the running was a large family of mixed race; well two of them were ginger. Bob got anxiety just watching them exist. Mum, Dad and four children. The youngest were twins (the ginger ones) and were fuelled by appeasement Haribo. The parents would be struggling to find a reason to live, let alone their car.

He had booked a cabin but wanted to mix with his fellow man for a while. He also needed a stiff drink; he had earned it. At the bar he could see that the inhabitants of the mobile Kibbutz had ensconced themselves in a corner. One of their number was next to Bob, ordering drinks, his French was excellent.

"I love your conversion" Bob directed at him.

"Why thank you, not many people appreciate its honesty" The man, who was sporting white-man dreadlocks, spoke with a lovely Home Counties purr.

"What are you plans? And is it powered by a wood burning stove?" Bob asked.

The man laughed. "No, but we do keep it alight as we travel, were you behind us in that mobile gin palace? Wow! What a bit of kit, however, you got stopped and we didn't!"

Bob smiled. "I know! I couldn't believe it. It was like you were too much effort. It's not my van, I am just driving it for someone, so where are you off to?"

"Well, most of the gang work in the smoke, but once a year we cash in our holidays together and go to France with our Border Morris troop, it is a right laugh I can tell you!"

"I bet it is" mused Bob "I hope you have a fantastic time scaring all the French children."

The dreadlocks smiled, not many people ever bothered to ask him what he did or even try to interact, he turned and headed back to the troupe.

"Oui Monsieur" Bob was next at the bar. He ordered a bottle of Cotes du Rhone with a single glass, and a packet of Marlboro; these he took outside to watch Devon fade away. He found a table and sat down. He poured out a generous measure, lit a cigarette, and drew back deeply.

What an adventure. His thoughts flicked through some key moments, and he exhaled.

If the people on this crossing realised what this non-descript man was about to become, they would be amazed, astounded, and probably try to get a selfie. These thoughts and the red wine gave him a warm glow inside and out. He drank and smoked until Devonshire disappeared from his eyes, then he went to bed.

Pam ...

The Breton cider marathon had worked. Several of the group had to be wrenched out of their slumber with a bang on the bedroom door. Some of the other hotel residents objected to this as they were not getting the god o'clock ferry. There were heated exchanges, slammed doors, and at last, 25 minutes after the agreed time, everyone was on board and Sheila got the coach moving towards the ferry terminal.

One of the last people to get on the coach had even brought the mini-kettle from the room in a vain attempt to ingest some caffeine before the off. He had actually switched it on before he went to sleep last night but during the succeeding five hours it had failed to take the water temperature above tepid.

Pam, who hadn't had too much cider, sat at the back and watched the dishevelled proceedings. In the dark, the coach approached the ferry terminal. Terry, still able to remember what had happened in Plymouth, let Jean do the talking. Someone from Brittany ferries got on and visibly tapped their watch. Jean handed over a mass of passports which were disregarded. Not even a head count was carried out. The ticket officer handed Jean several sheets of paper and then got off the coach.

Jean announced "Right folks, we are a little late so I am afraid we will have to wait until we get on board to use any facilities. I have your cabin tickets here and will issue them as you get off. It won't be long, look – the boat has nearly finished offloading."

Pam had already been keenly scanning the exiting vehicles for her first sight of Bob in what seemed like an age. Well, actually, she hoped she didn't see him – not yet anyway. At ground zero, the disembarking cars and trucks were thankfully quite far away. You couldn't read registration numbers or clearly make out the occupants. Especially in this grey, damp, early morning atmosphere.

Sheila was directed to move the coach forward to the customs booth. Fortunately for Pam, being this early meant a very thin number of staff, not that she had anything to declare but the fewer officials in general the better.

There was a dog and two armed officials circling the coach. Bill had got off, and, having opened up the luggage holds, stood back whilst torches and a dog's nose were thrust into the void. Nothing of any interest came to light. Another armed individual boarded the vehicle and this time did take the passports from Jean. He slowly made his way back through the coach counting slumped heads as he did.

Bob . . .

It was less than three seconds after waking that the Buckfastleigh Butterfly farm kicked in, in the pit of Bob's stomach. Even the melodic Brittany Ferries wake-up music didn't soothe him. All he could think about was the short stretch of tarmac that lay in front of him. He tidied up and packed his belongings, left his cabin and went to get his breakfast.

Before he was really aware of any of his actions he was sat inside the camper. He must have made it there on autopilot. For the first time ever he didn't even take in the conclusion of the 'find my car' event (which was won by the barely functioning Haribo family; the elderly couple were in their car before Bob).

Now that he was in the moment and away from his flow charts and lists, it dawned on him that this next small section was actually the hardest part of the last six months.

Bob sat at the wheel of the stolen campervan, watching as the vast bow doors opened.

The grey French morning light barely penetrated the car deck. He was less than 500 yards from his love, and, slightly more worryingly, the legal owner of the vehicle he was driving. Any minute now he would be waved forward on to the gangway and then on to French soil.

From the experience of his last crossing, he knew that he would be fully exposed for about 200 yards of open tarmac, with hardly anything separating embarkers and disembarkers.

It could all fail here. One casual look across from Terry at the exiting queue and his goose would be well and truly cooked. For only the second time in recent history a bead of sweat trickled down his spine.

And so, here he was. The bow doors had opened and there was no going

203

back. When prompted, he carefully manoeuvred the van out into the dull light. His peripheral vision caught sight of the waiting vehicles. For some pathetic reason he ducked his head down. Maybe he hoped that the roof of the camper would do the same.

He held back as much as he dared – screened by the large dock cranes, trying to get some gap between him and the Border Morris truck in front.

One of the Hi Viz got impatient and vigorously directed Bob to move forward up the gang plank.

Pam ...

Just as the armed border control officer got to the rear of the coach, Pam saw Terry's campervan drive up the slipway with, who she hoped was Bob, at the wheel. She got up quickly from her seat and just caught the arm of the official who proceeded to distribute all of the passports to the four winds.

"Monsieur, je suis tres desole, pardon, je suis une idiot!"

Pam started flapping about in an over exaggerated manner and dropped to the floor of the coach, carefully picking up and sorting through passports, until she found hers. Jean, Terry, and Peter rushed to the rear to see what all the fuss was about. Pam built the hysteria.

"Oh Jean, I am so clumsy" she shrilled "I went for my bag and hit this poor man, I am such a fool, so sorry everyone!"

"Don't worry Pam love, we are all a bit frayed and tired, it won't be long now."

Pam saw Terry roll his eyes at Jean as he said this. Pam didn't care, as the three of them picked up the last of the rogue passports and handed them back to the official.

Bob, driving Terry's van, disappeared from sight behind the terminal building.

Bob ...

This time Bob turned to look left. He could clearly see the waiting lines and the Twinning coach was not difficult to make out; not just due to its retro style but its strange tag line of 'Get the travel bug with us' scrawled along its length.

Back in Whiterock, as it had pulled away a few days earlier, Bob had thought that the marketing department might need to revisit its strategy; lest people linked it to the on-board catering.

He couldn't see any detail of the inside from this distance. He just felt very exposed. There were 200 yards of open ground and the Border Morris had been directed to stop in lane four; to await French border control. Bob took a deep breath and just did it. He drove across the no man's land, not at any great speed, but he put his faith in luck, the spirits and above all his partner in crime, Pam. She would provide some sort of diversion.

The fates and Pam's genius smiled on him as he was directed to lane one which was the furthest from his old neighbours. The one last hurdle for him awaited; French passport control. He was only five vehicles in the queue away from the window of the temporary porta cabin that had been there since 1977.

This time he was relieved not to be behind the Arkansas Chugabug as he was sure that they would create a lot of interest with the uniforms; who would be concerned that the occupants had created some new life form on board and were intent on unleashing it onto French soil.

He was now only three away. Half of him kept an eye on the queue in front and the other half was always conscious of a rear guard approach. If someone on board the coach had clocked Terry's quite large and distinctive mode of transport, they could have got off the Twinners' coach and alerted the Gendarmerie; who would be on their way over to feel Bob's now quite damp collar.

If that happened, Bob was already weighing up the chances he had of crashing through the barriers and making a run for it. He didn't think he would get very far; and would never leave Pam anyway.

Only two in front now, a smaller camper and a French caravan, nothing to worry about yet. He needed to calm down and try not to sweat so much; it was not a good look to have at passport control.

His thoughts turned to Pam. It was her big moment coming up and he knew she would be careful and brilliant. As he had suspected, the French caravan was waved through without it even coming to a halt. One to go.

The gendarmes had not come for him yet, so he could relax just a little and focus on the job in hand. The van in front had pulled up to the window and papers were handed over, words exchanged, all over in thirty seconds. Now it was his turn.

He carefully pulled forward and wound his window down. The very official looking official was about to ask for Bob's passport, when the final and greatest miracle was delivered. All staff were being directed as a matter of urgency to lane four to cope with a situation.

During the crossing, the Border Morris troupe had decided to save time and use all the on-board facilities to don complete costume and make-up associated with being a Border Morris. So they had all blacked up.

This was not only deemed to be racially inappropriate by the customs staff but also considered that it made passport photo identification almost impossible without the aid of some wet wipes.

Bob was hurriedly waved through with lane one being shut immediately behind him.

"I bloody love Border Morris" Said Bob aloud to anyone who could hear him.

He pulled forward, and again, checked that all was clear behind him.

It was.

He was home.

Pam ...

With Bob safely out of the picture and her passport not in the clutches of the French border control officer, Pam briefly sat back down to draw breath. She didn't have long until her next move was required. Timing was crucial, she only had a window of about thirty seconds to execute her extraction plan.

The by now quite flustered passport officer walked back down to the front of the coach with Jean. He handed back the stack of papers, and got off the coach. The door shut and the engine was running, ready for the signal, which by the look of things Pam didn't think would be long in coming.

Go! She got up and made her way sheepishly toward the front, apologising to anyone vaguely conscious. In the front seat, Terry was still not with it, and Jean was about to start counting the passports when Pam interrupted her.

"Jean, love, I am so sorry to be a complete pain and after upsetting the official but could I ask just one more favour?"

Jean, for the first time that Pam had witnessed on the trip, let her made up face fall. "For fuck's sake Pam, what now?"

"Oh, sorry Jean, bad timing? It can wait ..."

"Pam, no. I am really sorry. That's not like me at all, I am tired and have lost count of the passports and I am doing all this on my own as his bloody Lordship here snores off last night's excesses. Now what was it you wanted?"

"Look, after everything that has gone on, I would really like to be on my own. Please could I have my cabin card now so that I don't have to interact with anyone? I think everyone will be glad to see less of me."

"Of course they won't Pammy love, yes take your card now and lets all sleep on it." She handed Pam her card as the coach slowly eased forward. Time was running out.

Pam turned to walk back, and could see that the seats in row three were empty. She feigned a shoe lace issue and crouched down in the empty seat foot well.

From her pocket she took out a single cigarette that she had ponced the evening before from one of the smokers – who said they hadn't realised that Pam was one of the dirty folk.

She carefully lit it and placed the burning stick into the still fitted ashtray on the arm of the vacant seat. She got up quickly, and just before she was about to rush back to her seat, she clocked Peter's clipboard, unguarded.

She snatched it, and at a pace got back to her seat. Her clothing was already arranged in its mock human shape, and in less than five seconds she had donned her new Hi-Viz jacket. She grabbed her bag and the emergency door handle and waited. The coach was getting nearer to the ferry doors. 'Come on someone, smell it! No? Well it's up to me then' she thought. She shouted out in a non-descript accent.

"For Christ's sake, has someone lit up a fag? Can't you wait for five more minutes?"

Her words shot down the aisle just as everyone had started to get a whiff of the cigarette smoke. Sheila slammed the brakes on. Pam opened the rear door and climbed out.

Bob ...

As had been agreed with the French garage owner during his recent solo trip, Bob took an immediate right hand turn just after the port terminal building, which was shielding him from the embarking queues. Within 100 metres he pulled into the back car park of the Vasco De Gama pub; the one with no CCTV coverage.

There, leaning against an impressive looking Land Rover, was a pleasantly surprised Frenchman. He seemed suitably enthralled by the sheer size and splendour of his latest acquisition; and that the Englishman had actually turned up as promised.

Bob pulled up alongside the immaculate 4 x 4 and got out. All the relief and pent up emotion came out of Bob and turned itself into a big man-hug. The French recipient didn't recoil but embraced the moment and held onto Bob. They unfurled as close friends.

A tour of both modes of transport ensued, accompanied by numerous nods and smiles before an exchange of paperwork, keys, knowledge and handshakes took place. The new campervan owner helped Bob to unload his possessions and pack them into the capacious Land Rover. When this was done and they were about to go their separate ways, Bob turned to his new friend and with an earnest expression spoke.

"Monsieur, merci pour votre assistance et pour le transaction, mais, this campervan est un peu, how do you say? Dodgy, un peut etre 'illegal', comprendre?"

"Oui, oui, je te comprends, I suspect since the first time we meet, c'est bon. This campervan est pour ma Femme et moi pour vacances, don't worry Monsieur, I will say nothing. Au revoir et bonne chance!"

With that, Bob's third best French friend (after Raphael and the

Councillor) got into his new holiday home, fired it up, and with a wave pulled out of the car park and disappeared into his future.

Bob climbed into his new ride, took stock of all the refinements and changed his brain to LHD.

He took a deep breath. He was clear, in a legal car, completely invisible to anyone. Just a normal man, going about his business.

He started up the Land Rover. It indicated a full tank of fuel, 'good man' he thought.

He carefully manoeuvred out of the car park avoiding any cameras, and back down the slip road towards the port. This time he pulled into the normal car park reserved for people using the ferry terminal. He locked up his new vehicle and, after clocking where the security cameras were pointing, made his way to the nearest stretch of the harbour wall not restricted by security fencing.

He leaned against the concrete and felt the morning sun gathering strength against his skin. His eyes wandered over towards the queue of waiting cars. The Border Morris incident had clearly been sorted out as everything was starting to move. He saw the coach and it too had started to crawl forward. He sent every available part of his aura towards it and his love.

"Good luck my darling." He said on the early morning breeze. The words left his lips and blew away gently towards Pam.

Pam ...

As Pam hit the ground, the line of ferry-cleaning staff walked past. These poor souls were programmed not to interact with anything or anyone. They just shuffled untidily and without any motivation for either their employment or their lives. Pam joined at the rear; clipboard held in a 'recording of notes' position.

Pam didn't miss a beat. She kept in step with the rear of the cleaning brigade. She didn't overact. She discreetly placed her cabin card into the empty clear plastic pocket on her jacket.

The cleaners proceeded towards a staff exit which was guarded by two faux military personnel. At the gate the front member of the cleaning team showed her lanyard pass and one of the guards let her through; the rest of the living dead followed suit with the same procedure.

Pam counted them and kept her cool, she was so close to the gates of freedom. The last drone went through. She was working on the assumption that anyone wearing a Hi-Viz jacket and clutching a clipboard is without reproach. She stopped level with one of the guards and spoke abruptly to him.

"Douze?"

"Pardon?"

The guard looked a bit shocked and somewhat perplexed that he was going to have to do something that he wasn't trained for. Pam slowly looked at him in an up and down manner.

"Combien personnes?" Pam said assertively in her best middle management French.

"Oh, pardon Madam, douze, oui, douze personnes."

Pam thrust the clipboard and a pen at the guard and pointed to a place

213

next to a large number 12 that she had written on the list of the visitors to the cave complex.

"Signature s'il vous plait?!"

The guard, not wanting to appear a fool and question this totally new procedure which had probably been mentioned in an email or during that security briefing he had nodded off in, took the pen and signed his fellow security guard's name next to the number 12. Pam nodded with authority, took the clipboard and pen back, and added her signature next to his.

"Merci et bonne journee."

Pam nodded and walked through the now held open gate. The guard shut and locked the gate behind her, returned to his original position, and nodded at his co-worker; who returned the nod in an official manner also concerned that he too had missed this new security procedure update.

Pam didn't break pace and followed to where the cleaners had entered the terminal building. Inside they had turned left and entered a large cleaning cupboard, Pam turned right and went into the washrooms. Here she took off her jacket, which she ditched along with the clipboard, and within seconds she was in the terminal foyer heading for the main exit door.

Whiterock ...

The lit fag was found and stubbed out, and the nearest smoker was, despite being asleep, tried, sentenced and executed by verbal abuse.

Sheila shouted various incomprehensible words from the front and re-engaged the gears. Terry told everyone to calm down, and Jean told Terry what he could do with his advice.

The coach accelerated to make up the gap in the queue and disappeared into the mouth of the Armorique.

Pam and Bob – Reunited ...

Bob was just entering 'Scandinavia' into the search engine of his phone when he felt her approaching across the car park. He didn't have to turn to check, he just knew it was her.

She joined him at the wall.

"Hello sailor, looking for crew?" She pinched his bum.

"Actually, a position of first mate has just come up on a wonderful voyage of discovery, are you interested?" He chuckled.

"Count me in skip, count me in!" Pam smiled back at him.

They joined hands as the Armorique slipped its moorings and slowly left the berth.

As it moved around the end of the jetty, Bob took out his phone and, with his passport, placed them on the top of the wall.

Pam did the same.

As one of the large wake waves splashed against the rocks below them, Bob picked up the items and threw them all into the sea.

In silence they watched their old lives slip below the water and disappear forever.

As the ferry left the port and entered the channel, Bob turned to face Pam. He kissed her very gently on both cheeks.

"Come on gorgeous, there's this little place I know."

FIN